The Cleaning

By D.C. Reed

Publisher – Cowboy Bookworks San Antonio, TX
cowboybookworks@yahoo.com

ISBN – 978-09823158-3-5

Front Cover: ©BigStockPhoto.com; Kevin Kangas, Miraco

Editing for "The Cleaning" by Ruth Blaikie rblaikie@xtra.co.nz

All characters in this novel are created purely from the imagination of the author. No character is based on any real person, dead or alive. Any similarity is purely coincidental. Names are fictional as well and have no relationship to someone bearing the same name.

Other books by D.C. Reed are available on-line at

ReadReedBooks.com

The Cleaning

By D.C. Reed

The Cleaning

Prologue:

Richmond, Virginia: two years earlier.

Mira Stephens had eaten lunch earlier at the Zeus Gallery Café. Her life was finally starting to get back on track. Her affair with an up and coming Virginia politician had not turned out the way she had hoped, but that was all behind her now. Despite breaking off the affair, her lover had pulled a few strings to get her a better position with a software developer in the Richmond area. It had taken six months, but she was going to start her new job on Monday and she was really looking forward to it. She was relieved that she would not have to go back to Chicago and ask her father for money as she wanted no part of him and his family business. No, she had this job that was going to pay her good money—not that she would be able to buy a house in the Fan District or anything, but Mira did not have to have lots and lots of money. She was the kind of person who would be satisfied with good money, and then she could find a man—a man that had lots and lots of money.

The sky was a beautiful Carolina blue as Mira finished some shopping. She headed south on Highway 76 out of the Richmond Metro-plex, if you could call it that, on the way back to her apartment. She was within a block of the apartment and pulled into the alley that led to the back of the complex. The apartments faced a two-lane, busy street that management had already advised the tenants not to park on. Evidently, several cars had been broken into over the past few months. She pulled up to her carport, but could not pull in because her empty garbage can blocked the path.

She cursed the trash men who had obviously come by earlier that morning and inconsiderately dropped the can without regard for someone trying to pull in. As she got out of her late model Mercury, she was startled by a man that approached her. He was a sturdy looking man, about six feet tall and dressed in nondescript navy Dockers and a tan windbreaker. His hands were stuck in his jacket pockets, and he looked a little embarrassed. His smile was disarming, and Mira relaxed a little bit.

"Hi," he said, "I live next door and I locked myself out."

"Oh no! I've done the same thing myself. Don't you just hate it when it happens?" Mira said, smiling back with an empathetic expression and nodding her head.

The man nodded and said, "Could I borrow your phone to call someone to bring me a key?"

"Sure," Mira said and nodded.

She reached back into the car to get her purse. With her back turned for an instant, the man removed a Glock 31 pistol and clubbed her on the head. She collapsed into the running automobile and was lying over the front seat. Her assailant reached in the car door and expertly cut off her air supply. She came to and violently lashed out, but she was no match for his strength and weight. She finally succumbed, and her body went limp. Checking for passersby, he gathered her up with little effort and laid her on the driveway. To make sure of his work, he felt for her pulse. To his satisfaction, her heart had stopped. He got inside the car, picked up her purse, and removed the money and credit cards. He tossed the purse out the door. Its contents were strewn all the way under the carport. The man again looked around for anyone that might be in sight, put the car in gear and slowly drove off. He smiled to himself, satisfied with his work. The police would have no witnesses and no evidence.

The Cleaning

D.C. Reed

Chapter 1

Ben Thomas was staying in the Cincinnatian Hotel on 6th and Vine Street. The historic hotel had been in business for over 120 years and was a beautiful landmark with a marble indoor staircase in the foyer that led to the 164 guest rooms. Ben concluded his business too late to catch the last flight out to Dulles, his next stop. Besides, he was tired and decided to dine-in at the hotel's Palace Restaurant rather than try to battle traffic. He planned to sleep in the next morning, have a leisurely breakfast, and let the morning rush clear out. At 11:30am the next day, a porter arrived at the door to pick up his luggage. Ben tipped the man and told him he would go downstairs in a few minutes to check out. Heading out the door, Ben closed up his briefcase picked up his coat for the December morning, and took the elevator to the lobby level.

Ben used the opportunity to check messages on his ride down. Upon exiting the elevator, while going to check out at the front desk, he walked by a meeting room being used by a local men's civic club of some kind. He thought it was a Chamber of Commerce meeting, but it turned out to be a Rotary Club meeting. The local chapter had a monthly lunch meeting and like other such organizations, invited speakers in that might be of interest to the group. What caught Ben's attention while walking by the open door to the meeting room was the confident voice that was being projected over the speaker system and the phrase, "unintended result of government regulation." To his surprise, the voice came from a rather ordinary looking young man who appeared to be in his early thirties. No one seemed particularly interested in an uninvited guest, so Ben found his way in and sat down at an open seat at one of the tables. He asked a gray bearded man with thick glasses who the speaker was, but the man said he arrived late and did not catch his name. Ben noticed a nicely dressed young man in his mid-thirties, straining to listen, who was quite intent on hearing everything that was said. He seemed mildly annoyed at being interrupted, but enthusiastically gave Ben the speaker's name, Will Oliver, and quickly turned his attention back toward the podium.

Most of the audience was still finishing the remaining morsels of their buffet lunch, a medium slice of overly well-done roast beef with au jus sauce, which was ladled on to cover up any dryness. The $7.95 meal included a side of au gratin potatoes, coleslaw and tea. Many had skipped on to their slice of chocolate cake with a mocha icing. The few men at the head table looked on with polite interest, but were intent on finishing their lunch.

Ben listened to the passion of Oliver's voice. His genuineness came across in his easy-going presentation. He continued with his story of growing up in Arkansas, and then moving to a more civilized part of the world, Ohio. This drew a spattering of applause and several chuckles. He said he arrived in Arkansas as a third grader and left as a first grader. Again the audience snickered. His story was an illustration of how good intentions often resulted in unexpected consequences. The childhood story drew much nodding of heads and murmured comments as several men turned to their table partners and said, "He's absolutely right."

Oliver then dropped back into a statistical mode, recounting crime figures, unmarried pregnancies, and social disease rates. He quoted several government agencies that kept up with such things and then threw in a timeline of public education policies and the removal of prayer from schools.

"We need schools to teach the basics, such as reading, writing, and arithmetic," he said demonstratively and with force, "and get out of teaching our kids how to have safe sex and how the government has the answer to our problems. It is the parents' job to teach their kids about important life decisions, not the government's or schools'. And for those that say our parents are not teaching about condoms and homosexuality and government programs, there is a reason why we are not...We don't want them having sex, getting diseases, or relying on the government to solve our problems. We are not prudes; we are prudent. We are not sticking our heads in the sand; we are trying to protect our children from the very things that the 'know it alls' are saying we have to educate these kids about. From the statistics, these people were and are wrong! Every time parents rely on government rules to justify not allowing children to see a movie or drink a beer, we give up our authority. We must tell the kids that the movie is not worth seeing, and they cannot go. We must tell our children that they are not old enough to drink, and they cannot."

The audience was clapping and nodding with enthusiasm. Ben looked around and thought, *is this a normal Rotary meeting? Who is this guy? He has a certain, non-threatening appeal.*

Ben had the man's name and asked another guy on the way out, "Is this guy running for office or something?"

"No, but maybe he should."

Ben agreed and went out to the lobby. Arthur Means, the desk manager had taken notice of the unusual noise level and had moved out around the front of the sign-in counter.

When Ben exited the meeting, Means asked, "What is all the excitement about?"

"You mean it is not always this way?" Ben asked.

"No, they usually have people slipping out the back. Do they have some kind of entertainment?"

He looked worried. Ben deduced that Arthur might have thought the Rotary Club had brought in some adult entertainment to liven up the group.

Arthur said nervously, "I had better go and see what is

going on."

Ben, conversely, had seen enough.

Chapter 2

"I had Marley check Will Oliver out with some sources and it appears that he is a former business man, professor and several other things along the way," Ben told Ross Saunders on the phone. Richard Marley was an all-purpose employee. The former black-ops soldier was very reliable at all manner of surveillance and other more demanding matters. Ben continued on about Will Oliver, "He has a business degree and a doctorate in sociology or psychology or something. He has grown children, therefore looks much younger than he is, say ten years or so. He looked about 35, but must be about 45. He spoke with very good composure; related stories well; and seemed to have a very polished delivery. I didn't see him using any notes, so he was either well rehearsed or had a very good command of what he was trying to get across. I was just amazed at the level of excitement that he was able to generate amongst a fairly boring group of businessmen."

"Sounds interesting. We need someone in the pipeline," Ross said, and thought about that for a moment without saying anything. He stroked his chin and removed his glasses. Rubbing his eyes, he continued, "We could do a more extensive background on him, but we need to know what aspirations he has. We need to do a better job this time on the background; we cannot afford another misstep. We'll have to move fast—maybe get him elected to a congressional opening that is not too heavily contested. So let's move on Oliver. Find out everything about him and the best election we could get him in. I want to know the size of his short hair when you're done."

"Cleaning?" Ben asked.

Ross breathed out, "Well, we'll have to see. Cleaning ...within reason."

"What is the news on the Hill?"

"Parker and Swain, Swain and Parker, that's the news. Why Parker picked him still beats the shit out of me. Surely he doesn't want to throw away all that he's been able to accomplish. He must have found out something to make him just cut us out completely. But Swain, my God!" Ross thought about that and said, "What could he have found out that might have spooked him? All Smith would say, through a 'spokesperson' was that he did not know Swain was going to be his replacement when he agreed to resign. Now he won't talk to us at all. What could possibly be up with that?"

Brett Swain, an Illinois Senator, replaced a reportedly ailing Lancaster Smith. In reality, Smith had run into some problems with business dealings and many thought several of the top presidential advisors had been successful in railroading him out. President Parker went to Smith and offered him a way out. Among others, Brett Swain's name had been lifted up as a trial balloon by several more moderate congressmen to fill the open Vice-President's spot. Surprisingly, Parker seemed interested. In retrospect, Ben and Ross now realized it was Parker's way to end run the Matriculation Project. Never mind that the Matriculation Project was the reason he was in office in the first place.

The Matriculation Project had begun almost ten years ago, when a small group of men headed by the late financier, Algiers Banger, decided that the United States was in an untenable situation. Further, the politicians that were lining up for elections were the same old political hacks that were career politicians looking for the next buck. One might wonder why there are no plentiful candidates with outstanding bios. Truth be known, everyone has some skeletons. Politicians that have been around a while are usually given a pass, with most figuring that any bad stuff would have already come out. The newest candidates receive the usual once-over, but those that are running for major mayoral, state governors, U.S. Congress and, of course, the President, get the full proctologic exam. Those without political savvy or a sordid past usually cannot survive. Only those that were able to get into a significant office have the political clout to cover up past indiscretions or questionable activity. Algiers figured that the really talented candidates all had something to hide. He could pick his candidate that was the best fit for the job, clean up his past if necessary, and orchestrate his election. And it had all been working so well.

The Matriculation Project was created to fill the pipeline with candidates that would be discretely promoted and funded in such a way that the public felt they had discovered this new candidate and relished the outside the Beltway image. The candidates had to have been in the system for at least a few years, so each would have had an acceptable pedigree for the office. The candidate had to be new to the national scene to qualify as an outsider, but have enough experience not to set off warning bells. Background checks were part of it, so that had to be planned for. Several candidates were recruited, and the expected number of casualties had taken place. It was the recent unexpected derailments that caused the Matriculation Project founders to shake their heads in bewilderment.

Unanticipated stupidities had caused several candidates to become unworkable. Otherwise dependable and predictable people sometimes reacted to newfound attention in destructive ways. Ross Saunders thought to himself that some people just could not handle success. In fact, it may even be some sort of psychosomatic disorder or something—like the athlete that has the winning catch in his hand and somehow manages to drop it. After the success of Parker and Smith, Ross and Algiers were anxious to continue. Had they just experienced beginner's luck? They really only theorized about whether it could ever work, and then it just happened—everything fell into place. It was the classic case of the right place and the right time. *Unbelievable,* thought Ross. But was it over? Even if it only worked once, the fact that they were able to place the U.S. President was unthinkable. Not by stealing votes or election fraud, but by playing the system better than the two parties ever did. Sure, history contained some fixed state elections, but compared to the Presidential race, State races were small stakes. Certainly some candidates had been backed in the just the right way before, but it was more of the crowd following a candidate after they had proven to be successful. Was this different than the Manchurian Candidate? Ross and Algiers had watched that movie together once during the early days of the Matriculation Project. The idea of getting your candidate into an office was not a new one. Ross thought that most of the subterfuge had occurred from the other direction—namely, making sure that a particular candidate was not elected, thereby accepting the least intolerable candidate.

Now that Algiers had passed away, Ross wondered if they had just been very fortunate or whether Algiers had been the key to their success. Algiers Banger had always exuded confidence and optimism. Everything with Parker had seemed to just fall into place. Maybe it was blind luck. Parker could be a one-time wonder like some of the bands that have that one big hit, like Dexy's Midnight Runners with *Come On Eileen* or Tweet with *Oops* (*oh my*). Ross' mind returned to the recent failures of the Matriculation Project, like Karl Scott who was going to win the election for Virginia's Lt. Governor. The Matriculation Project had born and delivered Scott—and then, only 60 days before the election, he proceeded to lay a woman that he picked up in a bar after everyone was tucked in for the night. Of course, the word got out, and a jealous wife leaked his betrayal to the press. No, some people could not handle success, thought Ross. If the idiot had just waited until after the election, he could have had all the women in the city of Richmond and it would have all been very discreet. It was not a complete surprise to Ross, having uncovered Scott's previous indiscretion with Mira Stephens. Now her death seemed to be sadly unnecessary, and that fact was not lost on Ross or Ben Thomas. Another Matriculation Project candidate's previous life had been a problem. The fact that Satch Mitchell had some psychological counseling could have been handled if the Matriculation Project group had only known. It could have actually worked in his favor if everyone was made to feel he was a victim. Ross thought to himself that women always like a strong man that is a little vulnerable. But this came across as something that was trying to be hidden. The candidate denied that the counseling had occurred and then later had to admit it. Not so good—weak and dishonest is not a good combination.

Ross' mind shifted to Mike Robertson. Yeah, things were going well with Mike. The Matriculation Project had taken Mike Robertson from a little known county prosecutor and moved him along with great success. His short stint as a State House of Representative 120th district was just the thing to bring his name up as a possible appointment to fill a vacancy for the U.S. Congress—a vacancy that was created by the somewhat unexpected death of Congressman Morris Childs. The Florida Governor was all too happy to take President Parker's recommendation for Mike Robertson as a short-term appointment, particularly since the remaining term was less than a full term. Ross and Ben had more than once marveled at the possible timetable that would have Lancaster Smith take over when Parker finished. Smith would name Robertson as his running mate, and the Matriculation Project would just keep rolling along. But, now with Smith being out and Parker picking up Swain as the Vice President, those plans would have to be scrapped.

Chapter 3

President Richard Stone Parker had served admirably: first as VP, then when the sitting U.S. President fell ill and eventually died, as the Commander in Chief. Rich Parker went on to win a full term. In the previous election, the Democrats thought they had a winner in Hillary, but she had proven to be an unbelievable lightening rod and could not make it out of the primary process. Thus the White House remained in Republican hands for another term.

Parker was an unknown who had started in politics as a county prosecutor. He was the first Matriculation Project candidate and with their help he had moved up the political ladder, first as a State Senator from West Virginia and then as a U.S. Congressman. Algiers had masterfully guided Parker in the area of public relations. When Republican nominee became the odds-on favorite and went looking for a fresh face for his V.P. spot, Parker had an enormous war chest to go along with a high approval rating. Parker was the choice. Two years later, Parker took over for the ailing President. The Matriculation Project was ready for the VP appointment as well, and Lancaster Smith was introduced to the scene. How could Parker refuse when he himself had been orchestrated into the Oval Office?

The Matriculation Project was a success. The script could not have worked any smoother. Now the Matriculation Project was responsible for both the President and the Vice-President—and the Candidates were doing exactly what needed to be done. The national debt, which had previously ballooned to incomprehensible amounts, was finally starting to drop. The standard earmark growth had been replaced with zero-based budgeting. Many Federal programs had moved toward the individual states. The Federal income tax was eliminated in favor of a national sales tax. Trade policy had become predictable and consistent. Foreign aid was axed then reinstated slowly to those that were friends of the United States. Social Security was all but privatized for the next three generations. Middle East policy dramatically shifted when Parker announced that we were "staying out of business that is not our business." Long-term oil contracts were signed, but with the new technological advancements in energy, they were looking superfluous. Troops were backed out of the Middle East, except where the governments had specifically requested a U.S. presence.

Not all was rosy, but things were progressing well, and Parker's popularity numbers had never been higher. The crime rate, initially sky-rocketed in the wake of the social program reductions, and was still at an uncomfortable level. Abortion was again illegal and created a cottage industry that sometimes resembled M.A.S.H. units. The country's have-nots were at subsistence levels in the states that did not pick up the Federal programs. Immigration was another issue that had yet to be dealt with.

The China Fear had fairly much dissolved. As predicted by a little known columnist, Daniel Coleman, China went through the rise and fall, similar to that which the Soviet Union experienced. The only difference was that the China crash happened in just a few short years. The break up into regional governments illuminated the fact that there is seldom a homogenous country, particularly when you are talking about a country as large as China. In fact, China had over 50 distinct ethnic groups, each of which was anxious to give self-determination a try. The European Union had also run upon rough times. Coleman had again predicted—though a little less dramatically than actually occurred, a civil war of sorts. The smaller members began to see that France and Germany were clearly the winners in the economic arena. There were several pushes to pass increasing restrictions and requirements of the member countries. When the Lithuanians, Swiss, Dutch, and Portuguese raised objections they were blacklisted. The Italians were actually mediators until an incident left about 35 people dead when a small produce market near the border of Switzerland burst into flames. A Euro Force had been formed and had the unenviable reputation similar to the Gestapo during Hitler's tenure. Parker was a proponent of the European Union and therefore, the unrest raised an issue for the Presidential campaign. None of the negatives were going to matter; Parker won and won easily.

Ross thought that not only had Parker done a good job, but also he was benefiting from the inertia of being in office already. Parker's opponent was a relatively young, handsome former governor from the state of Indiana. Still, Evan Bayh needed some seasoning to become credible to voters. Maybe the gray hair that was added to his temples gave him the appearance of the gravitas necessary to be taken seriously, but it is was not enough. Against Parker, Bayh was as likable as his father, Birch Bayh, had been. But he lacked a real ability to define himself, stammering around; evidently unable to think on his feet. Birch Bayh had served honorably as Indiana's elder statesman, until a young handsome man ran a hard-hitting campaign to unseat him. The elder Bayh had lost his wife to cancer and had lost some of his political fight, but the allegations of incompetence by Dan Quayle were uncalled for and disingenuous. Today, knowing how Quayle's stock dropped just a couple years as the VP, Quayle's charges of Bayh's lack of acuity was, at the very least, the pot calling the kettle black. In reality, Quayle was not the dupe that the press made him out to be, but was the victim of the same type of misconceptions that he had used against the elder Bayh. Poetic justice one might suppose. In 1988, Bush 41 would reward Quayle for defeating Bayh.

Politicos are still baffled by the choice. Some believe that choice helped to get Clinton elected in 1992.

Algiers Banger absolutely loathed Bill and Hillary Clinton. President Clinton had benefited from an economy that was going through a quantum leap in the technology sector. Algiers knew that Clinton was a philanderer. Although Algiers did not approve of this sort of activity from the President of the United States, it was not that which caused bile to rise in his throat at the mention of Wild Bill's name. Algiers was a student of world history and understood the importance of international relationships. Algiers regaled his well-connected friends with stories of how Clinton practically armed the Chinese single-handedly and how China had unprecedented access to White Sands and our satellite technology. Banger always contended if China had not broken up like the USSR, the U.S. would have been reporting to the People's Republic.

Algiers considered Clinton a closet "socialist," an elitist and American Apologist, from one of the most unlikely places, Arkansas. He used to describe Clinton as a "floater" that you keep trying to flush, and the sucker just seems to come back to the top. His disgust for Hillary was just as visceral. When Hillary made her run for the Presidency, Algiers was inconsolable, contrary, and even maniacal. He poured money against her in as many organizations as he possibly could. He was fully expecting her to be the Democratic nominee, but to his surprise and extreme satisfaction, she pulled out failing to secure enough delegates and after internal polling showed she could not be elected. Algiers thought, *Clintons and their polls...if I could have somehow just "fixed" the polls a few times. I could have gotten the Clintons to invade China because they were performing abortions.* Finger in the wind politicians that had no backbone, always got Algiers' blood pressure up.

Chapter 4

When Parker announced that he would not seek another term it was a complete surprise to Algiers and Ross. It would not have been a problem had Lancaster Smith not resigned. Smith would have been a viable candidate for the next election. Then, Smith could have selected Mike Robertson as the new VP. Smith's resignation was a shock, and the Matriculation Project had to begin a quick regrouping. It was the fact that Parker put up very little fight to keep Smith that confounded Ross and Algiers. Shortly before his resignation, Parker cut off communication with Ross and Ben completely, and the Matriculation Project was left only to wonder what was happening. Parker announced that Illinois' Senator, Brett Swain would be his choice.

Popular with the congressional leaders, Swain was a complete departure from the fiscally conservative personality that Parker represented. Swain had his share of controversy, but he was a shrewd politician who had already shown he believed the end justifies the means. He definitely was a favorite of the media, which was dominated by the Left. He was as close to a moderate Democrat as a Republican could get and was generally regarded as soft on crime. It was even rumored he was tied to the Chicago Mob.

The challenge to have a candidate in place was now a long shot. With Swain the likely candidate from the Republicans, there was no chance that he would select Robertson. Maybe the next election would have to be written off, and the Matriculation Project would have to look at the next four-year term. It was possible that an existing Congressman or Senator could be backed in the right way, but the level of control would be practically zero. Ross and

Ben had discussed the problems that had manifested themselves. Of course, if the Matriculation Project ever became public knowledge, the repercussions would be very uncomfortable. The legacy of President Parker would be damaged beyond repair. Parker was not aware of all the support he gotten along the way, but no one would believe that he was not involved. Many would conclude that he knew and even planned the incidentals that needed to occur. Parker would never go public, but some of the candidates that had to be abandoned might be a risk. Smith was in political exile, but he knew to keep his mouth shut if he ever wanted to mount a comeback. Further, he was going to get fat and happy on the consulting tour. Following his resignation, Smith had sent a cryptic message to Algiers, thanking him for the political support and regretted his inability to make time for a personal meeting. Algiers had literally screamed, "What the hell does that mean?" and gave the command to get Smith on the phone or else. The phone call never came and the "or else" was never mentioned again.

Algiers Banger would pass away in his sleep two weeks after the swearing in of Swain as Vice-President. Banger had a bad heart, but Ross figured the Swain/Smith event proved to be the final slip of the grip. Other candidate failures also seemed to weigh heavily on the man who had accumulated billions in the finance industry. With a practically unlimited bank roll, Algiers had tried for years to influence politicians only to be disappointed time and time again by those that he thought had the backbone to make the tough choices. Parker had truly been a shining star, and Algiers considered the act of shepherding him into office one of his life's crowning achievements. At the end, even that victory had seemed to sour.

In Destin, Florida, looking out over a balcony in a rented villa in the San Destin Resort, Ross was marveling at Algiers' career and achievements. Algiers had always been quick to point out his shortcomings. He had accepted the failures of Karl Scott and Satch Mitchell, but he had taken the Parker incommunicado as a personal betrayal. Ross was amazed at how many people were not even aware that the man lived. There was virtually no one at his funeral. He had lived a life of prosperity and anonymity at the same time. He had been a recluse without the odd idiosyncrasies. To talk to him was a treat. Algiers told Ross not to give a bio for the paper. He just wanted to pass and go away, without any fanfare—and that is exactly what happened. How can a man worth billions in today's world just vanish without even an obituary to show for his life? Only Algiers could pull it off.

Since Ross was the executor of the estate, he was able to handle all the anonymous gifts and endowments. Several press people inquired, but they were put off when their calls were never returned. Many of the organizations were insistent that they knew who gave them several million dollars. Ross had explained that he would be able to tell them, but would need to rescind the gift. That deterred them from asking any more questions. It was actually easier for them. They did not have to name a building or street or a park after someone that they did not know.

Algiers had been a shrewd businessman who had considerable influence in his early life, but once he began to accumulate massive wealth, he began to withdraw. As a boy he grew up in an Austrian neighborhood and had witnessed the force that government could apply. He had seen boys, girls, women, and men killed with little regard to life. In some cases, it was the government doing the killing or those fighting for control over the streets. Algiers Banger had learned to kill as well. He grew up as a tough street-wise kid from a broken home. But, somehow he survived and made it to America. He cherished America and its freedom. He believed in the government and its rule of law. He was proud of the opportunities that America offered and even served a brief stint in the Army, but left after his enlistment concluded. Banger worked and earned a living. He started one business after another and each flourished, and his holdings became enormous. He invested in real estate as well as the stock market. This immigrant really had the Midas touch.

When Banger did not see something as fair, he worked to change it, but within the system of influence. He began to see the same corruption of government officials that he'd seen in his native land. In the name of protection of the people, the government was taking away right after right. He could see this inevitable evolution of the Federal government taking place. He gave large sums of money to candidates that he had individually met and talked to. He had agreements with them that were almost always reneged on once the person was past the election. Welfare reform, term limits, health care reform, Social Security reform, tax reform, political contribution reform, immigration reform, litigation reform, trade reform, debt reduction, balanced budget reform and on and on and on. Banger had seen politician after politician say whatever it took to get in, and then do whatever it took to stay in.

Banger sold all of his interests in the textile industry and pulled all of his holdings in a hundred different companies. It took Ross a full year to arrange all of his finances so that Algiers had punished everyone that he wanted to. Algiers Banger was a disillusioned and frustrated man. Ross was his lawyer and financial advisor for almost eight years and became his confidante. Ross had been working for a large investment law firm in the D.C. area when they met.

One day almost eight years ago, he walked out into the ornate lobby to borrow a pen from the receptionist/secretary. There was an elderly man out in the waiting area that appeared to be lost. He was dressed in tan Dickeys pants and a blue work shirt. His outfit had Sears written all over it.

"Who's this?" Ross quietly asked the receptionist.

She rolled her eyes and whispered, “He says he needs to talk to a financial advisor.”

“Did someone refer him to us?” Ross asked.

“I asked him that and he said he threw a dart at the yellow pages,” she said, slowly shaking her head.

Ross smiled. “Is someone helping him?”

Algiers looked up from across the room, apparently listening in on their conversation the whole time and said, “The answer to that is no, but I think you will do fine.”

Ross smiled at the thought of that meeting. What a pivotal day in his life that was!

Returning from his thoughts, Ross looked over at the clock on the side of the bed and went back inside the room off the patio deck. He reached in the refrigerator for a cold drink, but changed his mind. Instead, he closed the refrigerator and put some ice in a short glass. He picked up the decanter of Maker’s Mark and poured it over the ice. He took as sip and let the liquid warm his mouth then gave a little shiver as the bourbon crossed his tongue and he swallowed. Thoughts again began to race in his mind. *What had happened to make Parker turn so quickly?* He was not privy to the inner workings of the Matriculation Project. No one candidate had enough information to be able to put it all together. Ross thought his problem might lie in the failed candidates. Parker, of course, knew about Smith being part of the Matriculation Project and would have naturally figured that Robertson was as well. Parker and Smith would have discussed the Matriculation Project. It was too critical not to have been the subject of conversation. Had Robertson and Parker had contact after Robertson’s appointment by the Florida Governor?

Returning to the patio, Ross lit a pipe and sat in a padded deck chair. He blew a puff of smoke that was quickly dissipated by the coastal wind. He was really concentrating on the possibilities that had led to the apparent estrangement of Parker and the Matriculation Project. Could all this have a source that Ross had not thought about? Virginia's candidate for Lt Governor, Karl Scott, recognized that he'd made a mistake and gracefully bowed out, but maybe he knew more than he should.

Satch Mitchell, who had first denied psychological counseling, and then later admitted it, would not be taken seriously, plus his cleaning process had not been of any consequence. Anything that was done to smooth out his personal past had been accomplished without him being aware of it. Record cleaning had been minimal, and he did not have any skeletons in his closet—other than the psychological counseling, which of course turned out to be his undoing. Ross was not sure how they had missed it, but it was likely that the Satch had used a different name and thought that it would never see the light of day. Therefore, during the interview process, he decided to leave that detail out. He probably feared that his new-found friends, who were offering him a chance to move up the political ladder, might consider psychological counseling as a knock-out factor.

That was a tough lesson learned and would have to be accounted for with future candidates. Maybe a lie detector could be used. Prospects were not told of the full scope of the Matriculation Project or the extent of the help that was available. It just appeared to them that things were really going their way. Financing and positive acceptance usually would turn the crank of anyone looking to get into public office. The Candidates believed that they were doing much of the work themselves and that fate had finally swung to their side. Most would not be aware of how the problems of their past were going away. An indiscretion here or a minor arrest record there…just seemed to get cleaned up.

For Karl Scott, the cleaning was a little more complicated. It was discovered that Scott was involved with a young woman. Ross was fairly certain that Scott was aware that the woman was victim of an unsolved carjacking, but Scott did not attribute it to the Matriculation Project. He never gave the woman's name to the Matriculation Project and probably just chalked it up to good fortune. The Matriculation Project learned of the affair by virtue of having placed a listening device in Scott's office at his home. The affair was breaking up and as a payoff, Scott was arranging to have the woman set up with a new job. Upon finding out the identity of Scott's mistress, Marley was dispatched to eliminate the possibility of the story making it to the papers. The problem turned out that this would not be Scott's last dalliance. It was clear to Algiers and Ross that the "cleaning" of Mira Stephens had been unnecessary.

Despite being forced out of the race, Scott still considered himself to be quite fortunate. Even though his national political future was squashed, he'd managed to get a divorce that he'd probably wanted anyway. In addition, he did end up with a nice consulting job that paid him a comfortable salary. It was a job that he probably would like to keep. It was also common knowledge that the publicity surrounding Scott's infidelity and subsequent divorce had made him quite the popular guy in the highest social circles.

While any of the candidates could speculate in private about the Matriculation Project, anything of significance would be difficult to prove. However, Ross knew that in the public arena, proof was never needed for condemnation. The convincing evidence that Smith, Scott, Mitchell, or any of the others would need would be difficult to produce, but it would not stop speculation and inquiring minds if something were leaked. If one of them did know too much, Marley would need to go into action and quickly.

Robertson, on the other hand, had been a straight player and had little or no history that would have made a difference. If Bush 43 could survive the revelations of his early days, Robertson would have sailed through without much of a ripple.

There was a knock at the door, which interrupted Ross' ruminations. A hotel door card was being slipped into the lock. It was Ben Thomas carrying a flight bag of sorts, who already had beer in his free hand. Ross figured he must have stopped at the hotel bar on his way up.

Ross and Ben had to decide the most prudent direction for the Matriculation Project to proceed. Ben finished off the last of a sweating Heineken, tossed the empty into the trash can and joined Ross on the balcony.

"Maybe we can still get Robertson in," Ben said. "If he has a big issue that brings him to the forefront, maybe Swain would pick him. Swain is going to pick one of his cronies that will not overshadow him. He does not give a rat's ass about this country. He will reverse everything that Parker was able to do. How he ever got in, I will never know." Ross impatiently growled as his thoughts were rambling.

"Could Swain or somebody in his camp have found out about the Matriculation Project?" Ben said quietly.

Ross had been pondering that very idea. He looked out the window at a distant airplane that was circling the airport, waiting its turn to land at the nearby Egland Air Base. "You're thinking that somebody finds out and blackmails Parker into picking Swain. Why wouldn't Parker tell us? No, I think something happened with Smith and Parker. One of them found out something and panicked."

Both men were silent while in thought about the possibilities and the implication of those scenarios. They needed to find out. They needed to talk to Parker and Smith. They also needed to discuss the future of Dr. Will Oliver.

Chapter 5

Dr. Will Oliver had returned from lunch to the small faculty office in the back of the Economics Department of Wallen Community College. Wallen was located in the suburb of The Village of Indian Hill, which was just outside Cincinnati in a northeasterly direction. It was a short distance from Oliver's home in a nearby community called Blue Ash. Indian Hill was a tight-knit community that had luscious parks, country clubs, and a median house price of over half a million dollars. Legend has it that Indian Hill was named after an Indian horse thief who was shot on the run and found sometime later on a small farm atop a hill.

Oliver had become comfortable in the area. He lived in Blue Ash and traveled the short distance to Indian Hill each morning. Indian Hill was a city that was concerned about such things as sign proliferation and noise control at the monthly Council meeting. The predominantly White population of slightly over seven thousand was laid back in their approach to life. They had a quaint downtown area that had been relatively untouched by the normal overflow of a city the size of Cincinnati. Oliver liked the short commute from Blue Ash to his nearby college community. If the Village of Indian Hill was laid back, the city of Blue Ash was fully reclined.

Oliver had a comfortable teaching position in a college that lacked the competition that some schools regarded as healthy. He published out of intellectual curiosity rather than at the behest of the school. He made certain not to make a big deal of the articles that were published or the consulting that he was doing, so as not to create a problem. He liked the other professors and wanted to maintain that easy relationship. He had learned a while back to fly under the radar and attract as little attention as possible. He had turned down the position of Dean, which was offered up to anyone who would take it. The other professors had not wanted the additional duties either. He considered taking it, just to prevent the possibility of someone actually coming in there and messing up a good working relationship. The position had gone unfilled for almost a full term. No one seemed particularly concerned that it was not filled as the person that was there before had been in a sort of retired state for some time, working on a novel or some sort of literary pursuit with frequent long absences—presumably research trips. Will had the best sort of boss that one could have: non-existent.

Oliver was working on a report that was to put a price tag on government regulation in the beef industry. It was a brief that would be used by a lobbyist group hired by the American Beef Council in an effort to stem some of the negative public reaction to higher beef prices. The cost to producers of beef had nearly doubled because of the stringent government inspection process that was recently adopted. Each plant had to hire additional in-house inspectors that were required to have health training that was running into the thousands of dollars. Many said it was the price of doing business in the meat industry. The beef producers' cooperative was not in total disagreement with that statement, but felt they were getting nailed in public opinion because of the steep increase in the price of beef. All the Beef Council wanted was to present the case that these high prices did not translate into profits for the companies, but were going to offset the costs that were being dealt to them with increased regulation. If the public wanted to enforce extreme rules, the prices would have to reflect the increase in cost. Oliver was enlisted to prepare a report that would extrapolate the increased cost and translate it into the increases experienced in the grocery store by the little old ladies on a fixed income.

Oliver took the costs that were given to him and the recent grocery market figures and tried to make a reasonable correlation. He was able to determine that the increase in costs to the average processor was about six cents per pound. Cents did not sound significant enough, so it would have to be put in the proper perspective. The six cent figure would not be quoted. Six cents represented about a 22 percent increase in the cost of beef per pound that was the direct result of increased government requirements. Oliver would put in an editorial comment that would certainly be picked up by Scott Reyes, his contact with the group that was hired by the Beef Council. It would read: "This increase in government intervention into free enterprise in the name of public safety has caused a dramatic increase in the retail prices for beef and related products. These increases are the direct result of the extra requirement by the government of testing of processes in an industry that has been successfully regulating itself for over 60 years. No U.S. citizen has ever been infected with any of the diseases for which beef producers are now being required to inspect. Government requirements of training and inspection, while born of good intentions, have caused unnecessary suffering and deprived consumer of a free market." This sounded a bit exaggerated, so Oliver took out the last sentence and replaced it with, "If government agencies continue to require over-restrictive procedures in the testing of beef products, consumers may expect prices for beef and beef products to continue to increase dramatically."

Oliver had visited the National Cattlemen's Web site to get some of the particulars of testing that were available to the public as well. Beef must be inspected by a state inspector, or in the absence of state testing, it must be inspected by federal inspectors supervised by the U.S. Department of Agriculture. All of these additional inspections added costs to each pound of beef.

Oliver had previously been contracted to provide an outside opinion regarding the effect of government regulation. Each time he had become further convinced that many of the current economic problems that plagued this country were the direct result of government over-involvement. That is why his dissertation included a full chapter on the complications to the marketplace resulting from government regulation and the threat of litigation. Oliver wrote, "There are too many regulations and too much guardianship on the part of well-meaning politicians." He believed that the U.S. Government had no fiscal discipline, and no plan to develop any. It was full of politicians that were not even ashamed of a national debt that would have Bill Gates, of the now defunct Microsoft, blush.

Oliver specialized in uncovering the often unnoticed repercussions of laws and regulations. Unintended consequences of well-meant laws, taxes, and restrictions that some well-meaning soul dreamed up one day while coming to work in their diesel Mercedes or abroad on some political junket. Many laws and taxes were an effort to make a point about something or corral a group that seemed particularly offensive in some way. Someone had been offended by someone else or by something someone said. The politician sees it as an opportunity to make a statement. The whole hate crimes legislation was just political posturing about who could seem the most compassionate; the most likely to draw attention away from the fact that the very people promoting it were the most racist. All of it was public posturing for self-serving reasons. Oliver knew it to be true, but it was not a great strategy to call a spade a spade when it came to the Race Race.

The Race Race, was a term that Oliver had coined to describe the quickness that some politicians were likely to show when running to a potentially beneficial position regarding a race issue, or how fast they could run away from a possibly damaging race issue. Oliver thought to himself about the contradictions that existed in the U.S. political system and the media. President Parker had made a dent in the problem by insisting on sunset clauses on all new spending programs; but the battle had only begun, and Parker had named a liberal spending Swain as his replacement Vice-President.

His thought process was interrupted by the phone ringing. He wished that the school had caller ID. He could then feel good about not answering the phone. As it was now, all calls rang three times and then went to a mailbox. Many times Will had regretted answering the phone. Students usually did not call this number as Dr. Oliver gave them his cell phone number instead. He would rather give that out and caution them about trivial calls. Two rings. Three rings. He gave in and answered it.

"Dr. Oliver." The call had already forwarded to voice mail. He had that uneasy feeling that he should have answered it in time, but let the feeling pass and returned to his work. The phone rang again. *Okay, I get the point—someone is serious about talking to me*. Once again he answered, "Dr. Oliver."

A distant, but distinct voice with a slight New York accent said, "Yes, Dr Oliver, this is Thomas Ellerman. I am calling from Albany. I am the President of the N-PAC—Freedom Cause. I am not sure if you have ever heard of us, but we lobby Congressional Representatives to get them to try to downsize government."

"Yes, I think I've heard of you," Will lied. He could always say he was mistaken later. He scrambled for a pen to write the name down, but could not seem to find something—anything—to write with.

Mr. Ellerman continued knowing that Dr. Will Oliver could not possibly have heard of an organization that did not even exist. "Good, good. I was doing some research about the cost of legislation and your name came up in conversation. I was not even sure how to contact you, but I was able to 'noodle' your name from the Internet."

Oliver interjected an "I see" still looking for something to write with and trying to figure out if this guy was looking for a consultant or what?

Ellerman continued, "I was wondering if you have published any articles that I could review?"

"Well," Oliver said, "I have written quite a bit. Of course my dissertation involved the economics of government involvement in business in general, but that was just a part. Most of my work will not show up anywhere because I consult. The work often becomes proprietary. Does that make sense?"

"Yes of course." Mr. Ellerman stepped back in the conversation. "I would like to get some of your thoughts about the political process and your views on some current economic issues. Is there a time that I could come to you, say next week?" Without even waiting for an answer, Ellerman continued, "You see we are also interested in developing political talent as well as congregating a group of policy advisors. This advisory group would of course contribute in an anonymous way if necessary, but would have significant input to the direction this organization takes as well as candidates that it promotes."

Oliver had finally found something to write with and even though he had been listening carefully, he was now ready to give his full attention to this call. "I see, well that is interesting, and I would naturally be interested in meeting with you, but next week is not a good week because it is a mid-term week."

Mr. Ellerman shifted in his chair and looked over at the clock which had a calendar on it. "Dr. Oliver, I would really like to have one of our people interview you as soon as possible, but I don't want it to interfere with your work schedule. I tell you what, have you ever been to St. Thomas?"

"St. Thomas, Indiana, or Minnesota?" Oliver said.

"The Virgin Islands," Ellerman said as he smiled. "One of our directors is down there now and I would like you to meet with him. Could you free yourself up for the weekend?"

Will spun around in his chair and sat up. He was speechless. He took a sip of his coffee and set it down on his Dos Equis coaster. He began manipulating a pencil between his fingers faster and faster. It was a nervous habit.

"Well, I really could not just..." Will was interrupted by Ellerman.

"Dr. Oliver, I think that we have some common ground and some common goals. You could develop some good contacts and maybe gain a perspective of the potential of this organization. Our Assistant Director, Ben Thomas has given me the authority to make whatever arrangements are necessary in order to make this happen. I, unfortunately, am tied up until late next week, and you are busy as well. So I think that rather than put this off for a couple weeks, we could go ahead and get the process started this weekend. You could relax a little bit and also have the opportunity to give us some insight into your thinking about the cost of government."

Will hesitated.

"Dr. Oliver?" Ellerman said thinking, *come on now, St Thomas, Virgin Islands or Ohio—is it that tough of a choice?* Ellerman realized Oliver was being cautious, but he had to wait to see if there was at least some curiosity. There had to be curiosity.

Will was shaking his head in puzzlement and indecision. *Was this legit?* He finally said, "Let me check with my schedule and give you a call back later this afternoon."

"Dr. Oliver, I will need to go ahead and make the flight arrangements. We could cancel them if you are unable to work it out. Would a Friday night flight or Saturday morning flight work better?"

"Well, Saturday would work, and the return would be when? No, no—Friday would be better. No—better make it Saturday morning."

"Saturday morning it is. We could get you out Sunday late afternoon or Monday morning."

"Sunday, I think I had better get back," Will said shaking his head at the thought of making a trip to the Virgin Islands.

"We will use Delta. The tickets will be available at the counter. We will have a driver at the airport to take you to your hotel," Ellerman said. "With your permission, I will advance you some expense money. All I need will be a confirmation that you are going. I will make all the other arrangements."

Ellerman, otherwise known as Ben Thomas, smiled at the result. Who could turn down a quick, free trip to the Virgin Islands?

Chapter 6

From the restaurant overlooking Cowpet Bay, the setting sun could be seen as it just began to sink into the horizon. The colors were magnificent. The water was a light blue that captured anyone's vision. The temperature had begun to drop to a comfortable 70 degrees, and most patrons were dressed casually in island colors appropriate to St. Thomas.

Formal introductions had already taken place between the two men. Ben Thomas and Will Oliver were seated toward the back of the terrace eating area. Robert's, a restaurant and bar, was classy for an island that made a living out of being relaxed. The owner/operator was an extremely thin man who wore a shirt that said: "When it comes to good food, ask the skinny man." Robert's had an outstanding wine list and served a variety of American style cuisine. A black man came around the bar and greeted them. He had a big smile and a personality that matched his large size. He introduced himself as Paige, took their drink order and handed them a menu. Will looked out onto the water and thought that one could just sit there for hours looking out over the scenery. The sailboats were anchored out in the placid bay. A few tourists lingered in the water trying to get a last few minutes of snorkeling in before the sun finally set. They seemed to congregate over toward a bend in the beach that was lined with black volcanic rock. Evidently the fish all gathered there.

"The plane ride was not too bad I hope," Ben Thomas commented.

"No, not bad at all. I did have my doubts when the guy was landing the plane though. I could see nothing but water and we were dropping fast. I thought we were going to land in the ocean when at the last second we hit the runway," Will said, smiling.

"I think the pilots really enjoy doing that."

"This is a great place and it is nice to be away from the real world for a while."

"This is one of the best restaurants on the island. But really, there is not a bad view and most of the restaurants serve very good food. Service sometimes is a bit obligatory, but it is okay. Some of the other islands are really worth visiting. I think my favorite is Antigua." Ben seemed lost in thought for a moment and then just snapped out of it and said, "Dr. Oliver, I hope you…"

"Please call me Will."

"Surely," and Ben started again. "Will, I hope you won't mind that I get to the heart of the purpose of our meeting."

"Not at all, I am very curious," said Will as he took a sip of an Elephante dark ale from a tankard that had been expertly iced before serving.

Ben continued, "I am part of an organization that takes a keen interest in the political process. We have been purposely recruiting candidates for various elected positions. We are interested in people that understand the critical condition of our government. We see the U.S. as the greatest country in the world, but a country that has slipped because the political process has failed to produce candidates for public office that understand the constitution or don't have the backbone to stand by the founders' original intent. It is amazing how people can run for office and then once elected, simply do what is expedient in order to be re-elected. We originally tried the customary efforts of lobbying. That worked to some degree, but we felt that the candidates that were running were too engrained in Beltway politics to make any substantive changes. We were continually being let down when it came to critical votes and really felt that we had to get in the race at an earlier level. So, now we are trying to identify individuals who have the values and convictions that would make good candidates for public office. We have the financial resources that allow us to get behind an individual who we feel is a fit candidate and strategically promote them in races that we feel can be won. Our organization is seeking those people that have the qualifications to be elected and have a good command of what the government is supposed to do. You were identified as a person that we wanted to consult with in our recruiting process. You have a solid academic preparation, and you would likely be helpful in screening candidates for us as well as coaching potential candidates." Ben then took a drink from his Heineken. He waited to see what Will's response would be.

"Sounds like a grass roots type of effort," Will said contemplatively.

"Yes; 'grass roots' is the appearance that we would like to maintain," Ben smiled broadly as he said it. "Unfortunately, we have found that a true candidate from the grass roots does not stand much of a chance. So we have had to find a way to sow some of those candidates. Well, it might be better stated as saying we have to fertilize the grounds in order to get some of these qualified candidates in a position to be elected. We believe that there are many people out there that are good prospects for public service, but because the political parties are so entrenched in our system, they are not elected. Really, they never have the opportunity to even run."

"Again, this sounds like a noble cause. How has it gone so far?" Will took another pull on his ale. He accepted Paige's signal for another beer and gave the bartender a thumbs up.

"We have had some successes," Ben said, aware of the need to handle this just right. He did not want Will to have too much information too soon. "Some of the people that we identified seem to have good potential. Obviously, we try to screen those that are considered as candidates very carefully. We do exhaustive background checks and each person goes through extensive interviewing. We try to identify potential problems before we ever begin the promotion process. The problem with political unknowns is that there may be some baggage that rules them out. In some cases, we have been able to take rather obscure politicians and once they are identified as someone we want to back, they can be successfully guided to move along faster," Ben said as he settled back in his chair. He studied Will and allowed him the opportunity to express his thoughts. *Was he even mildly interested in their operations?* He was not giving a lot away in his expressions, but did seem to be thoughtful.

"So you are asking me to help in the selection process and help coach those that you have already selected?"

"Well, yes, possibly. We wanted to gauge your interest in something like this and see where you might fit in. That could be, depending on your initial impressions, in a variety of roles. You were identified as having the right ideas and the ability to express those views," Ben continued while casually evaluating Will's body language and reactions.

They ordered food. Both chose the fresh catch of the day—tilapia, blackened and grilled with sides of grilled squash, mushrooms and carrots.

Finally, Will ventured with the question that had been on his mind since receiving his initial phone call. "How exactly did my name come out of the heap?"

"You delivered a speech a few weeks ago to a Rotary luncheon," Ben said without hesitation. He figured the truth was the best approach. He did not need to mention that he was the one that heard his talk. That might bring up questions about why he was in Cincinnati. That was not a good line of questions for Ben to have to answer.

"You're kidding," Will said with his mouth slightly agape and his eye growing wide in disbelief and surprise.

"No, it is the truth. Our director received a report that you delivered a cogent and well prepared talk that was well received by a group of businessmen," Ben said carefully not to implicate himself. "From there, a search of publications revealed a consistent, well thought out and fiscally conservative view that we look for in our people."

"I am amazed. I guess you never really know who is listening. I am flattered…" Will stuttered and was shaking his head slowly, "and…shocked."

"My question is, do you believe what you are saying and are you willing to do something about it?" Ben asked as he leaned forward. He did not want to spook him, but wanted to see if this man had the balls that a run for office would take. Dr. Oliver could be the type that felt very safe preaching from the pulpit, but did not have the intestinal fortitude to actually run for office. The best scenario for Ben would be for Will to say, "hell, yes" he believed what he said. Ben was bringing him along slowly. He wanted to interest him in a consulting job, but then ideally have Will say that he had given thought to running himself.

"I absolutely believe what I write and what I say," Will said, not defensively, but rather as a matter of fact statement—and maybe with a hint of indignation.

Ben's gaze narrowed and he asked, "So what part do you see yourself playing in this?"

The silence at their table was complete. The rest of the restaurant carried on with the usual activity of a tropical dinner. The piano man was playing in the corner. Laughing and murmurs of conversations could be heard throughout the eatery. But at Will and Ben's table, the question brought the conversation to a halt. Will was contemplating his answer, and Ben was awaiting the reaction to his question. Ben knew that he had really shared very little and was asking the question just to get a clue as to what Will was thinking. How would he handle a direct question?

Comfortable with the silence, Ben waited.

Finally, Will was ready to answer, "Well I really don't have very much information, but as you describe the goals of the organization, the prospect of working with you is intriguing. I have often thought of running for office myself, but did not really feel that getting into the system was worth it. I hate asking people for money. So I figure I might be better use to your organization as some type of consultant."

"I think we should examine this from both sides: the candidate side and the consultant side," Ben was masking his excitement well. This is exactly the response that he had hoped for. He then continued, "If you were to run for office, have you scouted out potential offices?"

The conversation went on throughout dinner and a light desert of Key Lime pie. By the end of the evening Will was excited and feeling very little pain. Paige was only too happy to oblige Ben as he continued to order drinks. Will seemed to handle his liquor well, maybe from practice; but even then, Ben thought this to be a good sign. Everything he said seemed to be from the heart and honest. At 10:30pm, Ben paid the tab, giving Paige a nice tip and called for an end to the evening. The two of them agreed on a meeting place for breakfast the next morning and headed off in the direction of their rooms. When Ben got back in his room, he pulled out his cell phone and called Ross Saunders.

Chapter 7

Will received an 8:00am wake-up call on Sunday morning. He thought to himself that he was glad that he had requested a wake-up call because he was sleeping very soundly and probably would have slept another hour, thus making a poor impression on Ben by missing breakfast. He did have quite a bit to drink the night before, but he thought that he'd held his own. Ben Thomas had been more sloshed than he had been; he was sure of that. He mentally patted himself on the back for coming straight back to the hotel and going to bed. He had been tempted to scout out some of the island. He had never been to the Caribbean before and was interested in exploring it. He wanted to go over to St. John or St. Croix. He'd read up on the Islands on his flight over and found out that St. Croix had a casino that was recommended. He was not sure what Ben might think about him showing an interest in gambling, so would just see how it played out. Trying out his luck at the craps table might be a possibility if his afternoon somehow freed up. He showered and dressed, and decided casual would be appropriate—and he was right.

The beautiful island was casual for sure. Shorts and sandals would have fitted in quite nicely, if Will had a pair of shorts and sandals. He had packed quickly and only had a pair of light Dockers. The two met in the lobby of the Black Beard Hotel and went around the corner to a nice little restaurant that served fresh fruit and pastries, scrambled eggs and grapefruit juice. Ben served himself from the family-type platter of fruit that the waitress placed on their table. He also ordered a blend of orange juice and champagne that arrived in a carafe filled with crushed ice, orange slices, and maraschino cherries.

"You have had a chance now to sleep on our discussion, so what questions do you have?" Ben asked matter-of-factly.

"Well," said Will, "You mentioned that your organization has moderate success; can you be more specific?"

"Not too specific, but yes I can give you some non-descript successes. For instance, we have helped several individuals rise through the ranks. I can be more specific, once I feel comfortable I understand your intentions," Ben said.

He was starting to regret that he had lured Will in with the premise that he might be a consultant, as this opened up a bunch more of the need to know file. He was not completely sure how deep into this he wanted to go without Will's "buying in." He thought Will was very intrigued and probably ready to roll, but he needed a little more of an assurance.

"Will, I need to know how far to bring you in to this. Some of what I could tell you is confidential. Not because it is illegal," Ben said, then thought to himself, *although some of it has been*, "but because if the press or the Democrats or the Republicans, for that matter, get a hold on this information, it would not look good for those that have been promoted, by legal means, but nevertheless helped along by our organization and financial assistance. To many, it would raise suspicions about election fraud or meddling of special interest groups. It could be interpreted by some as the very wealthy using some type of subterfuge in order to get their person elected. Do you understand my caution?" Ben dabbed at his lower lip with his napkin and replaced it in his lap.

Will looked directly at him and cocked his head to the left. "Ben, you asked me here. By the way the hotel is beautiful and the food has been great." He paused and gathered his thoughts. Will did not want to come across as flippant or cocky. "You are asking me to join something that I have no previous experience with or knowledge of. It sounds great to be involved in a political campaign, but when you talk about subterfuge or being interpreted the wrong way, I just wonder what I am getting myself into. I would need to have an idea of the scope of this project in order to be of any use. But you intimate that you cannot tell me, because I have to commit before you can tell me. We seem to be in a Catch-22 situation here."

"Not really," said Ben. "The confusion is my fault. This is what I am looking at. I think you have good possibilities as a candidate we would like to pursue that. I can tell you that we have excellent backing and resources. If you are interested we would bring you in for interviews and strategize about what path to take."

Will shifted in his chair and asked. "What type of elections are we talking about?"

Ben took a sip of coffee, grimaced and reached for the sugar bowl. Digging in with his tea spoon, he shoveled a couple spoonfuls of sugar into his coffee.

"That sort of depends on you, Will. How high can you go? It is our desire to promote individuals that can have a positive impact in the United States. That requires that you be in a position where you have influence." Ben saw that Will's face had a serious look of disbelief. "It cannot happen overnight. In fact it takes several years and several elections. Sometimes it works and sometimes we might strike out. We are looking for the right people and believe that you could be successful," Ben continued.

"I am interested," Will said. "Actually running for office—I have never done it. I would not even know how to file. I have not really looked at any elections."

Will's mind was running from one topic to another. Ben saw a side of Dr. Will Oliver that he did not like for the first time. He thought to himself that when it came time for decisions, Will's ability to remain calm and handle ambiguity might get him in trouble. This would be something that would have to be worked on.

"Will, our organization can help you with all of that. We think we can be, better said, I think *you* can be successful. Do you want to move forward with this?" Ben watched him closely, trying to figure out what he was thinking. Will was obviously was thinking voraciously. Dozens of questions must be swirling around in his head. Ben hoped that was what the silence was about and not that Will was in doubt. Ben decided to give him a nudge. "You seem to grasp the significance of our organization and its influence. What are you thinking?"

Will refocused his gaze on Ben. "I am not sure what to say."

Ben stepped in. "I say we move forward. We will need to do some tests before we take the next step, which would be to actually scout possible elections. Our testing process will help you determine if you have some areas of weakness that need to be worked on or even could be knock out factors."

Will looked through Ben with an intense stare. Ben, though not intimidated, thought to himself, *now this is the type of look that we are after.*

"What type of tests?" Will said without breaking his eye contact.

"Some intellectual tests, some knowledge tests, and a background test," Ben said with a reassuring tone. "Nothing to worry about. We could get you started and finished in half a day."

Will then questioned, "And these tests will determine if I am a good candidate?"

"Exactly. All you have to do is be yourself and the rest is done for you. With your permission, I am going to get started making the arrangements. You will be contacted next week by one of our people. He will set an acceptable time and place."

Will was thinking about all of this and he nodded his head in agreement.

Ben continued, "Your flight out tonight is at 9:00pm. You

have the rest of the day to be a tourist if you like. I hear St. Croix is accessible by ferry and has some nice casinos." Ben paused, and said, "if you are of the gambling persuasion. I will be in touch when you get back to the mainland."

Will was almost dizzy when he arrived back at his hotel. This was like a freaking dream. Was all this for real? It was surreal. *Oh my God, who am I dealing with?* Will was moving in to high anxiety mode. He was in fact a calm, fairly even keeled man, who was not easily shaken. But now..."Wow," he said aloud again.

He went to the refrigerator and pulled out a Dos Equis. He pulled out drawers of the white cabinets until he found an opener and popped open the top. The beer was missing the obligatory lime, but Will slugged half of it down with one long gulp. He finished the beer in another long drink. He looked over at the clock. He thought to himself, *I just polished off a beer and it is not even 10:30 in the morning. How did the hotel have a six pack of my favorite beer in the refrigerator?*

Everything was just crazy. He sat for a moment on the bed. He reached for his laptop by the lime green writing desk accented with paintings of a tropical flower. He stopped for a moment. That seemed strange. A boarding stub was lying just behind the leg of the desk. Will reached behind the leg and picked it up. It was his stub from the connection flight out of Cincinnati. He was sure it had been in his wallet. Will thought to himself, I should not have left my wallet out in the open like that. Had the maid gone through his wallet? He quickly opened it and saw that all his cash was still there. He had taken out $200 from the ATM at the airport before his flight. He checked again for credit cards. Yes, they were all there. Maybe he had just accidentally dropped it. No—he had not gone into his wallet. He looked around for anything else that was out of place. His appointment book was where he left it on top of the desk. He was not sure if it had been moved. The room had been cleaned, the bed was made and the bathroom freshened up. He furrowed his brow and shook his head slightly in puzzlement. He momentarily put his quandary aside and pulled out his laptop and began accessing the Internet.

The cell phone rang and Will just about jumped through the ceiling. He admonished himself for being so skittish. It was his mother just checking in with him. He gave her the usual information, leaving out the fact that he was in St. Thomas. That would bring up just too many questions. After finishing the conversation with his mother, he returned to his previous line of thought.

The stub was inside the folded wallet. The maid probably knocked over the wallet and the stub slipped out and behind the leg of the desk. The maid probably did not even realize that something had come out, because you could only see it from the angle that he had been sitting on the bed. He thought back to breakfast. *What an unbelievable meeting that was.*

"Wow," Will said aloud.

He was feeling lucky and grabbed his coat. He tracked down the concierge, who flagged a cabbie for him and then he was on his way to the ferry and heading for the Divi Resort and Casino on the island of St. Croix. Will felt his luck had taken a turn for the better. He was confident and it showed. After two hours at the craps table, he extended his $200 in to a nice take-home of $650 dollars. Yeah, things were looking up.

Chapter 8

Will had been back on campus for a full week and had not heard even the slightest sound of moving forward with the candidate testing. He decided to ride his motorcycle in from Blue Ash. He was still learning to ride and considered himself a danger on the road to himself and others. He had to set the bike down one time when taking a corner. Fortunately, the bike, a three–year-old Honda Gold Wing, suffered only a little scrape. He liked riding the bike; it gave him a chance to think about all that had happened. He decided that he was a bit uncomfortable about the prospect of actually running for office. He was not sure if it was just fear or something that his intuition was telling him to run from. It really could just be the fact that he had grown accustomed to having a low risk existence. His ventures into speaking were not new for him, but did allow him to talk the talk without having to walk the walk. He often offered up a voluntary admission that it was easy for him to be a thousand miles away and giving all the advice but taking no responsibility for the outcome. He remembered one time that he gave a talk in which he offered up several tips on parenting. He figured that the audience, primarily middle aged couples were too polite to point out the fact that he did not have children and should not be giving parenting advice. He had only occasionally been in the hot spot where others were looking at him and telling how it should have been. He remembered calling someone on that very thing. It was easy to make predictions without any fear of someone actually doing what you are saying.

Will pulled in to the parking lot at the university and parked easily in a motorcycle designated area. Everyone was in the early classes by the time he walked inside, so he was not interrupted once. He went to his office and sat behind his desk, figuring he'd have peace for about the next 30 minutes before the classes finished.

His mind returned to his previous thought. The experts were not in positions of accountability nor would they ever have to actually make the tough decision. They would not have to face the wrath of the public or have their livelihood hang in the balance over a decision. Will thought of all those talking heads on the sports shows and how cocky they were. The coach should do this or that. The coach should be fired. The political official should do this or that. Will was often tempted to call in and start criticizing the host and saying how the host should be fired. All those pretend experts were annoying. Anybody that had an opinion and a way to get on the radio or television was an expert. He noticed that the real professionals seldom made comments about what someone else should do, but rather related the situation to something that happened in their own experience. Seldom outrageous, the real professional did not have to prove himself by showing how smart he was. Occasionally, Will had caught himself trying to sound too smart or be too insightful.

He realized that it just showed a lack of self confidence. Oliver's phrase, the Expert's Peril is the only thing that holds back the so-called experts. It is the possibility that someone might put the expert in charge and hold him responsible for what actually happens. If there is little or no chance of the expert being put in charge, the comments can be outrageous or even ridiculous, because no one is actually going to do what the expert recommends. Sometimes the advice or criticism is right on, but impractical when you find out the real consequences. Consultants are usually anxious to go into some company and have all sorts of ideas about what is wrong and what should be done. Then they leave. How many of the so-called experts ever go into coaching or politics. Oliver thought it was the equivalent of telling an astronaut how to pilot a rocket ship, knowing there is no chance of anyone asking you to do it. Oliver realized he could mull this over forever, but he really needed to grade papers and get his finals ready. He had to forget about running for office and St. Thomas and all of that. He needed to focus.

Just as he turned his attention to his work, there was a knock at the door. The sudden rap caused Oliver to jump in his seat. It was one of his students. Oliver sighed as the student came in and then smiled. The student needed a clarification on the final and quickly moved on to his next stop, wherever that was. Oliver thought to himself that he really had a good job with good students. He experienced very few problems. He taught three classes during the week and they were all classes that he enjoyed, which was not always the case for some professors. He basically taught just a few hours out of the day, and with the exception of a meeting here and there, had tremendous freedom to do whatever he wanted. He had vacations along with the students and had very little, if any, administrative responsibilities. He made just over $100,000 per year and he thought that was good for the most part. Of course $100 grand would not buy what it used to. He lived in a nice house that had been remodeled recently and drove a nice car. He once had a beautiful wife –deceased and three children that were out of the house and on their own. Should he give up his very safe and comfortable life for politics? It was a silly question, because he knew what the safe answer was and knew what he was going to do. He would march toward the unknown with trepidation, but would accept the job as he had always done. *No, Will Oliver did not look for a fight, but would not walk away from one either.*

He had been taught well to rise to the occasion, to fight the good fight and all those other clichés that had been lathed on in athletics and by others that were trying to get him to step out of his usually calm persona. People seemed to be puzzled by Will's potential and his seeming contentment with being a college professor. He was a college professor at a small community college that only attracted those with mediocre talent and few aspirations. Will had always told himself that he had been put where he was by design. He was a big believer in destiny. He was responsible for lighting the fire of students that would not ordinarily pursue anything with passion. And he did. Students seemed to appreciate him and even occasionally send him a nice note thanking him for his instruction or encouragement. He received very good reviews from his students.

He did enjoy teaching and even looked forward to starting new classes and was flattered when students signed up for his classes because they wanted to rather than because they had to. Oliver used his consultant business to have an outlet. He had always had some type of distraction from his main job. He had always written or coached or taught on the side. He thought it was smart to have several sources of income, but the reality was that he was unable or unwilling to give anything 100 percent of his effort. Maybe he just needed a release or a distraction. But it may be that release which caused him to not be a star among stars. He preferred being a medium fish in a small pond. He would rather excel with low expectations than to really take the chance of stepping into the big game. That bothered Will and he struggled with the idea of not living up to his potential. He knew people talked about it. He again wondered if Ben Thomas had decided that he was not a good candidate after all. That would probably be the best anyway. But the thought of being rejected was an insult. It seemed to work that way, didn't it? You wanted to be considered and even though you were not sure it was something you wanted to do, you certainly did not want to be turned down. Still, being turned down would eliminate the need to make a decision.

Some would say that he was hard to get to know. He

understood that he was not the most flamboyant person—his wife was the gregarious one. She had truly been his better half, but she was taken away. Will had not even thought about dating or getting married again; he did not have the need. And now, this strange opportunity presented itself. Could it be for real? He never considered himself lucky, but he had been fortunate.

Will thought about his cluttered past list of jobs. Would that be a negative for a political candidate? He thought about all the crazy stuff he did in high school. The brushes with the law had never been serious. He had been taken in a few times, but had never been officially arrested. He had a couple friends that had not survived their high school days unscathed. One had applied for law school, but was rejected because of one early morning drunk and disorderly charge. He was now a manager of a large chain restaurant. Will thought about the many times that he had been drunk and disorderly. Some would say downright criminal—certainly a mischievous juvenile delinquent would be an apt description. Would someone, somewhere, remember him as a partier or hell raiser? He had certainly been that, but it all seemed so harmless at the time. He came out of it all right it seemed. But now, could that be a negative or even a knock out factor?

Will's heart sank for a minute as he flashed back to a couple other skeletons in his closet. Oh man, he thought, *what about some of my other indiscretions?* Will had forgotten about some of the girls and even worse, he had in fact... Will's stomach curled, he could not even bring himself to think about that. No, he would not even acknowledge it. He would lie until his death. But what if one of those... He again cursed his youth. He could not get around the fact that he had screwed women. That would not likely be held against him, but the two "experiments" with his friends would be another story entirely. His friends would not say anything. They never had. Both of them had married and had kids. It was not like he was gay. It was just innocent youthful experimenting. Will thought that most people had done some of that. All the health books talked about it. Would Ben Thomas' testing uncover that bit of history? That was years and years ago. Surely, getting married and having a family superseded that. If it came out, the public embarrassment for his family would be unbearable. What about the girls that he had screwed? Would they all be coming forward to tell all, to some gossip magazine? He thought back; how many were there? He mentally went through his first sexual experience. He wondered where Deborah was. Did she have a family? *What if I have illegitimate children?* he thought to himself. Will was beginning to have one of those panic attacks.

Will started making a list of the girls. It seemed paltry at first, and he was glad. But then he remembered one and then another and another. There was high school and college and before marriage. And then Will's stomach turned over. His thoughts returned to his two friends Sean Henry and Mark Collins. How would he ever explain that? He couldn't. It could never come up. The thought of their shame made him nauseous. He was not going to let it happen. Maybe he should call Sean and Mark to feel them out about his running for office and just mention his concern. That might just bring it up all over again. They would be too embarrassed to bring it up. But, what if it just slipped out? Will thought about that and truly felt sick. What would his kids think? Was it sexual experimentation? He could have only been about twelve or so. Then, Sean and Will enlisted Mark into their sick little adventure. He could just see it now in the Enquirer headlines "State Senator Admits Homosexual Encounter as a Youth." *Yeah that would go over real well with a conservative constituency,* Will thought.

One of his peripheral friends, Jack, asked him one time if he was gay. Will did not have to act shocked. He genuinely was shocked that the kid asked and wondered what was being said. Jack was not around anymore; Will found out years later that he had killed himself. It was a really weird deal and still confounded Will to this day. No, this could not come out—he would just decline after further review. He needed to bow out of this whole deal gracefully, so he'd decided to tell Ben or whoever calls, that he was flattered, but not interested.

Just then the phone rang and caused Will to knock over the pencil stand near the phone.

"Dr. Oliver," Will said as he answered the phone.

The voice on the other end sounded so clear it was as if they were standing next to him. Will was given instructions on where to go for his testing. He asked to speak to Ben Thomas, but the person was either unsure of Ben's whereabouts or was not willing to give that information out. He apologized and said that he was only told to give Will directions. Will figured that he could talk to Ben when he took the tests.

Following his last final on a Thursday, Will headed out for Columbus. When he arrived at the appointed place and time, he was met by an elderly man in a white doctor's coat. Dr. Redding had a medium build and looked quite unassuming. He offered his hand and invited Will to come in the back of the modestly apportioned offices. Will asked the doctor if Ben was going to be part of the questioning.

He replied that he did not expect to see Mr. Thomas. "He does not take part in this. He will only get the results," Dr. Redding answered.

Will expressed his reluctance to go on with the testing and asked about other "candidates" that had been tested. Dr. Redding was rather forthcoming. He reassured Will this entire process was completely and absolutely confidential. This was done in order to find out about strengths and weaknesses of candidates. He described a couple of the others without giving their names. He told about some of the problems that were encountered and said those problems were evaluated. Many could be handled and others were not viewed as a problem. He was very confidant that if Will's answers were honest and forthright, it would be to everyone's benefit. He told Will about the candidate that had left out the fact that he had received psychological counseling several years earlier and how that had derailed his political career.

Dr. Redding unexpectedly looked directly at Will and said, "Dr. Oliver, are you worried about things that are in your past?"

Will blushed and felt like room was closing in on him. He was tempted to get up and walk out. He recovered and said, "We all have done things that we are not particularly eager to talk about. What I am concerned about is that I don't know you. I am not sure that I should be going through this process. There are a couple things that I don't want to share with anybody—as I am sure you understand."

Dr. Redding's demeanor had already changed back into the friendly doctor with a sensitive bedside manner. "You are exactly right. And what we are here to do today is in no way meant to embarrass you. We are trying to find out about your background so that we can determine whether there are knock out factors or just inconvenient facts that can be dealt with. If you have some past experiences that concern you, we can tell you whether you should be concerned." Will hesitated. He was really unsure. He did not want to talk about his private life and yet he knew that it would inevitably come out.

"Dr. Oliver, the most basic question is: Can you see yourself being a U.S. Senator or State Representative? Do you have ideas that will help the nation?" Dr. Redding paused, waiting for an answer.

"Yes," Will exhaled.

"Good. Let's start with the basics. Have you ever been convicted of a crime?" Dr. Redding asked in an emotionless tone.

The questions covered every possible area and started with

early childhood and worked toward present day. Where were you born and where have you lived? Where were your parents from? How many siblings do you have? What schools did you attend and what activities did you participate in? Who were your friends and who did you date? When was your last speeding ticket? Did you have any affairs while married? Have your kids been in any trouble? Have other members of your family been in trouble with the law, with the IRS or any other governmental agency? Have you ever filed for bankruptcy or defaulted on a loan? What kind of grades did you make? What colleges did you attend? What degrees do you hold? What jobs have you held? Have you ever been fired or laid off? Who are your current friends? How did your wife die? What was your reaction? Have you ever had any psychological counseling? Will answered one question right after another, for a solid two hours. He did his best to answer, which was strange because he had intended to just go in, thank Ben for considering him, and then politely decline. But when he got to Columbus, he realized that he actually did want to try running for office.

He had been in that office for almost an entire day. He had been hooked up to machines and taken written tests. He even had a short nap in order to clear his mind. Despite the intensity of the tests he felt invigorated, and even felt good about his answers. He felt reassured when he asked about previous candidates and their problems.

*****

"Ross, I just got word on Oliver. Appears to be a small bump," said Ben.

Ross leaned back in his chair and braced for the bad news. Every time there had been a problem in the past, it meant taking risks. He would have preferred that Oliver's past had been clear, but some cleaning was inevitable. If Ross were the candidate, he knew that his past would have required some cleaning. Now that Ross thought about it, he would have to have a sterilization crew.

Ben continued, "He's good on the credit stuff. We pulled his driving record using his license number and Social Security Card that we got in St. Thomas."

"All right; how does the rest look? Is it doable?" Ross said softly.

"Doable, certainly; we have two possible collaterals. Everything else was standard encounter stuff."

Ross started to scratch down some notes, but thought better of it and asked "How messy is it?"

"Just a coming of age deal, but it was on the wrong side of the fence."

"Oh," Ross said with concern. He then followed up with, "But it has not shown up again?"

"That's right. He had several pre-marital experiences with women, married and had children. He's not aware of any illegitimates. We got all the names of former partners and we will do a spook run on each. His kids are grown and he is a widower. Looks like he collected a nice insurance policy on his wife, but he split that among himself and the three kids. He paid off all of his credit and he makes a decent salary. He invests a lot of what he makes, probably has a net worth of about $250,000. Not much of it is liquid. He did pull a loan not too long ago to pay for one of his kid's college loans."

Ross leaned forward in his chair and placed his elbows on his knees as he listened. "What about his kids?"

Ben checked his notes and said. "Each one is self sufficient and married. They appear to be all-American. I think Oliver did a good job raising them."

"Do a background on each of them as well. Ok; what else?" Ross asked, while thinking through the next set of steps.

"Everything else looks really good. His health is very good.

He looks young and speaks well. He's got a good education and seems to be liked by his co-workers. He is not overly ambitious. We may have to keep someone close to him when he gets elected. Someone like Todd Reasons would keep him focused and look out for him."

"Yeah definitely Todd, but I would like a person a little closer."

Ben completely understood and said, "We could probably move Kay Moore out of Robertson's campaign for a while. I'll take care of that. Also, we have an election for him next fall. It is a State Senator's race. It's a good shot. The incumbent is retiring and there are several that will want the position. No one person has any real claim to the office. We can get some of his stuff published and leak that he is a dark horse. We can do it through an editor that we have worked with before in Columbus. We have set up an exploratory account for Will with about $35,000 in it. It will show a variety of donors, just in case. But it is not likely that it will ever be an issue. We will get him some clothes and start arranging for him to get invited to the usual events."

"Sounds like you're ready to go. Have you apprised Marley of your shopping list?" Ross asked.

"I was waiting for your go ahead. It is possible that these two would never show up. However, if they are going to be tidied up, we won't want the two events to be too close to each other," Ben said.

"And totally unrelated," Ross interjected. "Let's turn him loose on one of them. We will wait for next fall for the second. We need to get that done before the press has too long to look into his past. For a State Senator's race he won't get too much scrutiny."

Chapter 9

It had only been nine months since he had met with Ben, but what a nine months it had been. Will was looking at his calendar and trying to figure out how he was going to arrange his classes so that he could keep his teaching position and run for State Senator at the same time. He had been amazed at how fast Ben had been able to get the ball rolling. Will had filed as a candidate and set up an office from which to run the campaign. The funding had come from an account that Ben had set up to cover the basic expenses. Since Will had committed to run, things seemed to have turned 180 degrees.

Initially the university administration was not sure about his decision, but eventually decided that a State Senator could be in the best interests of the university. The students heard that Will was running and he was an immediate celebrity. The race was still a couple months away, but the excitement was effervescing. Will received a least a dozen invitations to social events and just as many requests for speaking appearances including the Kiwanis, the Rotary Club, the Methodist Women, and the Local VFW. Will knew that he could not have possibly done all this without the help of the Freedom Organization. They had fronted the money for campaign flyers that were about to be mailed to every registered voter that could vote in the senate election. He had signed the lease for the building that would serve as his campaign headquarters, but the money was coming from the account that Ben had set up. The last time he checked, another $15,000 had been deposited in the account. Ben told Will to make sure that he did not take money out of the account for personal purchases, but if he needed cash he just had to let him know. Will was actually fairly flush as one of the books that he had authored two years ago had been adopted by some northwestern university for a required economics class. The sales had rocketed up to around 500 copies. Not exactly a best seller, but the book company had taken notice and sent his royalties as well as a fresh advance for another book. He had also received a consultant's fee of $4400 for his work for Scott Reyes of the Cattleman's Association. That was about $2000 more than their contract stated. Will made a note to call Reyes to ask what was up with that. He had since forgotten to make the call.

Will's expenses had dropped dramatically in the last few years with all of the kids growing up and finishing up college. He had received well-wishes from all three of his children, and his mother of course was so proud. The three children were spread out throughout the nation and would not be directly involved in the campaign, but Will was pleased that they had taken the time to call and write notes. All of them seemed genuinely pleased and were very surprised. Will was surprised as well.

When it could not have seemed to get better, there was Martha Hall. She was a dedicated volunteer that he had just by chance met in a restaurant. He bumped into her almost knocking her over. She recovered quickly and when their eyes met, Will could not break off the stare—he was fixated. They each laughed and apologized.

When Will tried to introduce himself, she said, "I know who you are, I signed up to work your campaign."

The rest just seemed so easy. Will could not imagine an easier relationship. She had become more than just a volunteer. Martha was now one of his speech writers and advisors, and had become indispensable. And Will thought he might be falling in love with her.

*****

On the 13th floor of the Gray Scott building was a terrace that overlooked the city of Deer Park, Illinois. The ten-year-old office building was unique because it had a variety of businesses on the first 11 floors and a top scale restaurant on the 12th. The top floor was a private nightclub of sorts that could be crowded at times, but tonight the bar was empty—save one guy already at the bar sipping on a Tanqueray and tonic and talking on a cell phone.

For Mark Collins this was a Wednesday tradition. His wife always had late meetings on Wednesdays and there was no sense in rushing out only to get caught up in traffic. He stepped up to the bar. "Hey, I have not seen you before. Did something happen to Henry?" he asked.

The bartender looked up and said, "No—Henry is going to be a little late today, so I am filling in for him. My name is Tom."

Mark ordered his usual Bacardi and Coke and sat down to catch the market report on one of the six television sets that hung on the walls.

"Usually it's pretty crowded about now," Mark said the barman while running the calendar through his mind to make sense of the vacant establishment.

"It will be picking up here in a few minutes. Are you expecting anyone?"

"No, no, not expecting anyone." Mark shrugged his shoulders and came to the conclusion that the after-six crowd would soon be making its way into the club.

When the market report had finished Mark decided to go out on the terrace to take in the fresh air of a summer night. He also occasionally liked to smoke a cigar and this was the only place in the building that he would not get attacked by the smoking Nazis.

"Mark... Mark Collins?" The man who had been sitting at the bar appeared on the terrace just a few feet away.

Mark turned and said somewhat confusedly, “Yes, yes, I am. I’m sorry—do I know you?” He squinted through the puff of smoke that he had just exhaled.

“You probably don’t remember me, my name is Marley,” the man replied.

He reached out to shake Mark’s hand. With a questioning look, Mark took the man’s hand and began to shake. At the same time, Richard reached up with his left hand and gave a heavy pat to Mark’s shoulder. Mark winced at the prick in his left tricep and the look of confusion was replaced by one of disorientation.

Mark tried to get out the words, “What did you poke me…?”

As Mark began to tumble, Richard Marley called out to Tom, “Hey Tom, I think this guy is having a heart attack; you’d better call an ambulance, quick!”

Tom reached for the phone, and dialed 911, wiped off the phone and laid it down on the bar. Richard carried and half-dragged the limp body to a table near the bar and dumped him on the floor. Richard and Tom made their way out the door and down the hallway. They opened a control panel toward the left of a maintenance door. Tom disconnected the device that prevented the elevator from arriving at the 13th floor. Marley had already pressed the down button and within a few seconds the elevator door opened up. As the two reached the bottom floor, Tom pulled one sign off the wall within the elevator itself and then another just outside the elevator on the first floor. The sign read: “Harry’s Top Shelf 13th Floor Club will open half an hour late due to repairs. Thanks for your patience.” As the two exited the building, the sirens could be heard in the distance.

Henry, the real bartender for Harry’s Top Shelf, was headed out the manager’s office, down the hallway and to the elevator. He heard sirens and turned to the street, but figured the emergency vehicles were probably headed somewhere else. The signs that caused him to go to the manager's office had been removed. Confused, he stopped in front of the elevator

The manager had followed Henry and asked, "What sign?"

Henry was perplexed and said, "It was right here."

The manager frowned and said, "Well, maybe maintenance was doing something, but you need to get up there, the rush will be starting soon. I am going to see what the sirens are all about."

In Venice Beach, California, the hotel phone rang and Ben leaned over the corner of the bed and answered it.

"It's me. The restaurant was excellent. We dined alone, but the food was outstanding. Have you ordered the carry out?" Marley said over a secure cell phone.

Even though his conversation was scrambled, the operative still talked in code in case he might be overheard by a third party listening device or Ben had someone in the room that could hear his voice.

Ben listened and the replied. "No, do you still have a menu?"

"Yes."

Ben knew Marley had accomplished his mission without a problem; there were no witnesses or unexpected casualties and he was ready to go on the next assignment.

Ben continued, "Can I call you when I am ready to order? It should be around 9:00 or 10:00.

"Absolutely; I look forward to dining with you," Marley said and hung up the phone.

He jumped on his Italian made Aprilia Tuono motorcycle and touched the ignition. He slid the helmet down over his head and flipped down the dark-tinted visor. He slowly accelerated onto the entrance ramp of Highway 64 South, and headed out of Chicago.

Chapter 10

It was a late November Tuesday, at an extended-stay hotel. On a 7th floor balcony, Ben Thomas was looking out over the city of the Naples and Florida's I-75 from his luxury suite. His burgundy silk tie was loosened, and he had a Heineken in his left hand. Sitting just inside the sliding door at a mahogany crafted desk, was an elderly gentleman with a distinguished look. Ross Saunders was also looking contemplative, with his half-glasses perched at the end of his expansive nose. Saunders' gray hair was cut short, and everything about this man exuded style and class. Even his double-breasted jacket lay neatly folded on the corner of the bed.

Ben turned back to Saunders with a look of deference that only a student looking at his mentor could render. Ross loosened his tie, unbuttoned the top button to his shirt, and sighed.

The previous Sunday evening, Ross had received a call advising him that Florida Congressman, Mike Robertson, had been in an accident. Ross left immediately from Manhattan as soon as flight plans could be filed. On the flight he got word that Robertson had died. He moved to the front of the plane to change his destination from Miami to Naples and then called Ben, who had just arrived in Miami from Cincinnati. Ross directed Ben to unofficially meet with the authorities for a positive identification of Robertson's body, verifying that it was in fact him. Afterwards, Ben headed up to Naples to meet with Ross.

Ben had just given this multi-millionaire financier and politico a briefing of the preliminary police report, and the mood was somber. Ross looked at Ben and said in more of a question than a statement, "And it was an accident?"

Ben looked slightly taken aback before responding, "I don't see how it could have been anything else." He ran his fingers through his substantial crop of hair.

Ross stood and walked over to refill his drink and looked toward the younger man with his emerald eyes and said, "Cincinnati?"

"Went fine," Ben replied, "no problems."

After several quiet minutes Ross said, "How is Oliver doing?"

"He is doing well, and I'd say it is a good thing," Ben responded.

The elderly man shifted in his desk chair and took a sip of his Makers Mark bourbon. He liked it over ice with just a slice of lime. He finally spoke, "Oliver won by how much?"

Ben chuckled a little bit and said, "Three points."

Ross thought a moment, and then began crunching a piece of ice with his teeth. "I think we are going to have to move his schedule up. What kind of national exposure can we get him?"

Ben stood up and said, "I'll get started right away."

Ross let out a breath of exasperation and flipped on the television to catch the latest CNN Financial Report.

During the next twenty four hours, Thomas and Saunders had come up with a game plan, but it was not much of one really. They would keep working with Oliver and just have to wait until they got the final report on Mike Robertson. Ben was going to try to make contact with Parker and Smith. They were in limbo and needed to be very careful. He realized that the whole Matriculation Project was in jeopardy. They might just have to pull up stakes and disappear. Both he and Ross could do that, but what about the others? They would have to be paid a final amount and told to disappear as well. The two men, looking worn and bedraggled, shook hands. Ben would head to Washington, and Ross—well Ross would go somewhere; Ben never really knew where.

In Miami, Pat Lewis had arrived just in time to watch the bulk of the Coroner's Office head out to lunch. Lewis retrieved his expired U.S. Secret Service I.D. from his jacket and walked briskly into the Dade County morgue. As it would turn out, Lewis would not need the ID. In fact he walked right in without even being challenged. The only person that even gave him a look was a secretary in a side office. Lewis made his way down the hallway and opened the door that read Miami-Dade County Medical Examiner. He would meet his contact in the outer office of the morgue itself.

On the wall was a proclamation:

MEDICAL EXAMINERS; DISPOSITION OF DEAD BODIES, Chapter 406, Duty to Report: Prohibited Acts Public Health- Chapter 406

406.12 Duty to report; prohibited acts. It is the duty of any person in the district where a death occurs, including all municipalities and unincorporated and federal areas, who becomes aware of the death of any person occurring under the circumstances described in s. 406.11 to report such death and circumstances forthwith to the district medical examiner. Any person who knowingly fails or refuses to report such death and circumstances, who refuses to make available prior medical or other information pertinent to the death investigation, or who, without an order from the office of the district medical examiner, willfully touches, removes, or disturbs the body, clothing, or any article upon or near the body, with the intent to alter the evidence or circumstances surrounding the death, shall be guilty of a misdemeanor of the first degree, punishable as provided in s. 775.082 or s. 775.083.

Lewis had just about finished the quick reading of law. He figured knowledge of any kind might come in handy some day. About that time a young lady around 25 of Cuban descent, named Marty Prefilio, appeared. She came out of the back room, presumably filled with operating tables, cutting tools, refrigerators, and dead bodies. The thought made Lewis shiver a bit, but he would not show his disconcertion. You could tell that Marty liked the idea of having Lewis stop by. He had business with the Coroner a few weeks ago and made it a point to hold his gaze long enough for Marty to notice. He picked up her name from her name badge and said goodbye on his way out. Once again he looked at her a little longer than would be required. Earlier in the morning, Lewis had given Marty a call, asking a favor. She seemed happy to oblige. This information was not classified nor seemed even noteworthy. What could the Secret Service care about it? *Who knows,* she thought, *maybe it was just an excuse for Agent Pat Lewis to drop back by*? Regardless, it was okay by her; he was easy on the eyes.

"Hi Marty," Lewis said giving her his big confident smile.

Marty returned his gaze with a mischievous smile and pulled out the autopsy results that would be the official record forwarded to the police. Lewis gave no reaction as the coroner's assistant read him the findings directly from the report.

"Marty I really appreciate this," Pat said, "I can't tell you why I am checking this. In fact, I am not even here." He smiled while looking up and down her blue scrubs.

"This will all be available in a day or to, so you really don't have to make any excuses. It is not like it is top secret or something," Marty said through a smile. "Call me sometime when you need a real favor."

Pat Lewis's smile broadened and he said, "I'd like that very much."

On his way to Miami International, Pat removed a cell phone and placed a call.

"Mr. President, you have a call on line 6," a female voice said over the intercom in the Oval Office.

"Thank you, Doris," President Parker said over his shoulder.

He paused from the letter he was typing on a laptop computer and punched in the correct button for line six. It was a dedicated and secure line.

"What's the report?" the President said with no preamble.

"The report looks like it should. I don't see any connection to your information," said Lewis.

"I appreciate your efforts." The President breathed out and brought his hand to his forehead.

"Yes, Sir, if there is something else, just let me know," Pat Lewis said and ended the call.

He finished the drive to Miami International, returned his rental car return and proceeded to his gate for boarding. He removed his cell from his pocket and dialed his next call.

Nicky Topolo answered the phone with a quiet, husky voice. "Yeah?"

"It's me," Pat said.

"Just a minute—he's in the can."

Pat waited for about 30 seconds and heard a door bang closed. He could hear some of the conversation between two men, but all he could decipher was Nicky saying, "It's Miami."

Heinz Innsbruck exited the bathroom and unhurriedly walked to the phone. He was wearing an open-collar, white shirt and loose khaki pants with suspenders. He picked the phone up off the table and said in a raspy voice, "Tell me."

Pat said with little emotion, "Referee says it was an

accident. No mention of the players. There was one fan."

"Does she need her ticket punched?" he said, leaning back in his worn leather chair and gave a little laugh, as if he'd said something clever. Nicky was now standing across the room sipping on a glass of water. Both men smiled at each other.

"I don't think so. From what I am told, she did not see the event very well. But I put someone on her just case she gets questioned again," Pat said. "If someone is nosing around, I will hear about it."

"Okay, sounds like it went well. You will let me know if the fan gets her memory going, right?"

"Yeah, we are keeping up with that."

"And you relayed that back to the commissioner, correct?"

"Yes, he evidently got his information from someone familiar with the Freedom Organization. I told him what the coroner's report said.

"Did he seem to accept the ruling?" the man asked.

"He seemed to." Pat fidgeted in his seat and looked around to make sure no one was paying particular attention. He saw weary travelers going from one gate to the next and no one looked even mildly suspicious.

Innsbruck took a final drag on a cigarette and crushed it out in a nearby ashtray. "Okay, good. I only wish Banger would have hung around a little longer. I wanted to be there for that," the man growled, forgetting about his baseball cover.

"Yeah, well, it is just less exposure. I can be expecting a clean slate?" Pat asked evenly.

"I am doing it as we speak. I will give it to our scorekeeper. Wrap up a few loose ends and we will be square. Maybe you want to open a fresh tab?" the man said, gave a little laugh, and hung up.

Pat Lewis cursed, shoved the phone in his pocket. This was supposed to have cleared his debt. Lewis might just have to visit Innsbruck and punch his ticket. Lewis boarded the Airbus A31 jet, flight 1447 out of Miami for Dulles.

Innsbruck turned to Nicky across the room. “Can you believe that? That guy did all that for a lousy 35 grand in markers.”

Nicky shook his head and laughed. “Must be a labor of love,” he said.

Chapter 11

The morning sky was lighting up in Miami. The press had gotten hold of the pile-up story that killed Mike Robertson. He had been a high flying, novae politico that somehow blew to the top of Florida politics in a few short years. Charles (Chars) Reynolds, senior writer of the Miami Express, was sitting at his breakfast table reading the article that he'd written. His write-up gave a short bio on Robertson. Short was the operative word, thought Chars. This guy really was a political shooting star, quickly rising on the scene and then, poof!—gone.

Chars thought, *What did Robertson have that was so attractive to big donors and the common everyday person?*

He took a bite of his wheat toast and butter. Mike was a nice enough and normal-looking guy. His background didn't include the wealthy family or a long history of public service, which was so common of the current day candidates. Many thought that he would take a run at the governor's office or even the U.S. President. He was full of homespun wisdom and seemed to be liked by almost everybody. The Democrats could not find any dirt on him, and don't think they didn't try.

Chars had been up since almost 4:00am. It was usual for him not to be able to sleep. Often he would have a beer or two in the evening and that took care of any sleeping difficulty. When he woke up this morning, he followed his usual procedure. He got up, used the restroom and drank some water. If he could not get back to sleep in one hour, he would stay up. He could usually get some work done. This morning he was on his second cup of coffee and continued perusing all the major papers online. He leaned back and stretched to try to shake an uneasy feeling. His journalist's intuition was itching. Something was weird about this. He pulled out a stack of manila folders from his worn leather portfolio.

Something about this just seemed strange. Maybe it was the fact that a likeable person had been accidentally killed and nobody liked that. Robertson seemed on a mission and he was cut short. Chars felt sad, he was not sure why. He had only met Mike Robertson a couple times. It could not have been bereavement, but maybe it could be bewilderment at the unfairness of life. He looked again at his notes. The autopsy was all but too clear. No alcohol or drugs were involved. I was just a case of everyone in the wrong place at the wrong time. The witnesses or witness as it were, said that she thought she saw a blown tire on one of the vehicles. But the police were not going to spend a lot of time bird dogging out a flat tire. They would interview everybody and wait for the toxicity reports to come out, hoping for a scapegoat to blame the whole thing on. All the various groups would use the wreck to advance their own cause. The anti-cellular phone people would blame it on cell phone use. The anti-drinking crowd was looking for their angle. The cops would use any of the reasons as indications of the need for more officers. Everybody had their own agenda. When someone of note was involved, each group stepped up to the trough hoping for a nice drink. The insurance adjustors would be very interested in trying to come of with an explanation. Each company would be trying to limit their liability and assign blame somewhere other than their client. All the injury lawyers would be interested to see if they could sniff out a million dollar baby or two. The lawyers were licking their chops at the sight of a wreck of this proportion. Every family member would be hounded with letters and phone calls. Chars thought that it might be good to start with the insurance adjustors. The official coroner's report was in the hands of the police and evidently just confirmed that everybody was dead as expected. It would be a few days until the official police report would be made available.

Chars punched the remote and his Sony wide screen TV popped to life in bright vivid colors. Just as he figured the lead story was the follow-up by the on-scene reporter, Paul Gregory. The picture flashed to the capital building in Tallahassee. The reporter was getting a comment from the Governor's spokesperson. He would go on to say, "The Governor sends his condolences to friends and family of the late congressman." Of course it would be pointed out that the Governor appointed Robertson to his first state office. He too was looking for an angle to benefit from this tragedy. Chars thought it was all too predictable. Maybe he would just run up to where the accident happened to look around. *But what would be the point?* he thought. Everything had been hauled away long ago. Maybe it was a heart attack or something. "There were really no witnesses to speak of. I wonder if I could get a witness list," he said aloud to himself. Surely, someone had a list somewhere. Chars picked up the phone to call his contact in the police department.

On the second ring, a deep raspy voice answered, "Collins."

Chars smiled and said in his best Yosemite Sam impression, "What are doing you scurvy varmint?"

Jerry Collins, a 21-year veteran of the Miami Dade Police Force smiled, laughed lightly, and said, "What's up Chars?"

"Doing great," said Chars, evidently going past the superficial question and directly to the standard answer for the question that most people ask, How are you doing? "How's Melanie?" asked Chars.

Collins had a picture of Melanie on his desk and he glanced over to it and smiled again. "She's doing well—visiting the parents at Cocoa Beach. She won't be back for a few days. They went up for a little sun and the space launch. Why, you looking for a date?"

"Sure. I'd be the best date you've had and I'm cheap too," Chars said, as he leaned back in his chair enjoying the friendship and the usual banter that would go on for several minutes before the purpose of the call would unfold. "Hey, you want to get a drink after you get off?" Chars continued.

"Only if you let me in on the latest scoop that you are working on."

"And you'll catch me up on the dirge of society and their woes.

"Cherries at five?"

Chars smiled and said, "Works for me."

At 5:05pm, Charles Reynolds walked in to the Cherries Pub and Grub. It was a clean "hole in the wall" type of place. The sign read "Welcome to Cherries. Come inside and get you some." Chars always wondered about that sign, but never asked. The crowd was sparse this early as most of the Cherries' clientele worked in the city and had just gotten off work. They would not arrive for another half an hour. There was a large full length bar with storage area up above for extra stock of all the various liquors and such. The taps were plentiful, advertising an assortment of beers. Chars could just make out the brands from where he sat. There were a couple of women sitting off to the side, evidently enjoying an early afternoon. The grill was off to the side of the bar and the offered up the usual bar and grill fare. Mary or Margie was standing near the bar. Chars could not ever remember the middle-aged waitress' name. She was usually on duty most days that Chars had visited the pub. She could be the manager or owner, for all Chars knew. She seemed to be very confident, and probably did not take any guff off anyone. *Maybe she's the owner*, thought Chars.

About 20 minutes had passed when Chars saw Jerry's car pass the glass front door. He began sipping his second tanker of Samuel Adams' Summer Ale. A few moments later, Jerry bounded in through the door and Chars rose to shake his hand. Jerry was a stout man, almost six feet tall, with the gray encroaching on the bottom half of his head. Chars thought him to be a slight look alike for Fred Flintstone. He seemed a bit disheveled, but no more than usual. He looked the part of a cop—square jaw and barrel chest. He walked on his toes like he was always ready to tip over. When he laughed, you could not help but laugh with him.

"Sorry I'm late. Just as I was walking out I got a call from the Lef Lieutenant," Jerry said while breathing hard.

His apology was sincere; Chars knew that and it really was not needed anyway. This was, after all, the normal schedule for Jerry, maybe even a little ahead. Chars had learned that Sergeant Jerry Collins was habitually late and always feeling guilty about it. Chars knew this and just scheduled around it.

"Not at all—I just got here a minute or two ago," Chars lied just a little.

"Looks like you have been here long enough to throw down a beer," Jerry said, not believing Chars accommodation of his tardiness.

The two of them shot the "shit" around for a while, catching up on family stuff for almost 30 minutes. Each of them had made very good progress on their respective beers. Jerry had chosen a reddish brown brew from a tap called George Killian's Red. It was good to talk to Jerry. They had come to trust each other over the years, even though police and reporters seldom got along. They were definitely an exception to the norm. Jerry and Chars had a bond that just seemed to be mutual ever since they met almost 15 years ago. Their conversation was easy from the day they met at a murder-suicide scene. Their similar sense of humor seemed to fit real well. Chars could always break up Jerry and he seemed to enjoy telling stories and getting Jerry really belly laughing. They had both lost children: Chars had lost a son in the 2007 Iran conflict and Jerry had lost a son in a freak accident at home. Small talk, stories, and very little business of consequence ensued as the two loosened up, each consuming cold draught beers.

The talk inevitably turned to work. They had always felt comfortable in commiserating with each other about the difficult bosses they had or the screwed up co-workers. Their stories would double them up with laughter or leave them just shaking their heads. The news business and the cop business had so many similarities: investigations, witnesses, and often the seedy side of human life. They would often exchange stories and had also worked through some puzzling cases before.

Jerry seldom asked Chars to actually do anything, but did often ask what he knew or thought about something. Chars had very seldom asked for inside information and Jerry knew that it would always be off the record.

Sometimes when stories got a little too touchy, Jerry would say, “You know you can’t know this.”

Chars had his standard answer: “I have already started forgetting what you just said.”

When it was really sensitive, Jerry would follow up with an apologetic, “I know you know what’s what. I’m just letting you know that this is not on the streets yet and won’t likely be unless it comes from the inside.”

Chars never pressed and Jerry trusted him implicitly. Often Jerry would let Chars in on a little information that would allow the reporter to ask the right questions. It was a mutually beneficial relationship on occasion, but it was more than that too. Their families had spent time together over the years. Since Chars’ divorce, those family times had waned, but Chars would still occasionally eat dinner with the Collins family. They had laughed together; and they had grieved together.

Their food order had just arrived and Mary (or Margie) asked what else she could bring. Both men looked appraisingly at their feast and said “more napkins” almost in unison. The spry waitress had some in her waitress belt and set them on the edge of the table then moved on to the next table where a young couple had just settled in. Jerry plucked a hot wing out of the massive plate of hors d'oeuvres and took a big bite.

"Jerry, I wrote a bio on the Congressman that was killed in that pile-up on I-75. What's the skinny on that?"

Jerry wiped his mouth and said, "It seems like it is just like everyone is saying, it was just a bad accident and the guy was killed. Of course I think there were other deaths as well as Robertson. Have you heard something different?"

"No, it just seemed a real shame and no one has really explained what happened," Chars said and stabbed a spare rib with his fork. "What was the sequence that led to the accident? Has anyone said?"

Jerry shrugged his shoulders slightly, grimaced and said, "Well of course until the Investigation Unit has filed their report there won't be any information. It normally takes about 48 hours to get that in. Once that's done then all the pieces will probably start falling together."

Chars almost blurted, "But it has been seventy two hours; the accident happened last week. The report has not been filed yet?"

Jerry looked up and cocked his head. "Has it really been that long? Well maybe the report is in and I just haven't heard about it. That's possible. I would not normally be included unless it was a homicide. The only way I'd know about it is through the scuttlebutt—and, only then, if there was something unusual about it." He reached for another hot wing. "These are really good, have you had one?"

"No, try the ribs; they are good too. The case is unusual because Robertson was involved."

"Just goes to show when your time is up, it does not matter how much starch is in your shirt, it is your time," Jerry said as he sat back and took a momentary break from eating.

"I suppose," said Chars, not sounding too convinced.

"Well, when I go in tomorrow, I'll get you the scoop. But this happens all over Florida and everywhere else—shit happens," Jerry said and sat back looking rather satisfied with the appetizer. He wiped his mouth with a cheap paper napkin and polished off the rest of his beer.

Chars leaned back thoughtfully and said, "Well, I would be interested in what the I.U. says the sequence of events was, like who hit who, and whose tire blew and why it blew."

Jerry looked across the table no longer distracted by his eating and said, "Sounds like you know something."

"No, I really don't and I am not even sure why all this bothers me, but something—call it instincts or whatever—just does not seem right. This is a fairly high profile guy," Chars said.

"Well, I figure that I.U. will have to tie this up fairly neatly to avoid everybody second guessing. This one they will want to get right."

Nodding his head, Chars reconsidered his earlier thought about the police not wanting to snoop out a flat tire, and concluded Jerry was right. This would be handled by the book for the very reason that Mike Robertson was involved and there would be a lot of press attention. The conversation shifted back to their personal lives and families and the usual topics before the two men paid their bill and headed off to their respective homes. As Jerry left, he promised Chars he would call with information about the accident.

Chapter 12

The next morning, Jerry asked with a smile, "Hey Chars, did I wake you up?"

"No, I have been awake for a while," Charles said.

"Just got a little info on the pile up. First of all, this stretch of highway is not real busy and has no camera on it. What I found out really doesn't change much, but the initial report that it was a four-car pile up was not correct. It was actually two separate accidents. It looks like Robertson's car was involved in the first accident. He must have gone to sleep or lost control because he veered into an abutment. He may have had a flat tire. An alternative scenario was talked about, but it could not be proven," Jerry said hesitantly.

"Tell me."

"Robertson may have been cut off by another car, then hit the abutment and was then struck by the second automobile. In that scenario, there is a missing car. The I.U. is theorizing that Robertson was killed by the second impact. It all happened within such a short period of time that it is difficult to say. Robertson's car looked like it had been run over by a steam roller. He was evidently going about 85 when he hit the solid concrete. The second accident apparently occurred about 90 seconds later. An elderly man saw Robertson's car all messed up and stopped his car to help. A third auto, a Saab convertible coming up behind, swerved but still caught the old man, part of his car, and flipped into Robertson's car. The old man, the driver of the Saab, and Robertson are the three dead."

"So how come four cars were reported?"

"I know what was reported. It probably came off the scanners that the reporters listen to. The dispatch was probably just passing along info that was reported in the 9-1-1 call. The only live witness was a fruit vendor from the other side of the freeway's access road. She had stopped her car to pick up a sign that was advertising her fresh fruit stand at the next exit. She called in the accident. She was calling the police when she heard the second crash. By the time she looked back, the old man was dead on the side of the road. The Saab convertible hit the old man; then his car flipped and struck Robertson's car on the fly. It hit right on the driver's side where Robertson lay unconscious after striking the abutment."

"If the head-on did not kill him the flying Saab certainly did," Chars said.

"That's how the I.U. figures it."

"So, we have Robertson, the old man, and the Saab convertible driver. So what about the fourth car?" Chars asked again.

"Maybe the witness was confused or maybe 9-1-1 got it wrong."

"Do you have her name?"

Jerry grinned and said, "Of course."

Jerry gave Chars the name, Freda Learned, and her address and phone number. He mentioned that it was in the police report and that Chars would have to come up with a story of how he got her name. Jerry figured that was Char's problem because he couldn't use Jerry as the source.

"Thanks. Hey Jerry," Chars said, just catching Jerry before he hung up, "What about the airbags, were they deployed?"

"I didn't look for that Chars; I'll have to get back to you."

Chars had begun taking notes. He really did not hear anything that raised a red flag. He did, however, want to talk to the witness. If there was anything hickey, she would be the one to talk to. He picked up the phone and dialed her number. A sleepy voice said, "Uh hello?" Chars quickly checked his watch again to make sure he was not calling too early.

"Hello, is this Freda Learned?" Chars smiled to try to give that warm, reassuring tone.

"Well no, this is Freda's mother, Mrs. William Wilson."

"I am sorry if I woke you, Ms. Wilson," Chars interjected.

"Good Lord no, I have been up since 5:00am, milked two cows and pulled eggs. Good Lord no," Mrs. Wilson said with a bit of a nervous laugh.

Chars hesitated a second and said "I am Chars Reynolds from the Miami Express; I was hoping to catch Freda. Is she around?"

"No Mister…. What did you say your name was?" the elderly woman asked.

"Chars Reynolds."

"Right, Mr. Charles, Freda is at the produce stand down off the highway."

Chars figured that Mrs. Wilson had probably liked the arrangement that sent Freda off to the roadside stand. She could do her chores and get in a short nap without anyone being the wiser.

"You can stop by and purchase some vegetables and she could talk to you there." she said, ever being the sales person. "What did you need to talk to her about?" Her curiosity had been pricked.

Chars did not want to say a lot, but said, "I just wanted to check if she had seen an accident on the highway last Sunday afternoon."

"Oh, she did mention that. Must have been bad. But they got it cleaned up real quick. Shoot, by the time I came home at around dinner time, I did not even see it. I didn't even know about it until Freda told me. Sort of shook her up."

Chars was nodding as if the lady could actually see him. "I

would have been upset too. Those things are scary when they happen that close to you," Chars said.

"It was bad for business too," Mrs. Wilson chimed in. "Freda sold about half as much as she normally would on a Sunday. You know, people coming and going to church often stop by. And then you get the afternoon Sunday drivers. Accident must have dampened everyone's spirit."

Chars thanked her, hung up, grabbed his windbreaker and headed out the door, with coffee in one hand and his note portfolio in the other.

Chars exited when saw the first sign for Freda's vegetable stand. Freda evidently put up a sign to give potential customers the heads up fresh vegetables and fruit were ahead. Chars illegally backed up the frontage road to the sign and got out of his car. He looked across to the highway overpass. The concrete abutment that Mike Robertson had plowed into was not too difficult to identify. It showed the effects of the collision. The Lexus was no match for the concrete. Chars returned to his car and continued on down the frontage road. He pulled up along the fruit and vegetable stand that stood about 15 feet off the access road. It was strategically located so that a passerby could pull off the road and get out without worrying about traffic. The stand was fairly large and Chars guessed that it must be sitting on the front edge of the Learned or Wilson family ranch. He doubted whether the county government would put up with a private citizen setting up a permanent shop on public access lands. He also guessed that any customers that Freda might have were regulars that lived in the area.

As Chars was pondering these thoughts, a late model sedan with what looked like a Tennessee license plate, began to slow down and pull slowly off to the side behind Chars' 2008 Grand Marquis. The gray haired couple bounded out of the car with surprising agility and hustled over to the stand. Chars pretended to be looking for something on his passenger seat in order to let the couple arrive before him. The man and his wife did not have to look long before they found what they were after, paid and were on their way again. Chars hoped that he would be that spry when he was their age. He thought about that and sighed. It really was not going to be that long. He had hit 50 last June and probably was not as energetic as that couple right now. He thought to himself that he really needed to lose some weight and get regular exercise.

Chars introduced himself, while extending his hand. He tried to put Freda at ease by saying that all she said would be off the record. He informed her that he was merely doing a background piece on Mike Robertson and just wanted to make sure he got the accident information correct.

"Can you tell me what you told the police?" Chars said with a big smile.

Freda looked somewhat impressed that a reporter was coming to talk to her. "Well, sure. You look like you might need some vegetables in your diet; how about some of the fresh tomatoes or green peppers?" Freda said with a fair amount of sincerity.

Chars realized at this point that this was not a casual statement. If he wanted this conversation to happen, he was expected to buy some of Freda's produce. "You know I was just thinking that very thing. Just sack up what ever you think I need and that will be fine." Chars figured that yeah, he could probably use some fresh vegetables and fruit in his diet. Whatever he did not use he could always give to the pool secretaries at the office. They would be very impressed with his thoughtfulness.

Freda snapped a paper sack to attention on the counter and slowly started preparing Chars' purchase. Chars figured he had better get to his questions quick or he may be taking the whole stand back to Miami in his trunk and back seat.

“So what did you see happen… may I call you Freda?” Chars asked politely.

“Freda is fine. Well, I really did not see much. How did you know that I was a witness? Freda said, while faking a suspicious look.

Chars thought he detected the hint of enjoyment at the fact that she was getting some attention and she was making a sale at the same time. Chars thought of Mrs. Wilson’s comments as he hung up the phone: “You could stop by the stand and buy some vegetables—she will probably talk to you.” The emphasis that she put on buying came back to Chars.

“I simply saw the police report. I want to make sure I get this story right since Congressman Robertson was one of the accident victims,” Chars answered.

“Oh the police report. They didn’t ask me a lot of questions. Well I guess if it was me that…” she stuttered, “if that flying car hit somebody like me, nobody would have cared. But I can see your side, wanting to report the story correct and all. The police seemed to be in a hurry. They weren’t much interested in buying any vegetables you know,” she said, smiling at Chars.

She paused for a moment and Chars wondered if she was finished and then understood her veiled message. “Freda, are those squash?”

Freda gave him a nod of the head and said, “Yes, squash, Mr. Reynolds. You need squash; it will help your color.”

He started to prod her with a clarification, but she started into the story on her own while sacking up squash. She had probably told it several times in the past two days and had settled on the most dramatic version.

“I had stopped along the access road and was picking up my sign next to the highway. I suspect you saw it on your way in.” Chars nodded that he had seen the sign and tried to appear impressed. She went on in slightly disfigured English, “There weren't a lot of traffic, you see, going either way. I had a slow day and decided to pack up a little early. My momma was in town with a male friend of hers and she wasn't going to be home for a while anyway. She gives me a hard time if I am not out here all day."

Chars figured Freda left this part out when she recounted the story to her mother. "I heard a crack or a backfire or a popping tire or something and I looked right away. That Senator's car looked like it may have tangled up with another car and went straight into that bridge support. Smashed the living shit out of it. Oh, excuse my language!" Chars wanted to stop her there, but signaled that she could continue.

"I picked up my sign and hurried into the car. I was going to call on the cell phone and cross over a little ways down. You can't really cross over where the accident happened. You have to go down a little further; otherwise you might rip out the oil pan. In the wet season you can get stuck in the low areas. Sometimes I just go all the way down to the next exit and take the overpass. It is only about two miles."

Chars nodded his head in understanding, even though he was really hoping she would just get on with her story. Freda continued on without hesitation. Chars figured her story was now well-rehearsed.

"About the time that I got through to 9-1-1, I heard squealing tires and another crash. Whack!" She said with a bang on the table for affect. Chars jumped a little, not expecting Freda to add sound affects.

"This foreign sports car had whacked an old man and went flying through the air, flipped over and landed practically in that Senator's lap."

Freda took a short breath and began to continue when Chars interrupted. "Freda, was the car flying through the air a convertible?"

"Yes it was, and it had a young lady in it. She was a goner

for sure. Oh good Lord, I can see her hair hanging out the car. She did not even have a chance. Neither did that old man. He was sprawled out there on the grass, dead as a door nail," Freda said while sadly shaking her head.

Chars thought that this wreck was still bothering Freda a lot and he would need to be considerate of her feelings. "So there were four cars involved?" Chars clarified.

Freda nodded and paused, "Well, it did happen at quite a distance, but yeah I think that one and the other one and the old man and the lady. That's four, right?

Freda seemed to be struggling to remember. Chars needed to clarify a couple of the details, but he decided to let her finish.

"I could not even bear to go over there. Those people were dead and there was not anything I was going to be able to do to fix it. I could see blood and body parts and crushed metal. It makes me sick every time I think of it." Freda's voice trailed off.

Chars could see that she was reliving the experience. He let her think for just a moment before he continued. When Freda began putting apples in his bag, Chars figured he was on the clock again and began to clarify the account.

"Freda, you said that the Senator's car was tangled up with another car. What kind of car was he tangled up with?"

Freda looked at him and said, "It was the big SUV that they towed off first."

"Do you remember what color it was or what type?"

"It was the same color that the Senator's car was, white. I don't know what kind it was, but it was big and nice."

Freda again looked directly at Chars when she spoke to him. Chars noticed the direct eye contact and passed it off as a normal suspicion of city folks.

"And this car was towed?"

"Yeah, the SUV was towed first, probably because it was the easiest get to," Freda said contemplatively.

“Did you see the driver of the SUV?”

Freda thought about that and said, “No I don’t recall him getting out of the car. But he was up a little further, you know up under the overpass. He had those dark windows, so I don’t remember seeing the driver at all. But I do remember that his car was the first to be towed.”

Chars again interrupted politely, “Were the police around by that time?”

Freda looked puzzled. “Well they must have been; I guess so, but I am not sure.”

Chars pressed on. “So the accident took place and a tow truck showed up and took away the white SUV. Then the police arrived and began taking statements?

Freda was nodding. “Yeah, the police got there in 10 or 15 minutes.”

Chars knew that the response time had been clocked at slightly over 12 minutes, which was slower than the published 8-minute goal, but since the police had determined that everyone was dead, it probably had not turned out be a big deal. Of course since the Senator was involved, it could be turned in to a publicity mess. Nevertheless, response times were required to be entered into the police report just in case there was ever a legal question.

“Freda, do you recall if the airbags in the Senator’s car were deployed?” Chars asked.

“Deployed?” Freda asked slowly.

“Yes, deployed, fired, used, you know,” Chars fumbled around for a word that would help.

Freda thought back in her mind, replaying the accident yet again. “Yeah, I think they were, but he had those tinted windows too. Not as dark as the SUV, but still tough to see. I, of course, only found out that it was the Senator after the fact. I mean I did not know it was him until somebody told me it was him. I cried again after they told me.” She began to tear up again.

“I am just curious,” said Chars trying to keep her on track, “when I first heard about the accident, it was reported that there were four cars and four fatalities. With your story I count the four cars, but I only count three deaths.”

“Well, let’s see,” Freda said, “the old man that the foreign car hit, there was the one in the foreign car, and of course the Senator and whoever he was carrying with him.”

Chars stopped “The Senator had a passenger?”

“Yes. Now that you say that, I am not sure if he lived or not, but I guessed he got squished too when the foreign car plowed into the Senator’s car. But he must have been okay if they say there was only three deaths. Yeah, that probably explains only three deaths. Do you like grapefruit, Mr. Charles?”

“Yes, two please. I am sorry, but I just want to make sure I understand. Freda, you are saying that you heard a bang; you saw the Senator’s car and the SUV locked up. The Senator and his passenger ran head-on into the bridge abutment. You headed back to your car to call the police. During that moment the old man stopped, presumably to help. The convertible evidently did not see the old man until it was too late and hit him, hit his car, and flew through the air directly into the Senator’s lap. Are you still on the phone with 911 at this point?”

Freda nodded her head, yes.

“Did the operator ask you the number of cars involved?”

“Yes, she did. I said two and then whack!” she hit the table again with her open hand. Chars tensed in surprise and breathed out, slightly annoyed.

Freda said excitedly, “I told her that two more cars just hit the other. Then she asked how many people were hurt and I counted them up. One, two, and then three and four.”

Chars leaned on the table and said, “But when she asked the number of people hurt, you did not include in the SUV driver?

“I guess I did not figure he was hurt, because he did not

really hit anything," Freda said trying to remember back what she was thinking.

"Did you see anyone outside the cars at this point?"

Freda thought for a moment. "Not that was alive."

Chars now zeroed in: "Did anyone in the SUV get out?"

"If they did, I didn't see 'em. And the SUV was up a ways, you know up under the overpass, I told you that. But it did happen fast and I was trying to call and trying to get over there and all."

Freda was flustered now, having to give a detailed account of everything. Chars knew that was not unusual. Witnesses usually had to go through a scenario several times to recall everything. Details were often left out quite unintentionally most of the time. Of course, those that had something to lose or gain might deliberately leave out details so as to cover or protect. Chars did not get the idea that Freda was doing anything other than trying to honestly recount her memory.

He continued with his questioning. "Who was the first person you remember seeing outside the cars?"

"I remember the tow truck man pulling up probably about ten minutes after the wreck, but I guess it was not that long, since the police had not arrived."

Chars interrupted trying to get everything correct. "Did you watch the SUV get towed off?"

Freda thought about that for a second and said, "Well, I guess not, cause the tow truck showed up and I probably got distracted or something. Then I heard the sirens a-wailing; the police arrived and then the ambulances, 'cept what they needed were hearses 'cause, they was all dead."

Chars persisted with his questions while Freda was in the moment. "Did you see the bodies being loaded into the ambulances?"

"Well, I watched a little bit; I was fairly shaken. Let's see, I watched them load the old man. He was probably the first to be loaded up; then the convertible lady, then they cut out the Senator."

Chars jumped in. "What about the Senator's companion?"

"Well, I must have not been looking when they loaded him."

"Why do you think it was a him?" asked Chars.

Freda thoughtfully said, "I guess it was a him. I really did not see his face, but now that you ask... I really didn't see if it was a man or a woman, I guess. It is hard to remember. I am not really sure." As she was recalling the events, she became visibly upset.

"Just one more question, Freda. Has anyone else besides me and the police asked you about the accident?" Chars asked.

"No, you are the first one, besides the police of course. But, they didn't ask a lot of questions. They probably had everything about figured out and did not need much else."

"Did they ask you about the passengers or just the cars?"

"Neither one really. They just asked if I was the one to call in to 9-1-1," Freda answered.

Chars thanked Freda for talking to him and paid for about a sack and a half of vegetables and fruit. The bill came to $18.50, but Chars would have paid much more for the information that he'd just received.

Chapter 13

"Jerry, can you get a copy of the police report in front of you? Chars asked, not even bothering to say hello.

"Yeah, sure. And hello to you, Chars." Jerry feigned insult. "Have you got something?" Jerry asked.

"Get the report and I will know for sure." Chars said, keeping his cards close to his chest for the moment. Chars was on hold when another call came in on his line. He switched over using the flash button.

"Chars Reynolds," he said with his usual upbeat voice.

There was only silence. Chars quickly switched back over to the other line. Jerry was saying, "Hello, hello." Evidently not for the first time, because he sounded annoyed at be put on hold.

"Sorry Jerry, I had another call beep in." Chars said. "Jerry, does the report say anything about the people that were involved in the accident?"

Jerry perused the report and said, "Yeah, you have the Senator, male Caucasian, 58 years old, DOA; female Caucasian, aged 26, named Willty Simone, DOA; male Caucasian, 70, DOA. That must be the old man; his name was Blanchard Smith."

"No fourth victim and no fourth car?"

Jerry was thinking that Chars must know something that he was holding on to, "No. Was there a fourth car and victim?

Chars furrowed his brow. "I guess not."

"It appears that the Senator was dead on the first impact. The second one, well, it was just extra damage. The old man was hit and killed by the convertible. The convertible must have landed in such a way that the car fell on the driver after it smashed into the

Senator."

"What about the airbag deployment?"

Jerry cleared his throat in minor annoyance because the question had come up again and he had forgotten to ask. But he covered by acting annoyed and pretending like he just had not had the time to check every little detail.

"Chars, I thought you wanted to know about cause of death. This is the preliminary coroner's report, not the accident report."

Chars persisted. "Jerry, I need to know if the passenger side airbag of the Senator's Lexus deployed. I need to know if there were any scrape marks or collision marks on the passenger side of the car."

Jerry was alert now, because he had heard the tone of Chars voice and it meant only one thing. Something was up and it meant that there was a lot more to this story.

"Meet me at MPI in a half hour and we will find out ourselves," Jerry said referring to the Miami Police Impound yard.

*****

Paul Gallegos was sitting at his kitchenette table looking over the sports section. He wondered if the Zephyrs could ever win a doubleheader. They had won the early game against the Albuquerque Isotopes, but had lost the evening game, 6-2. He was still in his pajama bottoms without a shirt. He had slept in and really was not expecting anyone to be calling him today.

Nevertheless here was the phone was ringing, which he answered with an unintelligent, "Yeah."

Gallegos was anything but unintelligent, but he did not want to give anything away. He would rather have the underdog role when it came to his line of work.

The man Paul Gallegos only knew as boss, said, "Lego, we may have a slight problem. I am not sure yet, but there was a witness. I need you to go find out what she knows. Don't mess with her; just find out what she knows and if she has told anyone else. My contact told me she was interviewed by a reporter from the Miami Express, Chars Reynolds."

Gallegos finished the last of his Vanilla Cream coffee, which was his favorite and then asked, "What kind of reporter is she?"

"It is not a she. Chars is short for Charles. He is an investigative reporter and is like a bulldog; he won't let go once he thinks he got something."

Gallegos ran his hands through his disheveled hair and said, "Sounds like a pussy name to me. I'll go back over there, but it will be tomorrow afternoon before I can get there. Did Dish or Salvador say they saw the lady?"

Pat Lewis said in a patient but low voice, "It does not matter if they saw her or not, she definitely was there. Dish and Salvador have already left for their next job and won't be back in the country for another 13 days. The police report said the lady did not see the accident, but now she's talking to a reporter. I need to know exactly what she saw and what she is saying in order to know if something has to be done about her and, for that matter, the reporter. Get there as soon as you can and let's not let this situation go south."

Lewis finished the conversation by giving Gallegos the information about the lone witness to the accident. The last thing he said to Gallegos was "don't do anything till you get it cleared by me." He felt fairly confident that Lego understood, but sometimes he seemed dense and that bothered his boss.

Pat Lewis put in another call on his Motorola Cipher Tec 4000 secure phone to Carrie Hernandez.

"Carrie, did you see a lady across the freeway when you got out of Robertson's car?"

"I saw her, but I am certain she did not see me leave. If she saw me it would have been right after we hit the concrete. Did she tell the police that there was somebody else in the car?"

"It did not show up in the police report, but there is a reporter snooping around and asking questions. Are you still in Miami?"

"Yes, do I need to do anything?"

Pat Lewis thought about that and said, "No, just hang tight. We may have to handle the reporter if he starts asking too many questions."

Carrie sounded worried when she said, "Damn bad luck for the lady to be there."

He agreed and disconnected the call.

Lewis dialed another number and said, "It's me. Thanks for the heads up on the lady. I need a car to be claimed at the Miami Police Impound as soon as possible. You can take care of that right?

The man on the other line answered with a blunt, "Yes, Sir."

"Then, it needs to disappear, comprendo?"

"Yes sir, I am on my way," Ted Bostic said as he was getting up from his sofa.

Lewis said, "I am sending the paperwork by fax, as we speak, that you will need to claim the car. Make sure you look the part, because the papers won't hold up if they do any checking."

While waiting for the fax to come through, Bostic loaded his Glock 17 semiautomatic. Made of steel and polymer plastic, the Glock 17 model in earlier years was carried by the D.C. police. It was a lightweight but powerful weapon, able to deliver 18 bullets in 9 seconds. It required little maintenance and was very easy to shoot. Unlike many semiautomatics, the Glock has no external manual safety. The pistol uses a five- to six-pound trigger pull—half the pull of most other semiautomatics for their first shot. The feature allows a shooter to fire quickly in dire circumstances when getting off the first shot is critical. Ted Bostic was no longer on the force, but was still in the business of enforcement. He searched around and found his keys. From a locked safe he pulled out a folder of fake IDs. He pulled an insurance company business card and picture ID badge. He heard the fax come on and the official looking forms began filing out one by one. Ted looked them over and noticed that somehow, Paul Lewis had provided him with the license and the VIN number that he would most certainly need. He slung his coat on, holstered his weapon, and headed out the door.

Chapter 14

Jerry flashed his badge at the Miami Police Impound check in station. They located the 2009 White Lexus that was mangled. Chars looked inside and saw that driver side airbag was hanging limply and covered with blood stains. The passenger side airbag was also exposed, but had no signs of blood.

"Jerry, would the passenger side airbag deploy if there was no one sitting there?"

Jerry leaned in and looked for an airbag disarming device. "It might have gone off with an impact like that, but these cars are so smart. The seatbelt probably has to be engaged for it to deploy. I could get one of the IU guys to run a deposit analysis on the bag to check for bodily fluids. If someone was sitting there, there would be saliva or facial oil or something left."

"If the Investigative Unit starts running tests, will that raise red flags?"

"They will definitely ask questions," Jerry said raising his eyebrows and nodding his head, "but this is going to have to come out sometime. Is there something else that you need to tell me?"

Chars thought about the big picture and was not too eager to break the story too quickly before he had something solid. Chars went around to the other side and looked at the damage to the Lexus. There was a large dent and scrape on the passenger side.

"The lady that was there, Freda, said that there was another vehicle that was involved. An SUV was tangled up with Robertson just before the head-on," Chars said quietly.

"Well, there would be paint left behind if that were the case and I would see the damage, but I don't see any paint left behind," said Jerry.

"What if there is paint, but it is the same color?"

Jerry looked closely and said, "That would have probably gone unnoticed, but the paint would be different from the Lexus paint. It could be tested as well and if another car hit the Lexus, it would be different. The front end is so mangled it's tough to say one way or another."

Chars exhaled and said, "Likely we are talking about a hit and run. At worst, we have a deliberate attack. It is strange that Robertson's passenger, if he had one, would just get out and disappear. The other strange part of this is that Freda said the SUV was towed before the police arrived."

Jerry looked upset and said, "Freda must have left out some of her story when she talked to the police. If she told them about the SUV, or even if she didn't, it is shitty police work."

Chars thought back through his conversation with Freda, knowing that she had not been totally frank with the officers.

Jerry continued "She may have been in shock or may not have made it clear—or even left it out entirely."

Chars interjected, "When she was talking to 911, she said it was four cars and four bodies. The reporters must have picked up the four and four from the scanner. When there were only three cars and three bodies and since the SUV was gone when the police got there, they probably assumed that she was mistaken. Freda says she did not see the accident and the police aren't as diligent as they should be."

"That really is shitty police work. I don't believe that the cops would be that sloppy," Jerry said, visibly angry.

"Jerry, we don't even know what really happened," Chars said and then ran through the scenario again in his mind. "If this was deliberate, one: we have a conspiracy to assassinate an elected official; two: Freda could be in danger."

Jerry asked an obvious question, "Why would Mike

Robertson be a threat to someone to such an extent that someone would kill him?"

"Jerry, could we get the tests and keep it low profile until I can do some more work?"

"Yes, and in the meantime I am going to talk to the cops that covered the wreck." Jerry's voice was angry as he climbed into his car and slammed the door.

Chapter 15

"I yield the remainder of this time to Senator Oliver from District Nine," said Senator Harvey of Ohio's District Two.

"Clerk, please note the balance of time is two minutes," the President of the Ohio State Senate said.

"Thank you, Mr. President. I want to bring to your attention the decreasing morale and the high fallout rate of our public school teachers. Since last year, our education system has suffered a significant increase in those leaving the teaching profession for private business and private education. We are almost at critical status in terms of foreign languages, mathematics, and business education. We are in short supply of college level professors in business and computer technology. I am recommending an initiative that brings the Ohio teacher salaries up to grade with the rest of the country. In addition, I propose that all certified teachers that are inclined to further their education, be allowed to attend state funded universities for a free or at least a reduced rate. Third, I propose that teacher and other school personnel be counted as State employees and thereby including them in any available health programs that are currently available to other State employees," Will continued for speaking until the clerk interrupted in an unemotional statement of fact, "Time has expired."

The Senate President stood and pounded his gavel then said, "Thank you Senator. I assume that this will be introduced as legislation through the normal committee process."

Oliver started to leave the podium, but a voice from the left side of the chamber stopped him in his tracks.

"Maybe the freshman Senator needs a couple of minutes to

explain his funding program, since he has been the one that has led the charge to cut education funding," Senator Harwood Clanston said with a bit of disdain and sarcasm all rolled in to one.

The President cleared his throat and said without much commitment, "Out of order, Senator."

The President was thinking the same thing, but had to at least mention the rules violation or he would hear about it when others did the same thing.

"This would have to be worked out in committee and not on the open floor of the Senate," said the President.

"Mr. President, I apologize. I am sure the freshman Senator has it all worked out," Clanston said.

There was a ripple of laughter from those that still regarded Senator Clanston as a political giant in the State of Ohio. A giant of man he was—tall and stout. He was a formidable opponent for any legislation that needed to see its way through the crevasse of the Ohio legislature. Many an idea had been squashed by the two-term Senator from the influential 15th district representing the city of Columbus. This included the Ohio State University, which had in its attendance almost 60,000 students. Clanston had served in about every state office there was, including his full term-limit in the House and was serving out his final allowable term as a State Senator. He had his eyes on the Federal elections, but generally had little appeal on a national level. He could get away with his bullying tactics in Ohio, but he was not a real player in the national scene. Oliver knew that Clanston was trying "jump the issue" and thereby attracting a large block of voters. It was not a secret that Clanston had eyes on the Governor's office. But this education reform bill was Oliver idea and he would simply turn it over to Clanston. Oliver did have a plan for funding and the massive Senator from Columbus was not going to like it. Oliver was still not completely sure of the all the rules of the Senate, so he kept quiet and did not try to answer the bellowing bull. Instead, he returned to his seat, gave a confident smile and nodded his head. In response, Clanston gathered himself, pushed up from his chair and bumped his way through to the aisle. It looked like he was headed directly to Oliver. Oliver thought, *this guy is coming over and he is going to sit on me*. But when Clanston reached the midway point of the aisle, he made a 90-degree turn and headed up the incline toward the back of the Senate floor. Several aides scurried in his wake, trying to quickly fold up documents and close briefcases. A number of other Senators were talking amongst themselves, evidently amused at the blustery old man or at the prospect of a freshman Senator getting a dose of what they had all felt at one time or another. Oliver wondered when he would no longer be considered a freshman.

The President of the Ohio Senate, largely ignoring the exiting entourage of Senator Harwood, concluded the session with a quick rap of his gavel and dismissed the rest of the Senators.

Martha was coming up the bottom aisle and leaned into Will saying, "Did you touch a nerve with the old man?"

"Yeah, he sure blew out of here quick," Will said as he was shaking his head and smiling.

"The newspapers were here, but I did not see any of the television stations. I guess that this story will have to break in print. They might pick it up if someone comes out strongly one way or another. Any way that it plays out will be good for you. You will be seen as the champion of something that is needed and they will either follow or become the target of the teacher's unions in the next election," Martha said with a satisfied smile on her face.

"I think you were right to have this brought up on the floor first and not take a chance of it getting tossed out in committee before anybody hears about it," Will said thoughtfully.

Martha jumped in and said, "Or it gets thrown out of committee and then someone else picks up the idea and claims it for themselves."

“Clanston would have loved to have championed this wouldn’t he?” Oliver smiled back at Martha taking in the natural beauty of her face and bright eyes.

She had come to him as a surprise and had become a trusted confidante that he could not have done without. She had saved him from being eaten alive politically and socially several times. She was intuitive, resourceful and politically savvy. She was quite attractive as well. Will had realized that he had fallen in love with her by the second time he saw her. He considered her his good luck charm. She had appeared when his campaign had just begun. Since he met her, things had been going his way. She had seemed to be attracted to Will as well, but he did sense that Martha was holding back. He could not put his finger on it, but when they were beginning to get close, he sensed a bit of detachment. They had made love on several occasions, but it was a more of an act than a coming together. She was more passionate about the campaign and now the politics, than their relationship. Several times Will had started to bring up the subject of the future, not just his political future, but the future of Mr. and Mrs. Will Oliver. He had stopped short when he noticed the apparent apprehension that Martha showed whenever the conversation started going in that direction. He had felt the lack of commitment several times, but usually it involved the idea of meeting family or attending weddings or funerals. One of Will’s best high school friends, living in Deer Park, just South of Chicago, had unexpectedly died of a heart attack. Martha and Will had only been together for short time, but Will assumed Martha would have wanted to go and support him. He needed some emotional support—after all Mark was one of his best friends, but she seemed rather interested in not giving any. Will figured that the newness of the relationship was the reason. Technically, she was working for him and was not comfortable with traveling as the boss’ girlfriend. Then later Will figured that a political candidate was better off not having a public relationship with a campaign worker. He understood that. But now, even after all the nights spent with each other and the love that they had shared, she was still playing the role of employee. It was if they had a plutonic relationship; as if Will was the only one in love. It seemed that she screwed him because that was what the job required. It puzzled Will. Maybe she was in love with someone else? Maybe she had been dumped or had a bad relationship that was making her unwilling to commit? He did not really think that he was a means to an end, but it sure seemed that way sometimes.

Chapter 16

"Sergeant Collins?" the forensic technician on the other end of the phone said, "You asked to have a couple of tests run on the white Lexus?"

Jerry sat up uncomfortably. "Yes."

"Someone released the car to the insurance company."

"No!" Jerry was puzzled.

"Well, it is not here and the guard said that a tow truck picked up the car about an hour ago. They were taking it to the insurance people to be totaled."

"Shit, shit, shit!" Jerry slammed down the phone and grabbed his coat. He punched in a speed dial number for Chars Reynolds. "Chars, we've got a problem. The car has been released to the insurance company."

"Any way to get it back?" asked Chars, who was chewing on a toothpick; sitting with his feet propped up on a short filing cabinet.

"I suppose I could. Let me run the plate and I'll see what that turns up." Jerry said as he leaned back in his creaky old leather swivel chair. "I'll call you back. No—just wait for a second," Jerry said and turned to his computer. He plugged the number into the Miami Dade Police search. While patiently waiting on the information, Jerry said, "Hey, I checked with the cops that covered the wreck. Miss Freda told them she did not see anything. She drove up on the accident after it happened. She said she was calling in the first accident when the second one took place and did not see anything again."

He received the onscreen information on the Lexus. "The

car was a lease vehicle. The lease was in Robertson's name. I have an address if you want it. Oh, but wait, it is a post office box in Richmond, Virginia. It must be the lease company's address or something. Anyway, Chars, the first question that needs to be answered is: if the circumstances aren't Jake, where was he going to and where was he coming from?" Jerry said.

"That's a good starting point. Did you say his address showed to be in Richmond, Virginia?"

Jerry looked at the screen again trying to get some more detail. "Yeah, that's what it says. But this may just be some kind of billing box that gets forwarded somewhere else, you know."

Chars was silent in thought for only a second. "Give me the address and I'll get back to you."

He wrote down the information and disconnected. He knew at this point that he was in over his head. He picked up the phone and called Priscilla White in Washington's Bureau Research Department.

"What you doing, sweetheart?" Chars said in his best Humphrey Bogart.

"Chars, I haven't heard from you in a while. I thought you must have died or joined a monastery," Priscilla said with a wry smile.

"Not at all dear, just been busy that's all and spending most of my time in Miami," Chars said knowing that he should have followed up his lunch date with Priscilla a couple months ago with some flowers or a note.

"Is there something that I can do for you, Chars?" asked Priscilla.

Chars grimaced at the curt reply. He took a breath and unashamedly said, "Well, yes there is as it happens." He waited for a protest, but there was none. Priscilla was either waiting to tell him to go to hell, or she was not that upset. "I need some information about a post office box. There is a lease car that is registered in the name of Mike Robertson, but the address is a box in Richmond. Can you run it through your sources and see what you can find out?"

"Sounds simple enough. I should have something for you in a day or two," Priscilla said with very little emotion.

Chars gave her the box address and thanked her. The next day Priscilla had left a message for Chars to call her back. He was anxious to find out all that Priscilla had dug up on post office box. Priscilla answered the phone on the first ring and gave a quick greeting to Chars. Chars frowned realizing that she was almost frigid with her responses. She wasted little time with pleasantries and got right to the point. He thought to himself that something was up for her to be so short with him.

"The post office box belongs to an organization called the Right Way. The Right Way was chartered in 2004 as a non-partisan political action organization. The Right Way is a subsidiary of a group called the Freedom Organization that was formed in 2001. The Freedom Organization was created by the late Algiers Banger. It looks like they may have been quiet supporters of several different candidates. A NEXXUS search offered little help. The only entry was a Wall Street Journal article that mentioned that the Freedom Organization contributed to a television ad campaign that helped sink Hillary Clinton. Since there is no direct link I am not even sure if it is the same group. I searched in our newspapers databank, but found nothing there. I made a couple more inquiries to the county registrar and to another friend. Most of the Freedom Organization's expenditures have not been for or to a particular candidate. The Right Way organization does not appear to have any activity and therefore is probably just a shell corporation. I did notice that the charter for the Freedom Organization had not been amended following Banger's death. From the lack of information it is possible that the group just went away," Priscilla editorialized.

Chars thought a second and said, "There weren't any other officers listed?"

"I would have to get that from the state, I think there is a form that can be filled out to obtain public records, but that will take a couple weeks to get an answer back from them."

Chars was trying to piece all this together while Priscilla was giving him her report. He asked himself, would the Freedom Organization through the Right Way pay for Mike Robertson's car? He was sure that was illegal, although he figured that it would be difficult to pin down who actually paid for it. What would it matter anyway now that Robertson and Banger were both dead? The lease was probably paid for with a wire transfer or cashier's check arrangement. It could be traced to a point, but again, who would care? Robertson was dead.

"Chars, Chars!" Priscilla was trying to get Chars' attention.

"I am sorry Priscilla; I was just trying to put this thing together. Thank you so much for the information. I really appreciate it," Chars said genuinely.

"Sure, anytime Chars," Priscilla said and disconnected.

Anytime did not really mean anytime; she was upset. Chars pushed the button for a new line and called a florist to order the flowers that he should have ordered the last time he had lunch with Priscilla. She was a nice enough girl. She was tolerably attractive, but Chars was not going to pursue a long distance relationship and did not want to string her along. He just needed her occasionally to track down a loose end or two. He was not looking for a romance. Chars guessed that Priscilla had figured that out as well. That was why she was so short with him and the whole conversation seemed awkward. She had gone to a lot of trouble and the flowers were a good make-up. You never know when he might need her again. Chars sat back in his chair and pondered the situation. His instincts were telling him that something was up. He needed to find out where Robertson had been going to and was coming from. That might tell him who his passenger was. Until he found that out he had reached a crossing without a ferry.

Chars' cell phone rang with the usual Beethoven's 9th Symphony. It was the D.C. Assistant Editor, Thom Stanton.

"I need you at the Washington Bureau this afternoon, Chars. The Congress is going to pass another immigration reform regarding Cuba and I want someone from Miami here."

Chars always referred to Thom Stanton as the ASSistant Editor. Stanton and Chars had not mixed well when Stanton was full time at the Miami Express. Now Stanton spent most of his time in D.C., and that was just fine with Chars. Chars did not actually report to Stanton anymore. Chars had taken care of that a year earlier by turning in his resignation. The chief editor had interceded and coaxed Chars into staying. Stanton was promoted to the Washington D.C. bureau. Stanton had never forgotten Reynolds' insubordination. Chars wanted to say, "Go screw yourself, but in a magnanimous gesture on his part, Chars went along with the charade of Stanton's authority. He got the angle that Thom wanted and packed his bags for the flight that was leaving in three hours.

Chars checked his office e-mail before heading out and he saw 113 new messages. There were three from his office, each of them telling him to check in. Several more were comments from readers with various angles on stories that he had written. He quickly sent some innocuous thank you replies. None of the messages concerned anything he had an interest in pursuing. However, there was one that caught his attention. The subject heading said "Robertson info." Chars quickly called it up and scrolled down. The word "interested" was the only word typed. It was signed MR Friend. Chars' eyes narrowed, he thought, *that's strange*. Chars replied with "interested; contact me on my cell." He typed in his number, hit send and signed out. He gathered his stuff and headed to the airport.

Chapter 17

Will and Martha had decided to make a weekend of the trip to Cincinnati. Will was in a celebrating mood and had made reservations at the Smith and Wolensky's Restaurant. It was a festive dinner. They had ordered a bottle of Cedar Creek Merlot. It was one of his wife's favorites, but he did not tell Martha that piece of information.

"What do you think you are going to do next? Martha asked as she sliced off a piece of the 8oz petite rib eye.

"Well, I am not sure really, the education bill will be the breaker. It could be over real quick," Will said and leaned back, having polished off most of his dinner.

"Will, you have to think positive. You are doing a good job and the people are seeing that."

As Martha swilled her wine and appreciatively inhaled the wine's bouquet, Will said, "I am not being negative, just a realist. And, I just have a hard time believing that this is happening this quick. It has been a whirlwind."

The restaurant had an elegant feeling about it. The tables were spaced well beyond the normal distance to allow for more privacy. Waiters seemed to appear as soon as a need developed, but were never in the way. Will thought Martha was beautiful in the candlelight of their table. His heart was full of emotion.

Will pulled up close to Martha and said. "I am so fortunate to have you to share this with."

Martha gave Will a light kiss on his cheek, smiled and changed the subject. "Have you been looking over the material that Todd Reasons gave you?"

Will paused for a moment, with the interruption of his thought process. "Yes, I have been. I guess I really never thought about all the issues that have to be considered. There are all the different programs that I had no idea about. I am fairly up to date on the economic stuff, but still need to work on all the different social issues and all the laws. You know, a lot of the material was more national stuff than Ohio issues," Will said with some distress.

His mind was racing again. Martha smiled at him and calmly said, "Will, you are going to be fine. You are smart and have good intentions. And, you need to be up to date on national issues as well."

"I wish I felt the same confidence that you evidently have."

Will looked up at the ceiling and took a deep breath. The waiter came by and filled their water glasses. They declined desert and the waiter placed the ticket on the edge of the table.

Determined, Will returned to his original topic. "You really ought to meet my kids."

"I would like that very much, but our schedule does not leave much time," Martha said.

"The last time they came, you were conveniently out of town. Maybe this time you can schedule yourself to be around," Will said gently.

Martha put her hand on Will's. "That would be great. You think they would like the fact that you have an interest?"

"Now who is being negative?" Will said, through a sly smile.

Will signed the credit card statement and mused to himself that the meal topped a hundred dollars. He would have choked over spending that much money for a meal just a few months ago. He liked the idea of not having to worry about money. The two of them made their way out of the restaurant, buttoning up their coats and pulling each other close. Maybe Will had been misreading her. Maybe she **was** interested. Martha saw the two men walking nonchalantly on the other side of the street. Granted it was dark, and this was Cincinnati, not New York City or Chicago. Nevertheless she was tense while Will started up a conversation about the latest happenings in the Senate. She pretended to listen but saw another silhouette in front of them several yards away. Martha unzipped her purse and placed her hand on her P229 Sig Sauer 9mm pistol. They were just 30 feet from the rental car. One of the men reached into his pocket. Martha thumbed off the safety. The stranger pulled out a cigarette and lit it.

"Everything all right?" Will asked noticing that Martha seemed to have tensed, but was still oblivious to the men that were closing in.

"Yes, I am fine. Do you have the keys?" Martha said and moved around the back of the car to her door.

"Right here, let me get the door for you," Will said while moving around to open it.

She started to protest, but Will was already opening up the door and allowing Martha to step into the car. Martha knew that it was a mistake not letting Will get in first, but the men walked on by and got in to a nearby car. She took a deep breath and looked in the side mirror to see if the car was following them. She pushed the gun safety back on and zipped up her purse.

"Will, could we just go back to the hotel?" Martha asked in quiet but unemotional voice.

"Sure!" Will said with a knowing smile. He was thinking about sex and he thought to himself, *Martha is thinking the same thing.*

They pulled up to the hotel a few moments later and the valet took the keys and pulled away to park the car. When they were inside, and at the door to Martha's room, she turned and gave Will a long kiss. She then gave him the feeble excuse of being exhausted, then asked for a rain check on the rest of the evening.

Will was visibly surprised at the turn of events and said, "Sure. I will call you when it's time to get up."

He swiped her key for her and she disappeared into her room. Will walked two doors down, swiped his key and went inside his room feeling totally confused and bewildered.

When Martha got back into the room, she pulled out a cell phone.

Ben Thomas answered on the first ring.

"Hey, I just had some visitors," Martha (a.k.a. Kay Moore) went into the bathroom and turned on the faucet. She was just being safe, but that was how she was trained. She had learned to be careful following six years of covert work with the National Security Agency.

"Why would they be following Oliver? And, why would they let you see them?" Ben was saying in a puzzled voice.

"They did not show a weapon, but there were about four of them. They weren't hiding really. But when they approached, I had no doubt they were making a move on Will," Martha's pulse started to rise again as she replayed the events. "I almost pulled my weapon."

"Did you have to race away?" Ben asked. He was trying to get an idea of the magnitude of the problem and some possible explanations. If Kay Moore said that there were spooks; then there were spooks.

"No, she said with exasperation, "Will seemed oblivious to it all and just asked if I was alright." Martha was speaking while walking in a tight circle in the bathroom.

"Did you see any identification or maybe their car?" Ben was still hoping to narrow down who sent the men.

"No, it was dark and I was just trying to figure out an escape plan. I mean if they wanted to have hit either one of us they certainly could have," Martha said.

There was a pause as both Ben and Martha tried to solve the puzzle.

"I don't know who it could have been. They were pros, but they did not care if I saw them."

"They weren't there to harm Will, just scare him?" Ben was just thinking out loud.

Martha nearly jumped through the phone. "Scare him for what? He was not scared; he didn't even have enough sense to be scared," Martha was talking in a low, but animated voice.

"Martha, you have experienced much tighter situations than that. What's the problem?" Ben said in a calm voice.

"It is just that it was so unexpected. It really caught me off guard. I am all right now."

She felt a little embarrassed at her reaction to the situation. As it turned out she and Will were not in danger, and maybe she just imagined the walk by. No; she knew by their walk and how they were dressed. She had seen that type before.

"Ben, they looked like CIA or FBI."

Ben thought about that for a minute or two. "I am just not sure who they would be. I can't imagine why the FBI or the CIA would be interested in Will. Has anyone else shown up recently, in the campaign office; or has anything else seemed unusual to you?" Ben asked. He was searching for a clue that had to be there.

"We have hired an assistant or two in the past month, but they were just college kids. I don't think they would have anything to do with this." Martha was now sitting on the edge of the bathtub with her hand on her forehead. There was a knock on the door. Martha shot up and whispered, "Ben there is someone at the door. I will call you back when I get a chance."

She quietly tiptoed up to the door and looked out the peep hole. Will was standing there. He was looking at the peephole as well and could see the shadow move through the glass eye. He knew she was there, looking to see who it was. He decided to pretend not to know she was there and turned and walked away.

Chapter 18

"Jerry, the P.O. Box did not give me much. I want to contact Robertson's family and his staff to see where he was going. What is the status of the investigation?" asked Chars. He was leaning back in his chair making notes as he talked.

"There is no official ruling, but I don't think that it is even being investigated. No one has said anything that would make me think there was anything else to be determined. The papers are all reporting about the accident, but not a single article or news story for that matter have even hinted at anything be wrong. Do you have anything else that would help?" asked Jerry.

"The only other bit of info that I have is that Robertson had some kind of tie to The Freedom Organization or the PAC, called The Right Way. Neither one of those organizations seems to be doing much, but in the past they had some significant influence. The founder was Algiers Banger. He died a year or two ago and it seems the organization did also."

"Dead—except that they were still paying for a lease car for a potential Presidential candidate," Jerry deadpanned.

"Yeah, that might have been a catch in the zipper. I need to talk to his office and to his family. If they have heard of the FO, then I might be able to track down some other leads. There is nothing else on the passenger or the SUV?"

"They did not exist as far as we are concerned. The officers went back out to talk to Freda, but her mother said she had run off with some man. The old lady was really upset. She has to run the fruit stand now all by herself," Jerry said slightly amused.

"You don't think that is strange?" Chars jumped in.

"I don't know Chars; wouldn't you want to get the hell out of Dodge if your white knight showed up?" asked Jerry.

"Not if the knight was driving a white SUV. I'll get back to you in a day or two. Oh, I don't suppose anyone was able to track down Robertson's car?"

Jerry cleared his throat. "No, he said, "it seems to have gone poof. The person who signed it out was from one of the big insurance companies, and signed a fake name. Of course the car was not insured by them and they had never heard of the guy that signed for it."

"Damn Jerry, this thing is stinking bad, and the PI guys made it awful easy on them."

Jerry took in a deep breath and said, "It was a low-level guy at the gate and he did not have any reason to think something was wrong. I talked to him myself. We put out an alert on the vehicle with a description of the guy. It is being handled as a theft."

"Ok, I appreciate the information. I will let you know what I find out from Robertson's group."

Chars hung up the phone and began typing a search for a cross-reference of Robertson and The Freedom Organization into his computer. The two names didn't come up together. He typed in The Right Way and received no hits. He went to the Robertson website and looked up the staff. He stopped with the name, Marsha Lincoln. He picked up the phone and called. Marsha was not in, but he left a message for her to call him on his cell phone.

Within ten minutes his phone vibrated and he answered it.

"Chars Reynolds—it takes someone to die in an accident before I get a call from you?" Marsha said in a husky voice.

"Hey Marsha, how are you holding up?" Chars asked with true concern.

"Not good. This was a shocker. Mike was such a good guy. You know he was different from the usual politicians. He was honest and I really believed he was going to be our next President."

"I was so sorry when I heard. He did seem to be a bright man. What are you doing now, Marsha? Chars asked.

"We are not really able to do anything. We are paralyzed. I know he's gone, but we still come in to work and just move paper around," Marsha said through a sniffle. She was obviously still quite shaken.

"I'd like to do a nice piece on Mike. I am sure you are being bombarded by everyone, but could you give me some information?" Chars moved into the point of his call as gracefully as possible.

"I think that would be nice. You were always very positive with your material," Marsha said as she grabbed a tissue from her desk drawer and lightly blew her nose.

"First of all, where was he going to or where was he coming from when the accident occurred?"

Chars hit with the first question that he really was curious about. Normally that would be a question that was just to put the other person at ease. It did not work this time. Marsha sounded like she was going to break completely apart.

"That is just it, Chars—we don't really know why he was there. He may have just decided to take a drive or something, but that was not characteristic of him. We have not officially said where he was going to or from, because we really don't know."

"Do you have any reason to believe it was anything other than an accident?"

There was silence on the other end of the phone.

"Chars, do you know something that we don't?" Marsha's voice was one of genuine surprise.

"No I don't. I am just trying to close a few ends up and there were a couple facts that are just difficult to put together—like where he was going or where he was coming from? Would his family be open to some questions?"

"I don't know Chars. Obviously this is a very difficult time. Everyone is being directed to Justin for comments. The family has not talked to the press, TV people, or anybody," Marsha said while wiping her nose again.

"I'll be back in Miami in a couple days; could you set up a meeting for me?" Chars said and held his breath.

There was silence on the other end. "Let me talk to Justin Crawford, to see where everything stands and I'll get back to you."

"Thanks Marsha. I am really sorry about Mike." Chars gave her his cell phone number and disconnected.

He went down to the coffee area, loaded up a cup with sugar and cream. He poured in a steaming bit of coffee. He took a sip and grimaced. Some things had not changed since the last time that he had been to the D.C. office. He went down the hallway and caught an elevator to the sixth floor. The sign read "KR Research" and Chars entered the modern office that was flanked by cubicles and computer rows. There were only a couple of people in the office; neither bothered to look up when Chars entered. He went to one of the side offices and poked his head around the corner. Priscilla was busy typing away unaware that she had a visitor. The flowers that he had sent were on the side of her desk and still looked fairly presentable.

"Priscilla?" Chars ventured a greeting.

Priscilla stopped mid-stroke and smiled to herself. She slowly spun her chair around finishing one last keystroke before she said, "Well, look what the cat dragged in."

"Priscilla, it's good to see you too," Chars said, giving her a winning smile and moved toward her desk.

"The flowers were a nice touch," she said not giving an inch on the hospitable side.

She looks pretty good, thought Chars. She was wearing a white blouse that showed an appropriate amount of cleavage.

Priscilla looked directly at Chars and blandly said, “Chars, I am not mad at you. I just did not like being left up in the air so long.”

“I am sorry about that. It was just real...” Chars started to give an excuse, but she cut him off.

“I don’t even want to hear the excuse. We are friends, Chars. I was not expecting a long-term romance. We live a long way away. You are in Miami and I am in D.C. I just thought that we might have had a follow up conversation or something. So, what can the Research Department do for you?” Priscilla said looking directly at the reporter and taking a sip of coffee.

“I do need your help,” Chars said sheepishly.

“I know you do, Chars, and I am glad you are willing to admit it. What do you need?” Priscilla briskly said, putting down her coffee and picking a pen and small spiral notebook.

Chars looked around almost conspiratorially to see if anyone was within ear shot. He said quietly, “I need anything you can dig up on this Freedom Organization; who runs it now and anything else you can find out. It is the Robertson accident. There are several things that are not kosher. I think that the Freedom Organization had a tie-in with Robertson that few people knew about. There are a lot of loose ends with the accident. Robertson’s car has disappeared before some tests could be run and the only witness to the accident has run off with a new Prince Charming. We have an unaccounted car at the scene that was towed before the police had even arrived. We also have a possible passenger in Robertson’s car at the time of the accident. I am not really sure where to start, but the Freedom Organization seems to be the only thread hanging out there to grab. Can you do some work and let me know as soon as you can?”

From around the corner a man in his forties stepped in the office. Chars wondered if the guy had heard anything. He asked to borrow a printer cartridge, but then he stopped when he saw Chars.

He excused himself for interrupting and took a package that Priscilla offered up. He winked at Priscilla and then gave Chars a wary look as he went out the door. Chars' face crinkled in a "who was that idiot?" look.

Priscilla said, "Oh you don't have to worry about Marshall, he's harmless." Chars waited for her appraisal of the situation. "Sounds like you might have something there that could use my touch." Her ego had evidently been stroked enough and she was on the inside of possibly the top story in the news.

"Thanks Priscilla," Chars said and got up to leave.

Priscilla smiled and shook her head as if to say, "why do I do what I do for you?" Then turned back to her computer and began searching.

Over her shoulder she said, "Hey, I want a bi-line if this thing takes off."

"That's a bit unusual, but if you find me something, you got a deal." Chars was smiling at the girl's somewhat audacious demand. But he shrugged and turned to go to his office. He thought, *Let's just see what she turns up first.* He went out the door and almost ran into Marshall again.

"Oh, excuse me." Marshall said, almost dropping the cartridge and spilled a little coffee on the carpet.

He did look embarrassed and held up the package he had in his hand and said, "Wrong cartridge."

Chars smiled thinly and moved to the other side of the hall. "Not a problem, Marshall."

Chars had a suspicious look on his face as he walked down the hallway to the elevators.

Chapter 19

"Ross?" Ben asked on a stealth looking Motorola, PEBL6 cell phone. He was calling from his hotel room in Chicago, having just finished a light dinner...

"Yes, what's happening?" Ross Saunders answered the secure call..

He clicked on a light next to his bed. He looked over at his clock. It read 2:04. The spot in the corner of the digital display indicated it was A.M. He sat the rest of the way up in the bed and tried to clear his mind.

"Kay says she and Will had visitors. She was certain they were spooks, but there was no activity."

"What was Will's reaction?" Ross asked.

"None. She said it was like he was oblivious to the men."

"Gee, how alert is this guy—or were they just hanging back?" Ross was also trying to understand why Will wouldn't have noticed a walk-by.

As if reading Ross' mind, Ben said. "Looks like he would have noticed a walk-by, but he's not trained to look for that stuff. We don't know who it was or why they allowed themselves to be seen."

"Maybe they just wanted to see if they would bolt."

"But who? And why would they think they had a reason to run?"

"I don't know, but we need to find out."

"Could they have been after Kay for some reason?" Ben asked.

Ross thought about that and arched his eyebrows in

contemplation, "Well, she was in Mike's campaign and maybe there is a connection there. Say, speaking of Mike, I got a report back from D.C. that Mike's accident may have more to it than seemed possible before. My contact overheard part of conversation between a reporter and another research lady. He said it was quite by chance that he was just sort of walking through. He says he heard this reporter say that there was a passenger in Mike's car when the accident occurred," Ross said.

Ben was puzzled and not sure how to respond. "Mike was not alone in his car?"

"That's what this guy told me. He said that the reporter's name is Reynolds. Reynolds was in the D.C. office talking to one of their researchers. The subject was Robertson. He overhead the reporter telling the researcher that Robertson may have had a passenger with him during the wreck," Ross repeated.

"Who could that have been? Everybody on the election staff was back at the office. No one there seems to know why he was where he was. Shit! So what happened to the so-called passenger? Does he just get up and walk away from an accident that is serious enough to cause three deaths? How does he just get away and avoid the police?"

Ben was incensed at the prospect that he had not gotten all the details when he was down there. He was embarrassed and upset with himself for not digging in more. Ben felt sure that Ross must be thinking of him as incompetent.

"The police do not have it in their report at all. I don't know how reliable that information is, Ben. I was just passing it along. It actually makes a bit more sense if the accident was not an accident if you catch my drift. I just can't imagine who would go to that length to get Mike. If this is all true, the passenger may have caused Mike to run into the overpass. Maybe the second car was truly just an accident. It would have complicated things, but may have made the details more obscure at the same time. A second accident that killed additional people would cause a closer look," Ross was thinking out loud.

"Not more attention than whacking a Senator," Ben said.

"Yeah, I guess that is true," Ross was again thinking through some possible scenarios that could lead to the Robertson crash. "Can you get Marley onto the reporter?"

"Yeah, we won't need him for a while," Ben said while looking over a calendar and then over to a map on the wall.

"We should keep Kay in place to cover Will in case there is any move on him," Ben said.

"Yeah; if someone actually hit Mike, then we may need to look at some evasive action. We have to figure out who is on to us and see how much they know," Ross answered. "Ben, we need to be careful as well. You should really watch your back."

There was a pause in the conversation. Ben was obviously trying to put this new information into an equation that would answer some of these questions.

"Could we meet and just lay out some possibilities?"

"Yeah, let's do that. When can you get to New York?" asked Ross.

Ben again looked at his watch. "I can be there within a couple hours. How quickly can you be there?"

"Well the next commercial would get me there around noon your time. I think I pick up about five or six hours on the trip back. Let's run a spy sweep on Oliver's Senate office and his house. Better hit the election office as well," Ross said.

Ben wondered what part of the world that time difference would correlate with and raised his eyebrows. He decided not to ask and said, "Ok, I'll get someone over there right away. I will give Kay a heads-up so she doesn't shoot him."

"Good idea, Ben. I will call you when I touch down," Ross said, hung up the phone, pivoted out of bed, and put his feet on the ground.

Chapter 20

Chars moved out into traffic on his way to the hotel. He stopped off at a store on and made a purchase. He hustled back out to his car and continued on to his hotel. He wanted to try Freda one more time, but in the evening. He wanted to know if the mother had heard from her daughter yet. He forgot to check his e-mail at his last stop. His mystery informant had not called, but maybe had sent another e-mail.

He was staying in the Hay Adams Hotel. It was located directly across from Lafayette Park. The Hay Adams offered the city's best view of the White House and Washington Monument. The hotel was named after statesman, John Hay, and historian, Henry Adams, whose homes once occupied this spot. The architecture was Italian Renaissance, while the guest rooms leaned toward a Georgian or Edwardian style. The afternoon tea was a Washington favorite. For Chars, it was a nice treat. If he had to come back to the D.C. Bureau, he figured this was his little way of rebelling. No one in the accounting department had ever questioned his expense account even though his room was consistently $365 or more a night. He wanted to try out a new phone that he had purchased at a Radio Shack. The sales person seemed knowledgeable enough and was even able to give him some pointers about e-mail encryption.

Chars pulled a six pack of tall boys out of a brown bag. He had been able to stop and get some travel items that he was low on and decided it would be nice if he had a bit of beer in his room. The beer was warm, so he decided he needed some ice. He would check his e-mail again for the mystery informant and now he had his secure phone. He extended the deadbolt to block open the door and went down the hallway with ice bucket in hand. The ice machine was down one hallway, around the corner and all the way at the end of the next hallway. When he arrived he thought the machine looked ancient. It was one of those kinds that you stick the whole bucket in a cubicle of sorts, pulled a lever and the ice was supposed to fill up the bucket just right. Chars gave it a try. As had been the case in his previous experience with this type of contraption, the ice was dispensed in a quantity that could have filled a suitcase. Ice was going everywhere and did not appear to be stopping any time soon. Finally the machine shut off its flow. Chars kicked the scattered ice cubes on the ground under the machine.

As he was coming up the hallway the exit door on the far side was closing. It appeared that a guest had chosen to take the stairs instead of waiting around for the elevator. Chars thought that was strange since they were toward the top of the hotel. He shrugged at the thought and pushed door open with his foot. He was concentrating on the ice bucket, trying to make sure that he did not drop any. From behind the door a man stepped out and whacked him on the back of his neck with what might have been a club or the head of a wooden walking stick. Chars never saw it coming and immediately slammed down hard on the ground. Just as he landed, his head slung forward and cracked open his forehead on the bottom corner of the desk leg. The cut was clean and deep. Blood began to flow onto the hotel carpet and ice was strewn all over the room. The attacker tried to step around the ice to avoid crunching any cubes—and of course to not leave a footprint in the increasing pool of blood. The hotel staff may actually think that Chars slipped on a cube of ice and hit his head on the table, causing him to pass out.

That was a fortunate fall, thought Paul Gallegos. He was wearing gloves so as not to leave prints. The gloves were powder-free latex, the kind that surgeons wore. He could still have the touch that he wanted, but would not leave fingerprints or any other residue. No one would suspect that there had been another visitor to Mr. Reynolds room. Lego moved quickly and carefully, making sure he didn't disturb anything, and went through Reynolds' briefcase. The suitcase was on the bed. It had one of the cheap travel locks on it. What he needed would be on the computer or in the briefcase. He just needed a look at some notes and then he could get the hell out of there. He booted up the computer. He stuck a flash drive the size of baby carrot into the port. As soon as the computer started its boot up routine, Lego interrupted it with a quick keystroke. The computer flashed to a different menu page. He selected a couple different commands in succession and waited for just few minutes. He now had every file downloaded on his tiny little portable storage device. It could easily hold all the information that was on the hard drive with room to spare. It held a full two petabytes. Technology was truly amazing to Gallegos. All that information could be stored in a piece of equipment that was so small. A few moments later the task was complete. Lego shut down Chars' computer and replaced everything like he remembered. He had been careful not to disturb anything else while he was there; Chars notwithstanding of course. Lego exited out the down and down the hallway. His partner was just inside the doorway and had been keeping watch. It would have been a bit neater if Chars had been gone for a while, but he seemed to take that computer with him everywhere he went. The open door was just too tempting to pass up. In a matter a minutes they were both gone. Chars began to moan softly and seemed to be coming to. About the same time a hotel maid happened to be passing by and looked in through the half opened door. She gasped and immediately radioed the supervisor.

In the Metropolitan Hospital, the cut caused by Chars falling onto the desk leg received the most attention. But Chars' neck was killing him. The nurse told him that he was lucky. She had a patient just last month that tripped on a lamp cord and hit her head.

"I am sorry to hear that. I hope she is okay," he said, trying to ignore the pain. The pounding was horrific.

The nurse raised her eyebrows and said, "She died," and then walked out the door.

Chars felt bad that he had even commented. His head began to throb again. A different nurse came in. Chars said, "I may have upset the other nurse that was in here. I really did not mean to."

"Oh, she is just emotional over a patient that fell and hit her head last week," the nurse said conversationally while walking around to the other side of Chars.

She was about 4-foot 5 inches and weighed around 210 pounds. She was as black as the night—so black she was almost blue. She had a beautiful smile and her eyes seemed to glimmer. Chars thought she looked like a person he could trust. He tried to focus on her name tag, but there was still a white light that outlined everything he looked at. In addition, someone had removed his contact lenses or they had become foggy. The lens often did this if Chars accidentally went to sleep with the lenses still in.

"I am sorry, but what is your name?" he asked.

The nurse went in close to Chars' face and gave his pupils a real good checking over.

"You got a concussion for sure, Honey. My name is Katrina, but my friends call me Kat for short. I like that better anyway. There was a real bad hurricane down where I came from named Katrina. So I really don't like that name too much. Now you have had all the medicine you need, but if you get to feeling uncomfortable let me know."

"Kat…" It seemed to take an enormous amount of effort just to focus his thoughts and speak, "Kat, when will I get out of here?"

"Oh, that is above my pay grade, Sweetie. But, I would think you would be here at least through tomorrow."

I have got to get out of here, Chars thought. He tried to sit up and a wave of pain rushed through his head. Kat just stood there and watched him. She did not tell him to lie down or anything. She knew what was going to happen and she just let nature takes its course.

"Well, Mr…" she looked at his charts and continued, "Reynolds, I guess you are going to stay with us a while after all." She walked out the door, laughing.

"Cruel woman," Chars said as she went.

He heard her say to someone outside, "Mr. Reynolds does not feel like seeing anyone right now."

He could make out Thom Stanton's voice. "Oh, Charles will be fine; he's got a head as hard as rock."

Kat looked at him with a sly smile and said, "Go right ahead then."

Chars looked up and could almost make out Stanton's features. "I am honored, Thom," he said.

"Chars, how are you doing?" Thom sounded concerned and compassionate. Chars knew that not to be the case. Thus it worried him even more. "Chars," Thom asked "They say you slipped on a piece of ice and hit your head on a table leg?"

Chars could almost see the man begin to break into a smile. Chars thought, w*hat was this, Enjoy Chars in Pain Day*? Finally, Chars gathered himself for a retort and said, "You sound amused."

"I must admit there is some… now that you are okay of course… well everyone was of course concerned. You know. So that's why I came up to see how you were doing," Thom said. He studied the patient and knew Chars was not altogether there. He could see Chars squinting and shaking his head trying to get a clear look.

Finally Thom said, "Man, that must have been some kind

of shot you took. Had you been drinking?"

That pissed Chars off and he said, "NO! … I" and the pain shot through his head.

Thom stepped back in surprise and said, "Hey Chars, I wouldn't do that anymore. That looks like it hurt."

Chars leaned his head back and thought to himself, *No shit Sherlock. Why don't you come over here and let me show you how much it hurts.* Chars thought aloud, "Did I say that?"

Thom said, "Say what?"

Chars did not know if he was just thinking something or was he saying it. He was confused and decided he had just better rest.

"I didn't say you had been drinking, the police say they found some beer in your room."

Chars was still holding his head. "Yes I had beer, but no, I did not have any beer."

Stanton seemed to be smiling, but Chars was not sure. Everything still seemed so fuzzy.

"I see," Stanton said with a disbelieving tone. "Chars, have the doctors told you anything else?"

Chars looked at his former boss and tried to hold back any contempt that was left over from the last question. In truth, Chars had never really cared for Stanton. He had only come back to Washington because he insisted. One of the reasons he liked being in Miami was because he did not have to deal with clods like Thom Stanton on a daily basis. The fact that he was here meant one of two things: Chars had done something wrong and Thom had come to see if he was healthy enough to fire; or he was here at the hospital anyway and wanted to appear compassionate.

Chars just answered with a quiet "No."

"Say Chars, do you always stay at the Hay Adams Hotel when you come to Washington?"

Chapter 21

Senator Will Oliver lay in his bed at his home in Blue Ash. He could hear the birds chirping outside, but next to him was an empty space. He closed his eyes and remembered the past years. He missed his wife. They had become closer as the years went on. When the kids left home he was not sure if they would survive the empty nest, but they had. And then, the bad news hit. She was sitting in a rocker that her grandmother had passed down. He thought she was sleeping, but she had be waiting for him to come home so she could tell him the about the tests. He sat there in silence. He prayed in his mind and then held her for a long time. She went quickly—three months to the day. She had been such a cheerful and energetic soul.

The phone rang causing Will to jerk upright in his bed. Looking at the clock through uncorrected vision, he realized it was after ten in the morning. It took him another second to fully comprehend that he needed to find the phone. It was not in its cradle. He almost fell out of bed, but finally located the telephone, which he had been sleeping on. It was wrapped inside several layers of the sheets and bed covers, so he was unsuccessful in retrieving it before it stopped ringing. He punched the button for the Caller ID. It showed that it was a private number. Will had learned not to fret over the calls that did not get answered. They would call him back if it was important. He had in fact gone from the person that felt like he was being put off or ignored to the ignorer, "the big man on-campus" that everyone else had to wait for.

The phone rang again. This time Chris looked at the caller

I.D screen. Once again, the only words it displayed were "Private Number." Without further hesitation, he answered the call by simply saying, "Oliver."

"Good morning, Senator. I am calling to give you sort of a heads up." It was Todd Reasons calling from his Senate office.

Will ran his fingers through his bed-head hair and swung his feet out of bed. "Okay, what's up?"

"Well, I am not sure what this will mean or even how big of deal it is." Reasons seemed to be equivocating.

"Todd, what is it?"

"Evidently, you did some work for the Beef Cattleman's Association, a while back." He was not asking. "Someone has put the notion into a Senator's mind that they paid you double the amount of the contract as some sort of bribe."

Oliver was stunned. Not having been in politics very long, he had a very sick feeling in his stomach. "Well, actually all that is true except that it was not a bribe. I had not even filed for office."

"I guess you did not cash the check for a while and it showed up on some disclosure statement that our office filed with the ethics committee. You know who heads that committee, don't you?" Reasons asked.

Will thought and asked "Clanston?"

"You got it." Todd said. Will was still not sure where all this was leading and asked, "So what will happen?"

"My sources say that the paper is going to run a story whose headline says 'State Senator to be Questioned About Contribution'." Oliver's face reddened.

"Can they do that…without a comment from me?"

Reasons had not seen or heard Will while he was angry. This was likely to be one of those times.

"Will, this is about par for the course. Clanston is just trying to take some of the shine off your finish."

"That is absolute bullshit," Will was yelling in the phone.

"What I would suggest is to release a statement to the press, saying that this was a politically motivated charge. The work was done prior to announcing your run for office and the payment was based on your performance. This had nothing to do with Ohio politics and anyone who would suggest otherwise is attempting to distort, mischaracterize, and slander," Reasons said.

"It is absolute bullshit!" Will was incensed. "That fat son of a bitch!" Will lowered his volume, but his voice was angry.

Reasons figured he would just let him go until he ran out of energy. He was not sure how long that would be, but it turned out to be just a half a minute or so.

Reasons said in a calm but sincere tone. "Will, you are just going to have to let this be like water off a duck's back."

"No, I don't want to just take it. That piece of crap needs a little bit of his own medicine. I'll call you back."

Will debated what to do. He paced around the room and thought through his conversation with Reasons again. Will scrolled through his phone numbers and came to one that read, BTHOM, and he hit send.

The voice came on and said "Eleven twenty-two."

Will said, "This is ten twenty-two."

"Got it, eleven twenty-seven," the voice said and the line clicked.

"Yeah, he seemed really rattled," Reasons said. "He said something about giving Clanston some of his own medicine."

He paused for Ben Thomas to respond. "I wonder how he intends to do that," Ben said with a smile.

At that moment, Ben's secretary slipped him a note that said, "Call Will in five. Received at 11:22pm."

Ben smiled and shook his head. "Okay Todd, thanks. Senator Oliver will be calling you back and he will tell you to release a statement. Meanwhile I'll see if I can shake Clanston's tree a bit," said Ben. "He has a few secrets as well."

He looked at the clock, waited until it read 11:27 and dialed Will. "How's the weather, Senator?" Ben was smiling. He genuinely liked Will, though sometimes Ben knew that he became flustered a bit too easily.

"Weather's real nice. I was thinking about taking a walk later on this afternoon." Will was trying to be calm and not show how much he was upset over this Clanston deal. He also did not want to spook Ben by implying that this was a real issue.

"Hey, sorry to bother you, but Reasons called to give me a heads-up about an article that may or may not be written up in the Columbus paper. Seems one of the senators has a problem with sharing the limelight."

Ben was patiently listening. Will wondered for a moment if Ben was still there. Finally Ben said, "I see."

"A month or so into the campaign I filed a disclosure form that listed income sources and a variety of other things. One of the items is a consulting fee from the Cattleman's Association for the amount of four grand," Will said and hesitated, again wondering if Ben was listening.

"I understand," Ben said.

"For some reason, the amount they paid and the amount that the contract stated was different," Will said.

"What was the contract amount?" Ben asked.

"Two thousand," said Will.

"Well, sounds like a red herring to me. Clanston probably just wants to throw a little mud around, just to see how you and the press react. I would wait to see what the press actually reports and then respond. I would say something like: 'this was a private contract prior to my candidacy.' If it mentions Clanston's name, then follow up with, 'Senator Clanston is known for this type of attack. I am sure that he will get his facts straight and realize that this is an unwarranted attack. I give credit to Ohioans to see through Senator Clanston's attempt to muddy-up the political water.'"

Will was feverishly taking notes, all the while nodding his head, and just said, "Ok."

"Will, this is about par for the course. You have been real fortunate so far. This just means you are making some progress. People are starting to take you seriously," Ben said and leaned back in his leather office chair.

"Yeah, I suppose I should feel flattered."

"Absolutely, in fact you could put that in a retort if you like... 'Senator Clanston must really feel threatened to come up with a mischaracterization of the facts. You have faith in Ohioans' and all that—but no anger, Will; not with anger. Do it as you would if you were excusing an unruly drunk," Ben said.

Will was not entirely convinced, but felt better about the situation. "Ok, thanks. I will wait till this comes out in the paper."

"If the story appears to have legs, we will go on the offensive. Ok?"

They exchanged good byes and disconnected the call. Ben entered Marley's number from memory.

When Marley answered, Ben said, "I need you in Miami."

Chapter 22

After 24 hours in the hospital, Chars insisted on being released. Closing up the slit in his head required 25 stitches and as soon as he returned to the hotel, Chars removed the bandage. To hide his scar, he bought a baseball cap from a small gift shop in the lobby. Soon, he was busy packing his stuff and not long after, he caught the first flight out of D.C. back to Miami International. As soon as he arrived in the Sunshine State, Chars caught a cab to a drug store and picked up a pain prescription that the D.C. doctor said he was going to need. There was a lot more to do. He called Jerry to schedule a lunch with him. Chars still had not checked his e-mail and made a mental note to do so—hoping he could rely on memory. Staring ahead, Chars moved his head back and forth. He was still having some pain, but it was going to be a good day, he thought. After all, he was finally out of the hospital and back in Miami.

Chars' head was still a little cloudy, but he was having lunch at one of his favorite lunch spots. Inside the Sonesto Resort, the Purple Dolphin overlooked the Atlantic Ocean. He pulled out his prescription bottle and tried to read the directions. It was a little blurry; he tried to remember if his contacts were in or not. He shrugged and figured that it was usually two every six hours or so. He was going to ask the waiter, but he was embarrassed. He dropped down a couple of Percoset and took a gulp of water that the greeter had placed at his table. He did not usually take medicine, but the pain in his neck and head had returned. He was still wearing the hat to cover up his wound; as an added benefit it shaded the brightness of the sun. Moments later, the waiter arrived dressed smartly in a waist coat and bow tie on a starched white shirt. He seemed to remember Chars, but Chars was having trouble remembering him. Chars figured that by the way he was acting the waiter probably knew he was a reporter.

"Meester Reenolds, welcome back. I have taken the liberty of fixing your favorite, our Mimosa."

Chars said, "That is very nice of you to remember." He thought, *I wish I could remember who you were.*

Arriving about 20 minutes late, Jerry was his usual apologetic self. Jerry had agreed to meet at the Purple Dolphin after some convincing. This setting was a little too posh for Jerry. It was also a little too visible and a longer drive than Jerry preferred. He would have to make up an excuse about returning late from lunch and he did not like to do that. Chars, on the other hand, loved this place. They sat outside at a table next to the rail. Jerry ordered an ice tea and began looking over the lunch menu.

Jerry gave Chars a strange look. "Chars, you never wear a hat. What's up?" Chars removed his hat. "What the hell happened to you?" Chars started to put his hat back on, but Jerry reached up and stopped him.

Chars said, "Depends on who you are talking to. But the hotel people say I slipped on a piece of ice and hit my head on a table leg."

"That looks really bad." Jerry said having seen enough and allowing Chars' hand to return the cap to his head.

"I was in the hospital overnight," Chars said almost pitifully.

Jerry was shaking his head in disbelief trying not to smile at the thought of Chars slipping on a piece of ice.

"You should have called. I could have helped out," Jerry said.

"I was in Washington D.C." Chars said quickly and then grasped his head feeling the pain.

"My gosh; a little lower and… well that would have been bad news. We had a friend that got up in the middle of the night, tripped over a chord or shoe or something. Her temple struck the corner of a night stand. She was dead—just like that." Jerry said, and snapped his fingers for effect.

Chars sort of winced. "That must happen a lot, I vaguely remember this story from somewhere else. Well, I will tell you that I don't remember slipping or hitting the table for that matter. I just remember coming in the door and it was lights out," he said while taking another sip from his drink.

"Really? You'd think that you would remember slipping. And you did not see anybody or hear anything?"

Jerry was in cop mode now. Chars was shaking his head.

"Anything taken?" Jerry questioned.

"Nothing was taken and it seemed nothing was even moved."

"Well, it could have happened as they said it. Who found you?" Jerry asked.

Chars thought about that and said, "I believe they said that the maid was going by the room and noticed the open door."

Jerry was in deep concentration, trying to imagine the sequence of events.

"So when did the ice part come in?"

Chars responded, understanding his confusion. "I went to the ice machine and was coming back in to my room. You know, I did see a man headed down the access stairwell. I had forgotten about that."

Jerry played the story back in his head. "Ok. You check in, go up to your room and get settled. You need ice, so you block the door or take the key?"

Chars nodded. "Blocked it with the deadbolt."

Jerry continued, "And then went down the hallway for ice?"

Chars nodded again.

"The ice machine was around the corner?"

Chars again nodded and said, "Around the corner and at the end of the hall."

"When you returned, you see a man going out the exit door. You pushed open the door and went in?"

Jerry was completely engrossed and only was distracted by the fact that their food had arrived. The waiter was patiently holding the plates until Chars finally signaled him to go ahead and put the plates on the table. The waiter offered fresh ground pepper, which both men accepted. The waiter then asked what else he could get them.

Chars said with a wink at the waiter, "I'll have another one of your orange juices."

"Oh, very good, Meester Reenolds," the waiter said with a broad smile and made a rather exaggerated exit.

"Did the police question you?" Jerry carried on.

"No, from the moment I got to the hospital, I guess they decided it was an accident, just as they said. I slipped on a piece of ice and hit my head." Chars was sounding resentful.

"Well the cut could be from a table leg. The door was on your right?"

Chars nodded.

"Say for instance, you came in the door and slipped. Normally, your feet go out from under you and you hit something that is behind you. And, you say, all you remember is stepping through the door?"

Chars saw where he was going with this. He had tried to put it together himself and now it seemed so obvious, he felt a bit embarrassed. "I could not have received a cut on the upper right side of my head while falling backwards."

"And you would have had to be several steps into the room, but you only remember being just inside the door?"

Chars again nodded his answer.

"So maybe, you step out for ice, someone steps in. He has a lookout, which you see go out the door. The lookout tells him that you are coming and he gets behind the door. You step in with your bucket of ice and he gives you a karate chop to the neck. You fall forward and whack your head against the table. He does not have to hit you again, because you are already out."

Jerry took a bite of his sandwich. It was a fresh filet of sole, grilled and seasoned to perfection. He wiped his mouth. Jerry was forgiving Chars in his mind for dragging him to a chic restaurant. Chars was lost in thought, but finally took a bite out his lunch. He had ordered the red snapper. He did not normally see red snapper out of the Gulf, so he thought he would give it a try. Chars appreciated food prepared well and he let the fish sit in his mouth for a moment. The garlic and butter was outstanding. This is why he liked this restaurant so much. Every time he came here the food was just incredible.

"So what did you have in the room that was so valuable?" Jerry asked.

"Nothing that I can think of. I had my wallet in my pants pocket and they didn't take it. I did not have a lot of cash on me anyway."

Jerry asked, "Jewelry? Electronics?"

Chars said with mild exasperation, "My computer was sitting there on the table. Anyone could have taken that, but they didn't, thank goodness. I would have been lost if they had."

"What's on the computer?"

Chars was shaking his head. He was privately scolding himself for leaving his door open and being so careless. He answered, "All my work is on that computer. I really need to back it up."

"Was there anything on the computer that someone could have copied? Or I should say, was important enough to steal?"

Chars hesitated before saying, "I was in Washington, working on an immigration story. I guess someone might want to know what I was going to write, but all I did was an update. Old stuff you know, because there had been a delay in the legislation."

Jerry was patiently working Chars, the same way he would question a witness. Each question might strike a chord that would give some crucial bit of information. Jerry was good at this. He had almost 20 years experience as a detective to draw upon.

"Are there any other stories that are of importance?"

Jerry was now seeing if Chars was deliberately avoiding the obvious answer. If he was avoiding making the natural connection to the Robertson accident, then Chars really was holding out on Jerry. So Jerry just let the question hang out there. Silence was a wonderful tactic. So many people cannot stand silence. Chars, on the other hand seemed oblivious to the break in their conversation. Jerry took another bite.

Chars seemed lost in thought. "Jerry, do you think that this has anything to do with the Robertson accident?"

Jerry blinked in wonderment and said, "What makes you say that?" Jerry thought that Chars really must have taken a wallop on the head. He was usually the one that was quick to make inferences and had a good instinct. Today, he was slow and distracted and seemed to be getting worse. He was still in the moment of the accident or he was deep in thought. "Did you have anything on the computer that they may have wanted?"

Chars tried to think and said, "Not really, it was all the stuff that had already been published. My notes on the other hand, were in a notebook. That was in my suitcase, I think."

"Do you still have that?" asked Jerry.

"Yeah, I saw it when I was packing up." Chars was trying very hard to concentrate.

"Well, we could be barking up the wrong tree, but I think the part about it being related to Robertson is probably a good one.

I would suggest a couple things. First, check with the concierge and the bellman at the hotel. See if they remember anyone using the stairs. I would do it for you, but it is a little out of my jurisdiction. I doubt that an attacker would walk all the way down, but you never know. Secondly, take your laptop to a computer guy and let him see if you have some kind of a log that records activity on your hard drive.

Chars' phone sounded softly. He reached down to silence it. It was the Washington office. Chars frowned and decided to answer it anyway.

He said, "Reynolds."

A high nasally voice said, "Hey Chars, this is Maria."

"Hi, Maria, what's going on?" Chars asked while thinking he really did not want to know.

"I am calling for Mr. Stanton by way of his secretary, you know, Patti, right? You are going to get an e-mail, but Mr. Stanton asked me to call you specifically."

Chars sifting through all the information and names thought that he caught a hint that Maria did not think too much of Mr. Stanton. She held on to the "Stanton" just a little longer than needed. She probably had to deal with the pompous ass on a daily basis and had all she could handle. He knew that no one liked his secretary Patti. Charles winced every time he even had to speak with her on the phone.

Maria continued, "All hotel and travel arrangements now must be made through me. It says this all in the e-mail, but Mr. Stanton asked me to call YOU." She said this with added emphasis on the word you.

So, Chars thought, *she was upset with Stanton because he was an asshole, but she was also upset with me, because now she had to handle all the travel arrangements for the investigation division.* In reality, that was not a big job. Everyone Maria would have to deal with would be anchored to D.C.; those that had to travel were handled by the corporate travel department. Chars had really circumvented that by just turning in his expenses directly to Maria. He had a corporate credit card and therefore was able to make his own arrangements. He was now handing that very card to Simone, who bowed appreciatively and headed away.

Chars said, "I'm sorry that got dumped on you Maria, it is really my fault. But I don't report to Stanton."

Maria had heard exactly what she was after, a little sympathy.

"It's okay, Chars. I tell you what, when you get ready to travel, you just let me know and we'll make sure that the only available room will be where you want to stay. Say, I heard you were in the hospital, that's terrible."

"Well, yes, I was. Just overnight though," Chars said, trying to lessen the severity of his accident.

"Oh my goodness, Chars. You know you still sound groggy. What happened?" Maria said with the utmost sincerity.

Stanton had no doubt told everyone in the office and in the building for that matter that the great Chars Reynolds had slipped on a piece of ice and hit his head... while staying at the Hay Adams Hotel. Chars was sure that bit of information was well discussed at the water cooler and coffee pots. Chars decided to play along, even though Jerry was fidgeting in his seat, having finished the last of his lunch.

"Oh, I am surprised that you have not heard. It was quite the site I am sure. A nasty bit of luck—took nearly 30 stitches to close this old head up."

She did not ask what happened the second time. Chars knew that she had already been told.

"Oh my goodness, Chars. Are you all right?" Maria was going on.

"Oh yes, fine now. Had a good night's rest and feel much better now that I am home." Chars rolled his eyes at Jerry and Jerry gave him the 'hurry up, I am getting impatient' sign.

Chars finished up and thanked Maria for her help, not that she had actually done anything. But she did agree to book him in where he wanted to stay and that said a lot.

"Okay," Chars said turning his attention back to Jerry and the subject at hand. "I am going to get my computer looked at and what else? Before Chars allowed Jerry to answer he asked, "Could you try to track down Freda? I am worried about her."

Jerry raised his eyebrows doubting that he could do anything when the mother had volunteered that she went willingly with a boyfriend. He was also very aware that Chars was still suffering from the effects of a concussion.

"Okay; I'll give the mother a call to see if she has been in contact with her. I also want to see if I can get a drawing of the man that claimed the Lexus."

Chars chugged down the last of his Mimosa and gave Jerry a wide smile before saying, "Book'em Danno!"

Jerry's eyebrows raised in disbelief and amusement. He started to ask, "Chars, what is…?" but did not finish. Chars was already out the door and headed to the parking lot.

Chapter 23

"I am looking at him right now and he is talking to a man, who I think is a cop," Marley said.

Marley was in Dockers shorts with a flowery tourist shirt. He had his sunglasses on and was seated on the sand taking in the sun that had almost peaked in the sky. His baseball cap had the logo for some bank in the desert southwest.

"I don't know that he is a cop; he just looks like a cop or a maybe private dick. No, he's a cop; I just saw his badge when he pulled his wallet out."

Marley was talking into a microphone/headset that was positioned in his ear. To the casual observer, he was just another tourist. But Paul Gallegos was not a casual observer. He saw Marley in the obvious tourist outfit follow Reynolds into the parking lot and then stake out a place in the sand where he could observe Reynolds while he ate lunch. Lego fished out his cell phone and called his boss.

"Hey, our newsboy is meeting with a cop and he has a tail," said Lego looking around the large flowering pot.

He watched as Reynolds and the cop left a tip and were getting up from the table. He glanced back over to the other tail, Marley, but he was already gone.

Gallegos said, "I gotta go, I'll call you back."

Outside the restaurant, Chars and Jerry were headed their separate ways.

Jerry looked at Chars and said, "Are you sure you can drive? You look a bit woozy to me."

"No, no, no, I'm okay."

From his police work, Jerry knew that when a person repeated no, no, no, it usually meant the person was lying or did not believe what he was saying.

"I will just follow you back to your place and then I'll head back to the office. They already know that I am going to be a little late."

"Great now I will have two tails," Chars said and giggled.

Jerry looked at Chars with a look that spoke volumes. "What do you mean?" Jerry said looking directly at Chars.

"There is a guy that I saw in back of me on the road and he also showed up in the restaurant. He was looking at us. And he left when we left," Chars said so casually that Jerry did not know if he was serious or kidding.

"He's in a Pontiac, blue or black; I couldn't tell with the sunlight. I have an idea. Why don't you follow me to my place and then go back to the office."

Jerry looked at him and shook his head slightly as if not believing. Somehow through the mental fog that Chars was experiencing, he was still coherent enough to recognize a tail. Jerry thought that was strange indeed. Plus he would think Chars would be panicked by the thought of someone tailing him.

"Chars, you are not all right. Are you taking something?"

Chars reached into his pocket and pulled out the prescription bottle. "You should try a couple of these. Say hello to my little friends. Just a couple of these and I am feeling much better now."

Jerry just gave a laugh "Yeah I'm sure you are. How many did you take?"

"Just two."

"Let me see the bottle."

Chars shoved the bottle towards Jerry.

"Chars, the label says one every eight hours. No wonder you are loopy."

Chars seemed unfazed by the comment and started walking to his car.

Jerry asked, “Do you have your computer with you?”

“Yes, it is in my car.” Chars said.

“Where is your notebook?” Jerry asked.

Chars gave that some serious thought and finally said, “It is back at the house.”

“Okay, that is where we go first, but you are riding with me. Give me your keys. I will get your computer and we will go in my car.”

Chars said with a bit of a slur and a laugh, “I have always wanted to ride in a police car.”

Jerry took in a deep breath and let it out. He then went with Chars to his car, retrieved the computer and walked with Chars back to his black Mercury Marquis. Jerry sort of wanted whoever was following Chars to see him get into an unmarked police car. Maybe that would back them off a little bit. Jerry needed to think. He was thinking for two now, since Chars’ mental computer had not fully rebooted and had been fully medicated. Jerry thought to himself, *Who in the hell released this guy when it is obvious that he is not fully functioning?* Jerry did not see anyone following him out of the parking lot or on the highway.

“Chars, did you drink any alcohol at lunch?”

“Nope. Wait, Yes.” Chars said and gave a smile that caused Jerry to do a double take.

“How many drinks?” Jerry asked.

“Just two.” Chars said and smiled a dopey smile.

“Have you ever taken any painkillers before?”

Chars head rolled around on his neck and he said with a wide grin, “No, but I’m thinking this is fantastic.”

Jerry reached across the car and plucked the bottle out of Chars’ pocket and put them in his jacket pocket. He picked up his phone out of the cradle and placed a call.

"Hector, this is Jerry. Hey, I need a geek to look at a computer. I'll be back at the office in about two hours. Can you send him to my office at 2:30? Thanks."

When they arrived at Chars' house, Jerry went around to the back door, unlocked it and went in to look for the notebook. It was just where Chars said it would be. He looked around and did not see anything out of place. *Chars is incredibly neat*, Jerry thought to himself. He moved to the back door and caught a glimpse of light in a flower pot down in the foliage. He stopped and looked down into the plant, but could not see it again. He realized that he was now in between the plant and the sun. He backed up to where he was before. Jerry tried to position his head so that his eyesight would tell him where he saw the glimmer. It seemed to be gone. He returned to the car and got in. Chars was sleeping. *Not a good idea,* thought Jerry—but maybe it was.

"Hey Chars, do you keep a house key in one of your plants?"

Chars roused a bit and said answered. "Yes, under the marigolds."

"In or under the marigolds?" Jerry asked.

"Usually it is under, but if I get in a hurry, I will just stick it down in the plant."

Jerry sighed. "Okay, I'll be right back. I just want to check something out."

Jerry went around the back of the house once again. A voice called over the fence. "I called the police."

Jerry was a little startled, but was able to smile and say, "I am the police."

The voice said, "You look like Chars' friend; not the police."

Jerry smiled and realized that the neighbor had recognized him from the previous trips to Chars' house. "I am Chars' friend and I am the police," Jerry said. He tiptoed over to the fence. On the other side, a little lady stood about four feet tall. She was dressed in a gardening outfit and was wearing a floppy hat.

"I called the police about ten minutes ago," she repeated.

Jerry stopped and thought about that. "Ten minutes ago? What is your name?"

"Let me see a badge," she countered.

Jerry pulled his sergeant's badge and draped it over the fence for the lady to examine. She looked discriminatingly at the I.D. Then she stepped back.

"Ms. Wendall," she said with some pride.

Jerry smiled again and said, "Ms.Wendall, I was just picking up something for Chars. It is okay."

Around the front of the house, Jerry heard several cars approach and doors open and close. Jerry thought that the lady was just bluffing, but he knew now that she was not.

"Okay, Ms. Wendall, thanks for looking after Chars' place. I will let the officers know that you mistook me for a burglar and get it all straightened out.

The little lady started shaking her head and said under her breath, "Stupid dick. I did not call the police because you were breaking in. I called the police because there was some other man in a fake cable uniform, breaking in. If you had not showed up the police would have probably caught him in the act. You came along and scared him away. He was a clumsy son of bitch though. When he came out of the house, he lifted up the pot to return Chars' key, but he dropped the key in the bush. Then you came around the corner. At first I thought you were with him. How you did not see him going around the corner, I'll never know. You are not very alert to be a cop. He waited until you left, went back and replaced the key. Then here you come again. The asshole about broke an ankle getting out of here the second time. He hopped over the side fence. You could probably still get him about two yards down if you hurry. If he goes in that yard there is going to be a world of...."

In the distance, Jerry could hear a growl and a series of angry barking. He raised his voice so that the officers could hear him.

"This is Sergeant Jerry Collins, Miami PD. We have a possible 26 with the suspect in the direction of the barking dogs."

One cop had worked his way around the house, stepped out from the corner and lowered his gun when he saw Jerry's badge.

He yelled, "Clear."

The two from the front moved slowly around and also lowered their weapons. The barking began to subside and one of the officers radioed in that they needed back up "This is Delta 04-063, we have a possible 26 with suspect heading south on foot. Request a cut off. Sarge, is this worth a chopper?"

Jerry did not hesitate. "Yes, suspect is also a 40 for a 32 in D.C."

The cop immediately raced around the corner almost colliding with Chars. Chars was not moving too fast and was able to step aside. The officer excused himself, but barely broke stride.

One block away, a white panel van pulled up to the corner. A man of medium build raced out of a backyard. On the nape of his neck was a tattoo of the Japanese symbol for love. He was wearing a cable installer's uniform as he came around the back of a two-story, Tudor style house in full stride. When he reached the front yard, the man slowed his pace in order to avert any suspicion.

The tear in the back of his pants was significant. It was accented by a light trail of blood. The man quickly opened the door, got in, and the car accelerated down the road. The police had just missed their man. The helicopter would arrive shortly thereafter, but the Cable Guy was no longer in the neighborhood.

Chapter 24

"What did you get from the flash drive?" asked Pat Lewis.

Paul "Lego" Gallegos said, "Well boss, looked like he keeps all his stuff on the laptop. All his articles are on there, even the one we're concerned about. But that has all been published."

"And the notebook?" Lewis asked.

"If he has made any connections that we are not aware of, he has not written them down. He had the witness' name and the initials ROW and FO written down and Lexus–airbag." Lego said.

"So he's made the connection of Algiers and Robertson and he is wondering about the passenger airbag."

"Appears so," Lego replied.

"Anything else?"

"The cop is a friend of his, but he is Miami PD. I am not sure who the tail was, but maybe an FO guy."

Paul hit his hand down on the table. "Damn it. This is getting way too messy. If it was F.O., then they are feeling the heat."

"Maybe they will take care of the reporter."

"Why didn't the coroner's report list the cause of death as a heart attack?" Lego asked.

"It does. It will be in the papers tomorrow. It would have come out earlier if the other car had not killed him first. They focused on the obvious and the "tox" reports had to go through the normal process."

"Seems like it has taken a long time for that to come out, but when it does, won't that shut down Reynolds?"

"It might, but I think this guy does not just let things go.

We will have to watch how he reacts. If he drops it, I think that will be that, otherwise, we may have to give him something else to concentrate on. We are getting sloppy, Paul."

"The hotel deal was my fault. I should have been more patient," Lego said.

"And the house job?" Pat asked curtly.

Lego rolled his eyes. "Our man was seen, but not caught."

Lewis was incensed, but maintained his composure. "Okay Lego, but let's not have anymore slip-ups. See what Reynolds does after the news release."

Jerry had decided to drop Chars at his house and left an officer there to keep watch. He did not think anyone would come back, but Chars needed a keeper right now. Jerry drove another officer back to the restaurant and returned Chars' car back to the house. He found Chars asleep on the couch. Jerry left the officer there and headed back to the office. His computer expert confirmed that the log did register a system halt dated the first day of Chars' trip to D.C. The computer was not password protected and would not have been too hard to scan for the information that they might be looking for and even download somewhere else.

Jerry decided he would have to get some sleep before doing anything else. He called his wife to explain the situation as much as he could without giving anything away, then drove back to Chars' house and relieved the officer. Chars was still comatose, so Jerry locked all the doors and found a good place to sack out.

Chars awoke the next morning to find Jerry sprawled out on the guest bed. His computer was sitting on the kitchen counter and he flipped it open and booted it up. He checked the national news online while eating his breakfast. He did a double take when he read one of the headlines. "Senator's Accident Caused by Heart Attack." He was scrolling down to the story when his phone vibrated on the kitchen table. It was Marsha Lincoln.

"Hey Chars, I guess you heard about Mike's autopsy."

"I am reading it right now," Chars said as he read and listened at the same time.

"It is a moot point now, but I couldn't get anything set up with the Robertson family. They just want to stay out of the press. The mother made a statement a week ago and asked for the press to honor their request for privacy. The report has actually been sort of a relief to us all. At least we know why it happened."

"Yeah, I can understand that. Okay, I appreciate you trying, Marsha," Chars said and almost clicked off.

"Oh Marsha, what do you know about the Right Way or Freedom Organization?"

There was a silence, and then Marsha said, "I have heard of the Freedom Organization from somewhere, but really I can't recall where. Who are they?"

"I'm not sure, but they may be some type of special interest group."

"Does it have anything to do with your story on Mike?"

"I am not sure yet, but the group came up and I was just trying to close a loop. Could you check?" Chars asked. His neck was starting to hurt again and he began massaging it.

Marsha Lincoln spun around in her chair and began typing on her keyboard. "Hold on one second and let me see," she said as she accessed a list of contributors. "Don't see The Freedom Organization on here."

"What about the group called the Right Way?"

She scrolled down. "No, I don't see them either."

"Ok—last one: Algiers Banger?"

Marsha scrolled back up to the top of the list. "No, he's not here either, but I do remember that name." Marsha was running the name through her mind trying to place it. "I think that Mike did meet with him a time or two. But I was not the one that was handling that. The one that probably could help you is no longer here. Kay Moore handled some of the big boys that wanted to talk to Mike about policy or taxes or real estate law or whatever their area of concern was. I did not really get involved too much in that."

"Where is Kay Moore now, do you know?"

"I am not sure. The last time I heard she was going to work for some guy in Ohio that was running for State Senator. I think his name was Oliver something."

"Okay, thanks Marsha."

Chars typed Ohio Senator Oliver into the search field. Up came Will Oliver in several articles. He asked aloud to himself, why would someone move from a possible presidential candidate to a state senator candidate? Why would you go from D.C. to Ohio? He typed in Kay Moore. No hits. He went to the Oliver Senatorial website. A big picture of Will Oliver popped up. He was a handsome guy, but rather unremarkable looking. Chars read through the usual political goals and other bullshit. *This guy is an ideological clone of the President*, thought Chars. He pulled up his staff. There weren't any of note, and there was no mention of Kay Moore.

Chars began running all the facts back through his mind. Mike Robertson has a heart attack that causes him to wreck his car. Maybe he runs into the white SUV and whoever is driving does not want to be involved in an accident investigation, so they take off. But that does not explain the passenger—and Freda said that the SUV was towed. That just does not make sense. Maybe Freda was wrong or just making it up. But now she's gone and is no longer a witness. Then Mike's car disappears.

"That is just too convenient," Chars said aloud.

He picked up the phone and dialed Oliver's office. A voice on the phone answered, "Senator Oliver's office, this is Mary."

Chars thought could hear stress in the tone of Mary's voice. "This is Chars Reynolds from the Miami Express; I was trying to reach Kay Moore."

"A reporter from Miami? Hold just a minute," Mary said rather curtly.

Chars listened to the background music playing, it sounded like a country station. He gathered that his call was not all that welcome.

After a moment Mary came back on the phone and said, "I am sorry sir, we don't have a Kay Moore."

Chars said quickly, "You know, I am sorry, I may have the wrong name. I was told that Kay had moved from Miami to work for Senator Oliver's campaign."

"Well, it is possible; we have so many volunteers," Mary said briskly.

Chars thought that she was either under stress or she was a bitch. He was being as nice as he could, but she was frigid.

"I don't think she would be a volunteer," Chars continued, "but if you don't mind checking, I would sure appreciate it."

"Just a second while I put you on hold. I will check with the Volunteer Coordinator."

Mary did not put him on hold this time. Chars could hear her asking someone if he had heard of Kay Moore. There seemed to be a lot of commotion in the background. It was getting louder. There were lots of phones ringing.

Mary was talking to a man, and he answered, "No, I don't recall that name. Let me check the list." There was a pause and then the man said, "No, I don't see a Kay Moore. You sure he's not just trying to get a statement? They can get fairly tricky."

Chars heard Mary say, "No, he says he's from Miami." She had put her hand over the phone, but Chars could still hear. "Could be an old boyfriend or something." Mary was raising her eyebrows. She uncovered the phone and said, "I am sorry sir, but there is no Kay Moore connected here."

"Thank you so much for your trouble," Chars said in an

apologetic tone.

"Sorry I couldn't help," Mary said, a little more relaxed now.

He was about to disconnect, when he heard a woman's voice. "Mary, who was that?" and the connection ended.

Chars hit the back button on his computer and returned to the Oliver search. The second site was an Ohio newspaper site. Chars thought, *That's interesting, Senator Oliver has made the news this morning. The title of the article was Senator Questioned about Consulting Payment.* Chars said aloud, "So the Senator is taking a little money on the side, huh?"

Chars was headed back to get a second cup of coffee when he remembered he needed to check his e-mail. He could hear Jerry stirring in the other room. His e-mail showed 212 messages. He quickly went through and weeded out the bulk mail and other waste. There it was. It was from MR_FRIEND@hotmail.com. Its subject line read, "Lost interest?"

Chars said out loud, "Mr. Friend, no I have not lost interest. What do you have to say to me?"

The message read, "E-mail your secure number. I have information for you."

Chars had forgotten about the phone that he had purchased and did not immediately know where it was. He went into his bedroom to look. When he returned, Jerry was pouring himself a cup of coffee and came over to the table and began reading the e-mail.

"Who is Mr. Friend?" Jerry asked.

Chars was coming back from the bedroom with the phone in his hand and said, "Hey that is a violation of my privacy"

"You don't have no stinking privacy when you have cop sleeping in the guest room," Jerry said and took a sip of coffee. "So, who is he and what information does he have?"

Chars sat down and said, "I don't know who it is and I

don't know what information he has, because he wants me to use a secure phone so it cannot be traced. He thinks that everything is being monitored or something. Probably a wacko."

Jerry stretched his arms up over his head. "But still, better take what he says seriously; after all, you have been attacked and your house was broken into."

"I don't know that for sure. You can't take my neighbor's word for it, she is a nut case," Chars said.

"Chars, if you don't think this Mr. Friend has some good information, why did you get the phone?" Jerry said and took another sip of the coffee.

Chars was annoyed now at the early morning, cross-examination and said, "I just said that I did not know who it was and my neighbor is the nut case. Being the diligent reporter that I am, I am going to follow it through because it is the prudent thing to do." He gave a short nod as if he were punctuating his sentence.

"Ok, hot shot, send this guy your number and let's see what happens."

Chars had to look in his wallet for the number since he had not used it before. He typed in the number and hit send. A message came back almost immediately and said, "That is not a secure phone number. What did you do, get something at Radio Shack? I did not know I was dealing with an amateur."

Chars noticed that the email address had changed again. "How does he keep changing e-mail addresses?" he asked.

Jerry moved over where he could see the screen. "He is using a scrambler. Those were made illegal about three years ago, but they are not super stealth or anything. It just sends a false e-mail name as the sender each time. Makes it tough to prove in a court of law, who sent what. But it can still be traced and the guy knows it. That is why he trying to get you to get a phone that's encrypted. You know, using encryption." Jerry was looking at Chars and he could tell that he did not know what he was talking about. Where did you get this one?"

"Radio Shack."

"This guy is fairly sharp or he was the one that was tailing you back at the restaurant. Just e-mail him back and tell him it was the best you could do on short time. Tell him that the spook division at the paper is on vacation." Jerry said and laughed.

Chars typed that in and hit send.

"Have you found some connection between Robertson and this Ohio Senator? Jerry asked.

Chars looked at his screen and noticed the article was showing from behind the e-mail screen. "Nothing really. There was a lady that worked in Robertson's campaign and my contact there said she was the one that handled the Freedom Organization—specifically the founder, Algiers Banger. She supposedly left and went to work for Senator Oliver in Ohio. Which in itself is strange, but there could be a reason for it. This Freedom Organization is a mystery, because it's as if they don't really exist. I suppose it is possible that the Freedom Organization quietly backs different candidates, but stays below the radar. With the political contributions disclosure legislation, it would be difficult to not leave any trail, but of course, not impossible," Chars said.

Jerry took a sip of coffee. "And why is this connection so important?"

"I don't know," Chars said, shaking his head, "but somehow I think this is a missing link."

Chars' computer said, "You've got mail."

"Here's Mr. Friend again," Jerry said getting up from his chair and moving around behind Chars so he could read the message.

Chars clicked on the message. It simply read, "Smith, Scott, Mitchell, Robertson."

Jerry read the message. "Is that a law firm or something?"

"I don't think so. Robertson was a politician. Maybe all four are politicians. It might mean Smith as in Lancaster Smith."

Jerry scratched his head and seemed not to know who this was. Chars gave him a disapproving look. "As in the Vice-President that resigned a while back."

"I knew that," Jerry said quickly; a little insulted that Chars thought he did not keep up with things like that. "Who are Scott and Mitchell?" he asked, risking further embarrassment.

"I don't know."

He flashed to his home page and typed in the names. Scott hit over a 187 million sites. He typed in Mitchell. It almost hit over 59 million sites. He typed all four names. None matched, but there were several hundred that had some of the combination. He typed in "politician Scott". There were 400,000 hits, but near the top there was an article "Virginia Lt. Governor, candidate, Karl Scott drops out of race after infidelity charge."

"What does he have in common with Mitchell or Smith?"

Chars said nothing and typed in Politician Mitchell. Again there were several hundred thousand hits. "Here is a George Mitchell that was a Senator. But that was in the early 2000s. Looks like he was out of office by the late 90s."

"They are all dead, right?" Jerry asked.

"Mitchell did not die and Smith is alive. I don't know where Scott is, but there was a Satch Mitchell that I seem to recall," Chars said with a tone of don't-you-keep-up-with-anything?

"Hey, I don't keep up with that kind of stuff!" Jerry objected to Chars' tone and look.

Chars continued to page down. "Here's an article about Satch Mitchell. This is fairly recent. He was running for office and had to pull out when it was discovered that he had undergone psychiatric counseling."

"The only thing wrong with him was that he knew he was

crazy. Most politicians consider themselves quite sane," Jerry said wryly

"Jerry, you are not helping."

"Sorry," said Jerry.

Chapter 25

Martha went around the corner into a literature room and closed the door. She dialed Ben Thomas.

When the phone was answered, she said, "Hey Ben, Will's office got an inquiry about Kay Moore just now." She listened and said, "It was a reporter from Miami." She shifted her weight against the conference table that was piled with multiple stacks of flyers and other campaign literature. She paused, and then said, "Okay. I can do that. You know he has gotten fairly attached." She listened and said, "No I don't think the reporter would know me or could figure out that."

Ben was working through some possible scenarios.

Martha said, "I am not sure it is worth the chance of letting him put two and two together, do you?" She listened, and said, "Yeah, I saw the report. That could be good news, if it's true, then we may have just had a run of bad luck."

Ben asked about Oliver.

"Well, he is fairly dramatic at times. The Cattlemen's story may eat his lunch."

Ben reassured Martha that there would be another story that would help put this to bed and just keep Oliver from over-reacting.

"Okay, I will tell him." She listened and responded, "Yeah, he will listen." Martha listened for a few minutes and then said, "He won't sit by and just let me go." After a moment she said irritably, "I have done what I had to do."

Ben spoke in calm tones and finally Martha said, "Okay, I'll start working on an exit strategy. But if I up and disappear, the reporter, if he does show up, will be very suspicious. Is there any way that we can give him another story that will preoccupy him a bit?" Martha ended the call with an "Ok." She was sitting on the edge of the table with her feet crossed. She closed her eyes and thought through what she needed to do.

Ben dialed the number for Ross Saunders. Saunders was in London, England and Ben did a quick time calculation. He figured it was about 5:00pm and placed the call. Ross' cell phone began to vibrate. He reached in his suit pocket, read the caller information and put the ear receiver in his ear. He did not say anything, he just listened.

Ben said, "Is this a good time?"

Ross replied, "I have about 20 minutes before take-off. What's up?"

"The article about Will came out this morning. I think the afternoon news conference will help in that regard. Also, this morning, the Miami Coroner published the final report on Mike. Says he was having a non-fatal heart attack. It was the second car that killed him. Last but not least, the Miami reporter has somehow connected the dots between Kay and Mike to Will's campaign."

Ben knew that Ross liked a complete summary before they started and he would deal with each issue in the order that he wanted.

"What did Marley find out?" Ross asked.

"He says that Reynolds..."

Ross interrupted and asked "The reporter?"

Ben said, "Yes, Reynolds, the reporter, was in D.C. writing about the immigration bill that stalled. He had to spend a night in the hospital, because he slipped on a piece of ice and split his head open.

"Sounds like an idiot," Ross said.

Ben continued, "He also said that Reynolds was probably being tailed, but he was not sure."

Ross just shook his head and said, "Don't suppose we

know by who?"

Ben breathed out and said, "He thinks it was a retired Secret Service guy. He thinks it was Paul Gallegos."

Ross about blew a gasket. He started pacing up and down the aisle of the Hawker 800. There was not a lot of room to walk, but he stepped in between the large lounge type chairs and went from the back to front and again. "What the hell is up with Parker? What the hell is he trying to do? He is going to bring this whole thing down and he is going to go down with it."

"It may not be Parker," Ben said cautiously. "It could be Smith—or Gallegos might be working this on his own."

Ross turned and headed the other way. "I don't see Lanny Smith doing this. I don't even know what this is. But I need to talk to him. Where is he now?"

Ben pulled out a small leather notebook from his pocket. "He's scheduled for a vacation in St. Maarten. I think he bought a place down there. He flies out of Atlanta, later today. Well, actually he has already gone."

"I presume that we still have someone on him?" Ross said.

Ben again checked his notebook, and said, "Yeah, Tommy is tailing him."

"Is he following him to St. Maarten?" Ross asked.

"He was going to have to catch a later flight down there. He could not get on the same flight. For some reason Smith is flying commercial."

"And Smith will still not answer any messages?

"We stopped sending about three weeks ago and just kept watching,"

"Well try again." Ross thought for a second, "I have to take off here and they think that my little cell phone is going to cause this airplane to crash, so I have to get off. What they don't know is that we are about to file a new flight plan. Call off Tommy. If he has already left, tell him to go to another island and have a vacation until you tell him otherwise. I will need to know where Lanny is staying, so get your people on it. I am going to speak with the Vice-President whether he likes it or not."

With a maximum speed of about 425 miles per hour and a cruising altitude of up to 45,000 feet, the Hawker 800 made its way to Philipsburg after refueling in Miami. The plane had room for eight, but Ross was the only passenger. He went through customs without even a second look. The customs agent stamped his passport, and welcomed him in Dutch accented English.

"Mr. Mauer, welcome to St Maarten."

Near the customs counter a driver held a sign that said Mr. Nauer.

Ross smiled, ignoring the misspelling, and said with a perfect British accent, "You must be here for me. Have you collected my bags?" The driver understood what he said and gave him a nod and a smile. "I am quite exhausted and would like to go to the hotel straight away."

The drive to the Sonesto Maho took less than 15 minutes. The driver gave Ross his room key and dropped him at the front of the hotel. A bellman met him at the front door, gathered his bags and took the door key. Ross followed the bellman into the room, waited for him to place his bags and gave him a nice tip in Euros. Ross noticed that behind the curtains the patio door was cracked open.

"Is that you Ross?" a voice from the patio said. Ross' head tilted to the left, a bit confused.

"Lanny?" Ross pulled the curtain back and opened the door the rest of the way.

"Mr. Vice-President to you," Lancaster Smith said through a puff of cigar smoke and gave Ross a big smile.

The men shook hands and Smith poured Ross a drink from

a half empty bottle of Makers Mark.

"Lanny, you are looking good." Ross took a corner of the balcony and rested his foot on the edge of a lounge chair.

"Amazing what a decrease in stress will do for you." Smith smiled again.

Ross took a sip of the brown liquid and let it settle in his mouth. He swallowed and let the chill work its way down his body. "How did you know I was coming?" Ross asked.

"Still have the Secret Service covering my back. And Ben called."

Ross looked at him and just shook his head in surprise. "But you took his call, this time?" Ross reached for an El Fuego and a lighter. He snipped off the end with a clipper that was on the table.

"Yeah, I answered it this time. But this may have to be the last time, Ross." Lancaster Smith sat back down in his chair and propped his feet on the rail.

Ross looked quizzically at the former Vice-President of the United States and asked, "Lanny, what happened?"

Chapter 26

Will was watching the Columbus News at Noon from his senate office. On the screen, bigger than life was State Senator Harwood Booth Clanston. He was dressed in a tailored gray suit. His silk tie was knotted tightly and draped down along the expanse of his significant stomach. He had a matching handkerchief in his coat lapel pocket. He was getting ready to lower the boom on the young freshman Senator Oliver. Oliver's face was already a deep shade of red in anticipation of what the fat old bastard was going to say.

His little weevil of a press man walked to the podium and said, "Senator Clanston appreciates the members of the press being here for this press conference and will welcome your questions following a short statement."

Harwood dutifully, and with a grave face of purpose, approached the podium. Will thought that the dramatics were a bit much, but not unexpected from the pompous old asshole. Martha came into the office about the time Senator Clanston was clearing his throat and getting ready to say something very profound.

"I appreciate that the members of the press are here today and I would like to cover a few items of business that are in the works in the near future for the State of Ohio. We have an outstanding chance in front us to further the education of youngsters in our great state. I am putting my support toward the improved teacher benefits and improvements to the infrastructure. I will be leading the charge to see that this type of legislation moves forward so that our education system continues to set the example for the rest of the nation."

A reporter in the front row raised his hand. "Senator, we are used to you taking the lead in the important issues and this seems like you are jumping on the band wagon with Senator Oliver."

Senator Clanston was nodding, but still had the serious demeanor. He said, "Thank you, Andy, for that comment. I have never let politics interfere with a good idea."

Will was now sitting in a chair, his jaw had dropped and his eyes were wide. He said aloud, "How in the hell does he get away with this absolute bullshit?"

Clanston continued, "What is good for Ohio is good for Ohio. This is not so much of an issue, but a mission to improve the future of our children."

Another reporter raised her hand. Clanston acknowledged her with a polite nod and said, "Yes Andrea."

"Senator, in the paper today was an article that called into question…"

Will said, "Oh shit here it comes."

"…Senator Oliver's acceptance of a payment by the Cattlemen's Association that was in excess of the contract. The implication is that it might amount to some type of political contribution in the disguise of pay for hire. How do you react to that story, knowing that Senator Oliver seems to be the lead proponent of these types of educational reforms?"

Clanston again was nodding gravely, and after some sincere thought said, "Senator Oliver is relatively new to the political landscape and these charges are serious. However, knowing the Senator for the past few months, I am willing to give him the benefit of the doubt. I will leave this type of investigation up to those that are the watchdogs of this great State. I would of course be very disappointed if these charges implicated the Senator in any wrongdoing. Regardless of what results from that inquiry, this legislation is too important to be tied to the political career of just one individual. The Ohio State Senate will be working hard to concentrate on the task at hand."

Will looked at Martha with disbelief. "He has just stolen this issue. He set me up and then he stole the idea."

Martha put her hand on Will's shoulder and looked him in the eye. "Will, this is politics. Your issue will go away and eventually so will Senator Clanston. You will issue a statement that states the facts. You had a consulting contract prior to your candidacy. You performed the contract beyond the expectations of your employer. You were compensated fairly and the payment could in no way be construed as anything other than what it was, payment for quality work. Any attempt to make this more than that is an unveiled political ploy."

"And you think the story will be put to bed?" Will asked in a shaky voice.

"Sleeping like a baby," Martha said.

Will's face showed that he was not convinced. "Martha, babies wake up four times a night."

Chapter 27

"Maria, I need to go to Columbus, Ohio." Chars listened a moment and then said, "Okay. Thanks." He called Jerry but there was no answer, so he left a message on his voice mail. "I am headed to Ohio to track down any connection between Robertson and Oliver. Call me on my cell phone if you have something for me."

Chars' cell phone vibrated, he saw that it was Maria and he answered it. "Chars, Stanton was in here when I was making your reservation. He said he needed to know why you were going to Columbus before he approved anything."

Chars covered the phone and muttered an expletive. "I don't work for him. Why is he approving anything I do?"

"Stanton was made overseer of reporters' expenses, company-wide," she groused.

"Not a problem, Maria. Go ahead and make the reservation and tell him that I am following up on the Robertson accident."

"I am not sure that will work. He wanted to talk to you."

Chars covered the phone again, and worked to control his anger. "Okay, put me through to his highness."

Maria let a little laugh through the phone before saying, "Please hold."

Stanton's voice mail came on and informed the caller that they had reached someone very important and he would try to get back to them if his busy schedule permitted him to do so. Chars pulled the phone away from his ear and flipped the phone off. He called the airline and booked the flight with his corporate credit card.

His phone immediately began to vibrate. It was Jerry.

"Hey Chars, two things: we found the car. It was in a compacter at a junk yard. The owner filed a report with the VIN number and the computer issued an alert."

"Can the airbag be tested?"

"I have a team out there that is going to try to recover the airbag, but it is not a good bet. Certainly nothing that would ever hold up in court," Jerry said and took a breath. He was walking while he talked.

"And the second?" Chars asked.

"Second what? Jerry was getting into his car and Chars heard the engine start up.

"You said there were two things," Chars said.

"Oh yes... I talked to Freda's Mom. She received a postcard from Puerto Rico. Freda is enjoying the sun and fun."

"Well, I guess we can assume she is alive assuming that she wrote it."

"Yeah, I thought the same thing, but the mother was convinced," Jerry said and then asked. "Why are you going to Ohio?"

"I am looking for the lady that worked in Robertson's campaign," Chars said.

"Don't you think that is a long shot?" Jerry asked.

"Just following a hunch, but my thinking is that if the Freedom Organization was connected to Robertson, they may be the common thread between Smith, Scott, Mitchell and Robertson. This group could be sabotaging candidates instead of helping them," Chars said.

"Why don't you just call those three and ask them?"

"That's a good point," Chars said as he was taking notes in his notebook.

"And Chars, watch your back. You are definitely at risk—

the hit on the head and the guy breaking into your house. If Robertson was actually killed, these people are not to be taken lightly. You may still be being followed," Jerry said. He paused while he was taking a turn and then continued. "There is someone very interested in what you are doing and I would recommend a little misdirection," advised Jerry.

Chars thought and asked, "Make them think I have started on a different story?"

"I would say that is a good idea. And be on the alert. Do you have a gun?" Jerry asked.

"No, do you think I need one?" Chars was now really concerned.

"Just watch your back. I am at the office, and I have to go. Check in with me every day and let me know where you are."

Jerry closed up his phone and walked toward the police station.

Chapter 28

Chars was not able to get on the last flight to Columbus and would have to fly into Cincinnati. He liked that better anyway. The Westin Cincinnati overlooks the historic Fountain Square and was a short distance to the Ohio River. He said a nice little thank you to his corporate credit card. He waited for his room key.

When he received it he said. "I am sorry to be a pain, but I need a room on one of the lower floors. Would that be possible?"

"Oh certainly, Mr. Reynolds," the desk clerk said with an understanding bow of the head.

He retrieved a new key card and typed in some information into the computer. He smiled and asked what else he could do for Chars. Chars thanked the clerk and assured him that he needed nothing further. Chars looked over the printout noting that the Media Rate was well below the normal $399 per night. *That should make his Stanton happy*, Chars thought sarcastically. He looked over at the lobby and noticed a man holding a newspaper. He made a mental note of the top of his head, stature, and clothing. He did not want to be paranoid, but his last visit to a hotel was not a good one. He went up to his room and cautiously opened the door. He turned on the light and checked the room thoroughly. He would check his e-mail and take a quick shower. Then he would be ready for a late dinner and a drink at the Albee Restaurant. His favorite dinner was the basil-coated fillet of salmon. The Albee was named after the grand theater that used to be located on site. The terraces allowed for a spectacular view of Fountain Square.

Chars booted up the old lap top and accessed his web mail

account. Sure enough, there was a message from MR_ Friend.

It read, “What’s in Cincinnati? The story is in Miami.”

Chars sent back an e-mail and asked: “If you are trying to tell me something you are going to have to be clearer. Who is the Freedom Organization?” He hit send.

Within a few moments he heard the familiar, “You’ve got mail.” He opened it up and read: “How did you find out about the Freedom Organization?”

Chars e-mailed back, “This is silly, can you instant message?”

In another minute, Chars had a message that MR_ Friend was signed on to AOL instant messenger.

Chars clapped his hands together and said out loud, “Now we are making some progress!”

He typed in who is this? Then he erased it. He is not going to answer that and I should not ask such an obvious question. Chars message box printed the message, “Are you there?”

“Yes I am here, dick weed,” Chars said aloud.

He typed: “Yes, I learned about the Freedom Organization through my investigation into the Robertson accident.”

The message came back: “Are you still referring to it as the Robertson accident?”

Chars said out loud, “I knew it. I knew it.”

He was up from his chair and pacing now. He went back to his computer, but did not sit in the chair. He leaned over the keyboard and typed in: “The official report is that Robertson was having a heart attack when he was killed by another vehicle. What am I supposed to call it?”

The instant message came back: “If you are going to play games with me, I don’t want to waste the time.”

Chars let out a little, “Damn.”

He needed more time to think about his questions. He needed this guy to give up what he knew: “I need more help to figure this out. Why are you doing this?"

MR_ Friend wrote back: "The question should be: why are they doing this?" Up came another message: "I can't be bothered with questions like that. Where did you find out about the Freedom Organization?"

"I told you. Who is the Freedom Organization?" Chars wrote back and hit send.

The screen said MR_ Friend is typing. Then a message appeared: "I can't help you if you are not going to answer my questions."

Chars typed back: "I am usually the one who asks the questions."

Again a pause: "That is not going to work here. I am in danger and I have to play it my way."

Chars typed in: "In danger from whom?"

The message came back: "The same one that attacked you in your hotel, and broke into your home. They want to know what you know and if you know too much, you are in danger too. Now how did you come across the name Freedom Organization?"

Chars sat down and ran his hands through his hair. He did not know who this could be and he was not sure what he should tell him. He did not want to compromise his sources, but then he thought *what sources*?

Finally he took a deep breath and typed: "I found a link to the Freedom Organization through a car title trace."

The screen again showed that MR_Friend was typing: "Which car was traced to the FO?"

Chars thought aloud, "Which car? What does that mean, which car?"

Chars asked himself silently, I am about to give something up here that I can not get back? This is really a key part to all of this. No one else has made this connection yet. Or maybe this person is simply fishing for what I do know. Maybe this is the person that was in the hotel.

The person was typing again. "You are going to have to trust someone. What car was traced to the FO?"

Chars typed: 'Trust someone? I don't know who you are. You could be the person that attacked me, particularly since no one really knew about that."

The person was typing again: "I know about the FO. It is not what it appears to be."

Chars typed: "It does not appear to be anything. No one seems to know about it at all and yet you obviously do."

The person then answered: "I need to know if you are getting your information from someone else—if you are, I could be in extreme danger."

Chars thought, "Well, I can answer this" and typed: "I have received no information on the Freedom Organization other than a car title trace. I cannot locate anyone that knows about the Freedom Organization."

MR_ Friend wrote: "I can help you, but you will have to proceed carefully. Why are you in Cincinnati?"

Chars let out a sigh and typed: "Here you go again. I guess we are at a standstill. You are not willing to give up what I need to know and you want to know what I am not willing to give up."

The person was typing again: "What could I tell you that would make you trust me?"

Chars typed in: "Why are you doing this?"

The person was typing and the message came across: "They stole the White House and they killed Mike Robertson. Who are you in Cincinnati to see?"

Chars typed in: "The FO killed Mike Robertson?"

The message came back: Why are you in Cincinnati?"

Chars typed in: "I am going to Columbus to see a Senator Oliver."

The person was again typing. Chars waited, still thinking

about the comment 'stole the White House'.

Chars' computer sounded again and the message came in: "Was there some link between FO and Oliver?"

Chars typed: "I am not sure I want to answer that."

The message came back: "You don't have to, but if there was, and you want to stir things up, ask Oliver about the Freedom Organization. Then watch your back; they will be coming after you. I'll be back in touch."

And MR_Friend was gone.

"That was the second time someone has told me to watch my back. Maybe I do need a gun," Chars thought aloud.

He shook his head and thought, *this is crazy.*

Chapter 29

The next morning, Chars drove to Columbus, Ohio. He pulled up his rental car to historic Capital Square. He made his way to what used to be the Judicial Annex that was remodeled in 1993 and now held the offices of State Senators. The rooms were decorated in reproduction furnishings and were quite exquisite. Chars identified himself as a reporter for the D.C. Bureau of the Miami Herald to the rather large security guard. He looked at his press identification and seemed rather unimpressed.

"Is Senator Oliver expecting you?" he said in an obligatory tone.

"Yes," Chars said, even though he was not sure that was exactly true.

He did speak with someone in Oliver's office to find out that the Senator would in fact be in the office. Chars had also placed a call to the Washington Bureau and asked for the secretary to set up an appointment with Oliver. He was given a light blue identification badge, not unlike the ones that are issued at the Washington capital building. He knew that it was a temporary pass. Once it was exposed to sunlight, the pass would change colors and therefore be void. He placed the pass on his lapel and allowed a second security person to escort him to a set of stairs. He was given directions to the office and followed a corridor past several other Senate offices and what appeared to be a large conference room. Chars hoped that his office had called ahead and made an appointment for him, otherwise, he might just be thrown out. When he arrived at Senator Oliver's office, he opened a large, wooden door with a full length glass insert. An attractive lady was busy answering phones, typing information on a computer and nodding to people as they crossed in front of her desk. Chars waited politely until she noticed him and held up one finger to indicate that she would be right with him.

She stopped, looked up, and gave Chars a big smile. "Mr. Reynolds?"

Chars was surprised, but then figured out that the security guard probably had already called ahead. "Yes, I am," Chars said and gave a winning smile. The receptionist was probably about 28 years old and wore a light blue dress that was nicely conservative and held on by two spaghetti straps. She was tanned, well proportioned, and Chars immediately took a liking to her.

"Senator Oliver has about 15 minutes before he must go into session. And you are here to get information about the new education bill for a report about the U.S. Department of Education?" Mary asked.

This was the first he had heard of this but smiled nonetheless and said, "Yes."

"Great. Lucille, the Senator's personal assistant will take you back."

Chars wondered who in his office was astute enough to come up with the Education Bill angle. He would have to send whoever that was a nice order of flowers. A new woman appeared and introduced herself as Lucille. She accompanied Chars down a short hallway past a couple of offices. Both had their doors open and as Chars passed by, a lady looked up and smiled. Chars noticed the name on the door, it said Martha Hall. She looked like a classy woman. He passed the second open door and the man did not look up, evidently preoccupied with something of extreme importance. Chars did not make a note of his name. The largest office was flanked by a series of office dividers, each with the top of a head showing. Senator Oliver was seated behind a large walnut desk and immediately rose when the young lady walked in and moved around the desk to shake Chars' hand.

"Thank you Lucille," he said.

The girl nodded but said nothing and closed the door behind Chars.

"Mr. Reynolds, I understand you are doing a story about the Department of Education and you want some information about our upcoming legislation here in Ohio."

"Yes sir. That is a story that I would like to discuss with you. But first, could you give me a little history on you and your recent climb into politics?" Chars asked while taking a seat in front of the desk.

Oliver took a second seat in front of his desk rather than going back around to his regular seat. Chars thought that was a nice touch.

"Well, I don't have a lot time to give you the full story, but I was a professor at a community college. I have always had an interest in politics, but was not really inclined to run for office. A speech I made and some of my writings caught the attention of voters and I was elected. I have an obvious interest in education and I have sponsored legislation that will encourage teachers to stay in the field of education and make it possible for them to further their education. The idea is that they will be better teachers and be more satisfied with their career. We are looking at restructuring the way that our schools are funded and cutting out the bureaucracy that has jammed up the system and caused the excessive costs that weigh down our schools." Oliver said with a serious look, but a manner that signaled he was pleased with his synopsis. He stopped and waited for Chars to respond.

While Oliver was speaking, Chars was trying to figure out a way to throw out the Freedom Organization's name and see how Oliver would react.

"Sounds good. Are you finding that there is resistance to

your plan?" Chars asked.

Will liked the idea that it was labeled as his plan. "Well, Mr. Reynolds, the people that are entrenched in the education system will certainly perceive this as a threat. There will be those who object because they will think that this is just another way to cut education spending, but the reality is that the education of our children needs to be run like a business. As with any business, you are going to go through some streamlining." Oliver said and paused again for a response. He was looking directly at Chars as if he was trying to see which side of the issue the reporter was likely to be favoring.

"Sounds like you are looking at the whole system rather than a quick fix."

Oliver nodded his appreciation for someone who could grasp the big picture.

"How do you think the teacher's unions will react?" Chars asked.

"I think we will get the usual resistance, but I think when they see the carrot that is being offered to them, they will become the biggest supporters," Oliver said earnestly.

"Do you have the details of this plan in some sort of proposal form?" Chars asked.

"It is still in the early stages and there are lots of details that will have to be hammered out in committee. I am waiting to put out any specifics so that detractors will not get a head start or start rallying the usual opposition," Oliver said—and then thought better of saying it. "I hope you will not put that in your article."

Chars smiled and said, "Just between me and you, Senator. I understand the political process and it sounds like this has to be taken in small steps."

Will smiled and was nodding his head. Chars thought, *this guy is way too trusting for his own good. Who believes reporters these days?*

The Senator glanced down at a silver watch on his wrist and was obviously calculating how much time he had left. Chars knew that if he was going to get what he wanted he was going to have to move quickly.

"Senator, what political ambitions do you have on a national basis?"

Oliver was taken aback. He said nothing, but was obviously unprepared to answer that question. Chars decided that was not a productive tact and quickly added, "I am sorry—I did not mean to catch you off guard."

Will recovered and said, "Honestly, I have not given that any thought."

Chars knew that when someone used the word honestly, it means what they are about to tell you is anything but that. He knew the truth was more likely, "I am embarrassed to say that I have thought about that quite a lot, but I am not going to admit it."

"Again, I did not mean to spring that on you, Senator. Did you have the support of any of the well-known lobbying groups when you ran for office? In other words, are your critics going to have ammunition that you are doing this as the result of some special interest groups?" Chars said and then immediately regretted the way it sounded.

Again, Oliver just looked at Chars with a face that showed disbelief. Oliver was trying to make sense of these last two questions and then finally realized that this guy was here because of the Cattlemen's article.

Will smiled and said, "I guess I was a bit naïve to believe that you would come all the way from Washington to find out about our education legislation." He gave a thin smile, brushed off his pants as if he were trying to brush off dirt that Chars had thrown on him.

Chars, meanwhile, was starting to get the idea now that Will had moved from a trusting soul to someone who was starting to dislike him very much. Chars was used to that routine but that was not what he needed right now.

"Senator, that did not come out like I intended." Chars was looking at Will with a pained smile that said 'I have made a bad mistake.'

"Mr. Reynolds, I have a session to attend. I have given you all the time I intend to," Will said as he was standing. "My secretary will see you out and please, the next time you want to interview me," Will stopped and smiled, "On second thoughts, there won't be a next time."

He walked out the door and told Lucille that Mr. Reynolds would need an escort to the exit. Lucille evidently understood exactly and called security. While Chars waited he pulled out a business card and wrote on the back, Freedom Organization. He quickly placed it on the Senator's desk. The same security guard that checked Chars in came in the door and looked around like there was a terrorist in the room. Chars thought, *at least the officer's weapon was still holstered.* Chars held up his hands in the surrender pose and shook his head to say that he did not understand what just happened, but that he was eager to cooperate.

Lucille gave him a dirty look as he went out and several other people stuck their heads up over the cubicles to see who the scoundrel was. In response, Chars gave everyone a curt wave as he was escorted out the door. He left the building under the watchful eye of the security detail that was assigned to make sure he left. He sped off toward Cincinnati. He pulled out his cell phone and checked messages. There was one to call Jerry, but that was it. He placed a call to Mike Robertson's office in Miami and asked for Marsha Lincoln.

"Chars, is that you?"

"Yes, Marsha, it is. How's everyone doing?" Chars asked.

Chars hit the cruise control and plugged in his ear phone. He missed some of what Marsha was saying, but caught the main idea.

Chars interrupted, “Marsha, I am headed toward Cincinnati to try to locate Kay Moore. Can you give me a description?”

Marsha stopped for a moment trying to figure out why Chars would go to all that trouble to find someone who had been long gone from Miami, especially after the report that linked Mike’s heart attack with his accident.

“She was about 5’7” I guess. She had shoulder length hair. She always dressed real conservatively, but sharp you know. There was a rumor that she bought her clothes at Saks. We could not figure out how she could afford the price.” Marsha was speaking quickly.

Chars interrupted again, “Marsha, hang on. So she is about five seven with shoulder length hair. What color is her hair?”

“Well she was thin and she had a natural dirty blonde look, but always looked nice. A real classy lady,” Marsha said and closed up an appointment book. She was about to head out for lunch.

Chars put a mental picture of this woman in his mind. He wanted to remember the description so he could recognize Kay Moore when he got back to the election office. He traveled till he got hungry realizing that he had not eaten lunch. He pulled off at the Middleton exit and found a restaurant that advertised Real Texas Barbeque. Jeb’s was clean and the sliced brisket was, in fact, delicious. Chars was not sure about the Texas part. He had not been to Texas in quite some time and he did not believe that he had eaten any barbeque. He had been tempted to order a beer, but thought better of it. Sometimes a beer and a big lunch would put him out for a nap. He started out again on Highway 71 South. He thought about his conversation with Marsha. He replayed the description. “She said dirty blonde, and a real classy lady.” Then Chars said out loud, “A real classy lady. Chars, you idiot.”

He pulled over to the side of the road, made a u-turn across the median and headed back to Columbus.

Chapter 30

On St. Maarten's Island, Lancaster Smith said, "I had this place checked for bugs. There were none...seems like no one gives a shit about a former Vice-President."

Ross Saunders was tense, but still able to smile at the humor. Smith continued, realizing that Saunders was not in the mood for any levity.

"Everything I am about to tell you is from my limited base of knowledge." Lancaster Smith said through a puff of Coahuila smoke. "Last year or earlier, somebody started talking about Freedom Organization and the Matriculation Project."

Ross took a sip of his drink, but his attention was clearly undivided.

Smith continued, "I am not sure who, but I think it may have been either Karl Scott, or somebody in the Secret Service, told Parker that the Matriculation Project poisoned the President to move Parker up and make room for me. This person went to Parker not knowing that he was a Matriculation Project. He—whoever he is—told Parker of his suspicions. This informant planned to go public and it seemed that I was the most immediate threat."

Ross cleared his throat and said incredulously, "He would go public with a poisoning that did not happen and reveal your appointment by the lawful President?"

Lancaster shrugged and said, "This person also had some incriminating information about some other Matriculation Project operations and candidates. This was what spooked Parker. He confirmed that there were several people that were made to 'go away,' shall we say. In the meantime, someone had done a number on me and a business deal that I did—granted, it was a little questionable in hindsight, but I did not even think about it being smelly at the time. I think it was a set-up. One of the partners turned out to be a Chicago mob boss. Then Parker got a message that either I resign or they go public with all their theories, some of which had teeth. By this time, Parker was beginning to realize that Matriculation Project's other candidates were or had been sabotaged as well. He got a retired Secret Service agent to start checking things out. I think it was Pat Lewis—a good guy and someone Parker trusted. Parker cut off communication from you because he thought that the Matriculation Project had been compromised or infiltrated—or even worse—gone black ops. He happened to run into Mike Robertson. He confidentially met with Mike to discuss all the things that he knew about the Matriculation Project without telling him anything. But then Mike got killed. He now really began panicking. He presumably got the same Secret Service agent to check on Robertson's death. The report came back that it was an accident. Parker was relieved, but is still wary."

"Why did he pick Swain?" asked Ross who was now sitting on the edge of his seat and looked ready to leap at someone.

"Beats the hell out of me. I have not talked to him since the day I walked out of there as the former Vice-President. Maybe he was told who to pick. Maybe Swain's backers are behind it all. Maybe, maybe, maybe. I just don't know. You know more than I do."

Ross looked up at the sky and slid back into his seat. "We would not have killed Robertson. He was going to the White House. And Algiers was not an impatient man. He had nothing to do with the death of the President. That's ludicrous." Ross was shaking his head and Lancaster gave him a dubious look.

"Ross, you and I both know what you are willing to do for this country. I could not give Parker any reassurance about all the collateral damage."

Ross was visibly angry now. "We did what we had to do. An arrest record here or a business deal there that needed cleaning up."

Lancaster took as sip and said, "Or an affair that needed to be erased?"

Ross looked at Lancaster with a piercing stare that was borderline malevolent. Ross asked himself, *Now how in the hell did he know that*? Ross got his emotions under control and looked intently at Smith.

"Lanny, people die for this country every day. Good people sacrifice. Algiers was a good man. He was willing to give up his life as well."

"I know how you see this Ross," Smith said, smiling, "and I am sure that history will someday cast you and Algiers as misguided visionaries. But misguided will be the judgment. Because once you crossed the line in your cleaning, you became fanatics. All this may not come out. I have tried to distance myself from it. All my records and conversations have been expunged. You see, I did my own cleaning. You and Ben are my only two liabilities. I trust you because I know either one of you would fall on the knife before allowing this to go public. But Ross, there is a rat in the kitchen and he is taking a shit everywhere. Robertson was killed, Ross. 'They,' whoever they are, were taking him out. It had to look like a heart attack because he was so popular. Rumor was they tried to get dirt on him, but couldn't. Your boy, Karl Scott, he was seduced by one of their people and then they leaked it to his wife. The same girl that screwed him was taking a shot at old Mike. I guess he had some real scruples or morals or whatever. Shoot, if a good looking girl just went after me, I doubt I'd turn it down, unless I knew it was a set up, of course."

Ross was now shaking his head. He was incensed at himself. He had known something was up all along and he did not listen to that little voice. His bad luck was not luck at all. Someone had been working very hard to undo everything that the Matriculation Project had done and intended to do. "What about Satch?" he asked.

"No," smiled Smith, "he did that all by himself." He shook his head in mild amusement and sorrow. "But if he hadn't done it, they would have done it for him."

"They could not have known about all that. There just aren't that many people involved," Ross said. He was visibly shaken. This was a man who was normally calm under pressure. His mind was racing and he stood up and walked inside the room.

"Ross, we are talking about some people that swing a sharp and mighty sword. Algiers must have slipped somehow and told somebody. Maybe it was one of his confidantes that only someone like Banger could have," Smith said and stood up.

He went inside to fix another drink and to relight his cigar. The fresh smell of a match lingered and then was taken over by the smell of burning tobacco.

Lanny continued, "I think the only thing that saved Parker was they did not know about him. But you can bet if they did, he would be on the scope. And Ross, that includes any other candidates you got coming up the pike."

Ross asked, "Lanny, how did you know about all this?" Lancaster Smith stood and moved toward the balcony and looked out over the ocean. There was an American 757 landing on the runway just a couple football fields away.

"Ross, you failed in compartmentalization. I am not sure how Karl Scott found out about me, but he knew. And I think that he was the one that probably needed public office the most," Smith said and leaned against the balcony railing.

He continued, "He was still seeing that other lady when she got cleaned. When he was "outed" by the mystery date, that cleaning was not a necessity."

Ross had a pained expression on his face. He was

experiencing the full recognition of underestimating the fallout that he and Algiers had been oblivious to. What to do now was the question. He gathered his thoughts.

"There is no way to put this genie back in the bottle is there?" Ross asked rhetorically.

Smith had already given this some thought and tossed out the first idea. "If you know who is behind all this, then your chances go up dramatically. It may be that there is nothing you can personally do, other than to pick up camp and disappear. The fact that all your candidates have been stymied or eliminated, what else is left for them to accomplish?" Smith said.

Ross kept his eyes focused on the ocean, not giving away any hint of another candidate.

Smith continued, "You and Ben are certainly possible targets, but that would be a battle that may expose these people to more risk."

Ross took a long pull on his drink and then returned the cigar to his mouth. "Who is your best guess about who is pulling the strings on the sabotage?" Ross looked directly at Smith trying to detect any sense of disingenuousness.

Smith raised his eyebrows in a look of not knowing, shook his head and breathed out, then said, "You have to start with the resources that this person has at his disposal. He has several that can arrange for an operation that is sophisticated enough to take out Robertson, set up Scott and cause the sitting Vice-President to resign. He has a connection at least to the Secret Service. He could be high level government. He could be someone who knew Algiers, someone who knows Parker or someone that came across one of your candidates."

Ross maintained eye contact with Smith and said, "Lanny, who have you talked to about this?"

Smith smiled and said, "Parker and I discussed it privately, before I left. I have not discussed any details with anyone."

"And why haven't they gone after Parker?"

Smith shrugged. "Too big a fish maybe. But I have not gotten the feeling that anyone knows about Parker."

"How did you find out about all the information you are telling me?"

Smith took a sip of his drink and looked dissatisfied. He leaned over and added some ice and a couple fingers of bourbon to his glass.

"Parker told me that he was having someone in the Secret Service check out the claims of an informant. Scott told me about his deal. Again, I don't know how he knew about me, but he must have picked up the information from someone at the FO. He also knew about Saunders. I guessed that Robertson was one of yours when Parker recommended him for the Senate seat."

"How did Scott know about Robertson?"

Lanny was not sure and shook his head to indicate that he did not know. "I guess it is possible that they already knew each other. Who did the background on Scott?"

Ross went inside and pulled his flip phone out of his jacket, which was lying neatly on the corner of the bed. He speed dialed Ben.

Ben answered, "6434."

Ross said, "Hey, how's it going?"

"Not too good. Martha is going to have to relocate. The reporter was there and had a meeting with Will, then Will called in a bit of a panic. The reporter left a business card with the words 'Freedom Organization' on the back. We are going to have to start thinking about what to do about this guy if he keeps sniffing around," Ben said and paused for any reaction.

Ross said, "We may not have to. The people that killed Mike Robertson have got to be getting nervous. I will find out who it is and then I will know what to do. Ben, did Karl Scott and Mike Robertson know each other or have some kind of history?"

"You think that Karl Scott had something to do with Mike's accident?" Ben asked quite shocked.

"No, but I am just trying to figure out some puzzles and one of them makes more sense if Mike and Karl knew each other," Ross said, looked over at Smith and shrugged as if to say, you never know.

"I'll ask Marley, he did the background on Robertson, but I think Kay did the background on Scott," Ben said and wrote himself a note in his organizer.

Chapter 31

Chars arrived back at the Senate Offices in Columbus, Ohio. He pulled in to an open spot that had an Official Senate sign in front of it. He was sitting in his automobile, trying to decide what to do next. He called the Senate office, but received a message that "the Senate offices are closed, but if you know your party's extension, enter it now. If you need a directory, press star." He followed the directions of the telephone voice and successfully managed to get Martha's office number. When he called, he did not get Martha, he got a receptionist that evidently screened Martha's calls. Fortunately, even though Chars gave his real name, the lady put him through to Martha's office anyway.

He was expecting a voice mail but Martha answered. "Hello, this is Martha Hall."

Chars did not want to blow this. He had thought about what he wanted to say. "Miss Hall, this is Chars Reynolds, I am a reporter from the Miami Express."

Martha interrupted, "Yes Mr. Reynolds, everyone knows who you are. You've had quite the exciting morning, haven't you? Senator Oliver will be issuing a '*persona non grata*' tag for you. I would not try to slip back in to the Senate offices again. Have a nice day, Mr. Reynolds," Martha said with little emotion, but she was feeling good about her tone.

She was just about to hang up when she heard Chars say, "Kay Moore said it would be a good idea to contact you."

There was a silence on the phone, with neither one of them knowing what exactly to say. Chars thought silence was a good tactic at this point. Meanwhile a police officer had moved around the side of Chars' car. He tapped on the window and gave him the roll down your window motion.

Chars said, "Can you hold on just a moment, a police officer is trying to tell me something."

Martha said, "Seems like you are having a lot of trouble with authorities today, Mr. Reynolds."

Chars rolled down the window and looked at the cop and said "Just one second officer."

The police officer raised his eyebrows, mildly amused but losing his patience.

"I need to meet with you." Chars was trying to think where his license and insurance card was located.

The officer was speaking to Chars, "Sir, you need to hang up the phone."

Chars looked up at the officer, "Yes sir, just let me finish this. Martha, can you meet me?"

The officer was now visibly agitated and said, "Sir, you can hang up now." It was not a request but a demand.

Martha said, "This evening, 7:00pm at the Brickyard. See ya."

Chars repeated the place and time and folded his phone and gave his full attention to the officer. The officer's name badge, read Sergeant Read.

"Sir could you step out of your vehicle?"

"No, no officer, I was just moving."

The officer repeated, "Sir, step out of the vehicle, now."

******

Outside the Columbus Police Station, Pat Lewis sat in his rental vehicle, speaking on his cell phone. "No, it does not mean that Oliver is one of their boys. But it looks very suspicious. It is not likely that Kay Moore could have just out-of-the-blue gone to work for Oliver," he said to the man on the other end of the cell phone call. "Yes sir, she could be the one that is feeding the reporter information," said Pat. He listened for a short time and then responded, "It appears that he met with Senator Oliver. I am not sure how he got in there on such short notice, but if he named-dropped the Freedom Organization, and Oliver is part of that, bingo he gets in." He listened a little bit more and said, "Yeah, but why would Oliver meet with him and then throw him out? Why not just say that you don't have time and refuse to meet?" Lewis said with conviction, "Well it sure looked like he was thrown out. There were about four security guys there at the door when he left and they were not doing a come-back-again-soon wave."

The voice on the other end of the call said, "Oliver is one of them and I want him too. We don't have time to be clever, so just get the job done."

Pat agreed. "Hey, hold on just a second, we have some activity."

Pat Lewis was waiting for Reynolds to exit the police station and return to the rental vehicle that he had parked in a reserve spot for CCDP Official Vehicle ONLY. In small letters the sign read, Unauthorized Parking Prohibited by the Columbus City Police Department. A traffic officer stopped at Reynolds' car and checked for a parking permit. He then pulled out his ticket book, wrote the ticket and placed it. Pat thought this would be ticket number two for Mr. Reynolds. Back at the Senate building, Pat had witnessed the police officer approach Reynolds' rental vehicle and stand with his hands on his hips. Pat was laughing to himself, because he could see Reynolds on a cell phone. When Reynolds parked, he was either ignoring or unaware that he was parked in a restricted spot. Pat figured that the police officer had noticed the car had no State identification and he was asking Reynolds to move. Pat had already run Reynolds through a Secret Service database that he had maintained access to. He had no priors and seemed to not show up at all, although he did have press clearance for the White House, which was impressive in itself.

Pat was puzzled, because the officer looked pissed, got him out of the car, but did not frisk him. He started to write a ticket, but never appeared to finish. He then allowed Reynolds to follow him back to the station. When Chars pulled in to the parking lot, he had the nerve or stupidity or the authority to park in another reserve spot. Pat had waited for about thirty minutes, when the second officer ticketed Reynolds.

He then remembered that he was still on a call. "I'm sorry. Honestly, I don't know what is going on with this reporter. He has been in the police station for almost half an hour. I guess they could have booked him on something." Pat listened again, and then said, "Yes I am trying to find out what he knows." Another pause, "I understand that he is getting too close and we will have to act." Another pause, "Yeah the same guy has been following him, but I don't know who he is working for. Okay, I will take care of it."

Inside the police station, Chars said, "Thanks Jerry." Chars hung up and finished with the police officer. He walked out the door of the Columbus Police Department onto Marconi Boulevard.

He was playing the previous hour back inside his head. He was thinking to himself that nothing else bad could happen because everything that could have must have already happened. The Sergeant had explained that there was a possible terrorist, an angry White man that had tried to get into the Senate building earlier that day. Chars just happened to fit the description. Chars left out the fact that he was in fact the angry white man that they were referring to. He was able to convince the police to let him call a friend in the police department in Miami to vouch for him. Upon hearing that Chars had been confused with a terrorist, Jerry was laughing so hard that he actually teared up. Chars, of course, left out the part about actually being the angry White man that had been escorted out of the Senate offices.

Chars had said quietly under his breath, "Jerry, this is not funny," but failed to stop Jerry's laughing spell. He tried again in a very low but commanding tone, "Jerry. These people are seriously considering holding me overnight. I know that you think that this is hilarious, but it is not. Please regain your composure and talk to the Captain."

After a short conversation, the Captain had gotten a number for the Miami Police Department, called the number back and verified that it was in fact the Miami P.D. He then got Jerry back on the phone and continued his conversation. After a closed door session with the apprehending Sergeant, the Captain came out and returned Chars' personal effects.

Without apology, Chars was summarily dismissed with an impersonal, "Mr. Reynolds, here are your personal belongings. Please sign that you received everything back."

Chars narrowed his eyes and started to engage the Captain in a conversation, but decided that if he hurried he could probably still make it to his meeting with Martha Hall.

Chapter 32

Martha Hall had agreed to meet him away from the office. He understood that because he was, after all, *persona non grata*, as she put it. Chars made his way down Vine Street and arrived at the Brickyard Grill and Bar. As he parked his rental vehicle in the parking lot and got out he noticed that the temperature had dropped several degrees and there was an ominous looking cloud toward the north. Chars went inside and looked around the restaurant, but did not see her at any of the tables. He told the hostess that he was expecting someone and that he would just sit at the bar and order a beer. The place looked like it was set up to host live entertainment. Chars made a mental note that he might like to come back here later when the action started to liven up. The sign said that the New Amsterdams were playing tonight at 10:00pm. Chars had never heard of them, but he was sure they were a group that appealed to people much younger than he was. Nevertheless, he thought it might be worth a try. It appeared that there was an outdoor stage as well.

Chars had about finished his Sam Bass Ale, when he noticed a lady walk in through a rear door. She casually looked around and evidently did not see Chars. She walked to the restroom and disappeared. Chars was sure it was her and decided that she had just gone to freshen up. In fact, she did return from the bathroom and sat at a table that was in a corner almost out of sight of Chars—but not quite. Chars sat there trying to figure out what to do next. He finally polished off the rest of his beer, ordered another and slid down from the bar stool. He motioned to the bartender that he was moving over to the lady's table and the bartender gave him a wink.

"Hello, I'm Chars Reynolds," Chars said cheerily.

Martha looked at him over her perfectly stylish, round glasses. She was watching him with a somewhat of an amused look on her face. Chars read it as saying this guy has the balls of an elephant.

She finally spoke. "Mr. Reynolds, I assume you know that there will be a reprimand on your editor's desk by 8:00am tomorrow morning."

Chars stopped, tilted his head slightly and said, "I am pleased to meet you Ms. Hall."

He sat down across from the lady and once again appreciated her look of class. She had the look of someone who was in control and he admired her togetherness. She was perfectly put together and was dressed in a way that people would immediately notice, but not gawk at. *Classy, real classy*, thought Chars.

"Where would they have sent the note?" he asked.

Martha stared with a narrowing gaze. "To your editor, Mr. Reynolds; Thom Stanton," she said.

Chars' eyebrows raised in a mild surprised look. "Wow, I thought you were bluffing. But I keep telling everyone that I don't work for him. It does not seem to be doing any good."

"Mr. Reynolds, you wanted to meet, so here I am. What do you want?" she asked making it clear she was not going to sit here all evening.

She had plans and this moron was wasting her time.

"You only met with me because I mentioned the name Kay Moore," Chars said with the intention of getting a reaction to the name. He wanted to see for himself if she flinched.

She did not flinch or anything. She just stared directly at him with a look of growing impatience. “So what is your point?” she said icily.

“You are Kay Moore.” Chars decided to just go in for the kill. It was more of a statement than a question.

Martha looked at him with a “is that all you got” look. Martha waited for him to say something else. Chars was uncomfortable with the silence. He felt a bead of sweat on his brow, but he did not want to let on that he was feeling a bit intimidated by this woman. She was really good looking he thought, but c*old, cold, cold.* The waiter arrived with his drink and asked if the lady would like a drink. It broke the moment and Chars was able to regain some of his composure.

She smiled and said, “Just a Perrier and lime for me please. This is not going to take too long.”

Chars eyebrows arched again, but this time a smile cracked and then went all the way across his mouth. He really liked this lady. She was tough and gritty, but classy.

“Scott,” Chars addressed the bartender.

The bartender dutifully turned back upon hearing his name. That was one of Chars’ favorite tricks was to notice people’s name and then use them to make an impression.

“Bring the lady a martini; it may take longer than she thinks.” The bartender glanced at the lady, who now had an amused look and slightly nodded her assent.

The bartender gave a knowing smile and said, “Very well.”

Martha turned her attention to Chars once again. She still was looking at him with a trace of disdain, but with a little more respect. She finally said, “And Mr. Reynolds, you were telling me who I am.”

“I want you to tell me who you are.”

Martha was not giving anything up. Chars thought that she would be a good poker player.

"Mr. Reynolds, what is it that you are looking for or trying to find out?"

Chars looked at her in wonder and said, "I am trying to locate Kay Moore."

"And if I knew who this Kay Moore was, what would you ask her?"

With what must have been the quickest preparation of a martini in history, Scott had returned with the libations. Martha's drink was gigantic and had three olives on a huge swizzle stick resting along its side. Chars did not notice a man that entered the bar and shut down an umbrella, but it did not escape the trained eye of Martha. The man surveyed the bar and then climbed up on a stool at the end of the bar.

Chars returned his attention to Martha, "I would ask her if she liked martinis."

Martha did not answer, but instead took the stick with the olives out of her drink and delicately used her teeth to pull one up on the stick. She then covered it with her lips and began to caress it with her tongue. Chars was mesmerized. She was turning him on beyond belief. Chars looked away to break the spell.

What was that? he asked himself. He quickly took a sip of beer. He was fighting off a rush and finally felt that he had to say something or this was going to get pathetic. He actually felt a rise in his pants.

"I am writing an article about Mike Robertson. I think you are the last person that could help," Chars said.

He was thinking, *Damn it! She is just going to sit there.* The silence was really uncomfortable for Chars. He tried to remind himself that he was the one that caused people to squirm, not the other way around.

"Are you just going to sit there, Kay?" He was losing his composure and searching for anything that would change the control of this conversation to his side.

"Why would you try to see Senator Oliver, if you were in fact looking for someone else?"

"I had to get in to see him in order to find you," said Chars.

"What does this have to do with Mike Robertson?" Martha asked.

"I have suspicions that someone killed him," Chars said.

Again Chars looked for any clue in her face. For the first time Kay showed a slight reaction. It seemed to be sadness, not disbelief.

"What have the police found?" she asked and then took a long sip of her martini.

Chars again looked probingly at her, but felt that his statement was news to her.

"The police have put out a report that it was an accident," Chars replied, then popped a small pretzel into his mouth and waited again for her reaction.

"But you know better than the police?" she asked in a rhetorical fashion.

"I have several facts that don't make any sense. One item that I think you can help with is why the change of name?"

"Mr. Reynolds, are you not familiar with the custom in America of the woman assuming her husband's name when she gets married?" she had a condescending look on her face, but Chars actually thought she was loosening up a bit.

"Congratulations," Chars said merrily, "but you changed your first name and your last name."

Kay took in a breath in a slightly impatient way and said, "My name is Martha Kay Moore. In Florida, I was Kay Moore. When I married, I did not like the sound of Kay Hall. Sounded like a college dorm. Since I was starting a new job, I just decided that Martha Hall sounded better. Now Mr. Reynolds, I don't know that I owed you that explanation, but I did so in hope that you would tell me why you came all the way up to Ohio to find me. And now

I want to know if and why Mike Robertson was killed," she said and tented her hands in a way that suggested that she was about to deliver some type of judgment.

"Kay," Chars stopped and asked, "May I call you Kay?"

She looked at him in a rather bewildered way. "Sure," she said through a thin smile that had a bit of a contemptuous look.

"Did you ever arrange for a meeting with Mike Robertson and The Right Way organization?" Chars asked.

"I don't recall ever hearing of the organization called the Right Way," Kay said earnestly.

"What about the Freedom Organization or Foundation?

"What would the Freedom Organization have to do with Mike's accident?" asked Kay.

Chars figured that he had scored a hit. She did not say that she had not heard of the Freedom Organization. This, in his mind, was the same as admitting that you knew who it was.

Kay lied, "I recall the Freedom Organization, but they were more of a lobbyist group not a political entity or anything very impressive. I simply arranged the time for the meeting after checking with Mike to see if he would keep the appointment. I think you have wasted your time as well as mine."

She wiped her mouth off with the damp napkin.

Chars felt like she was going to walk away so he blurted out, "Would the Freedom Organization want Mike Robertson dead for any reason?"

He took another sip from his frosty mug.

"I can't think of anyone that might have reason enough to want Mike Robertson dead. I heard he was in a multi-car accident and that it was just that—an accident. So Mr. Reynolds, I think that concludes this meeting," she said and began to stand up.

"Kay, please. I am not trying to dig up dirt on him. I am just tracking down some very intriguing inconsistencies in the police's public statement. You will have to believe me when I say that there is some fairly damning evidence that this was not an accident," Chars said.

"Then I would suggest that you go to the police."

She lifted her drink to her lips. Chars noticed the peachy red lipstick for the first time. Her lips left an imprint on the side of the Martini glass. He again felt a tingle go down his body. He tried to clear his head, but there was something about her that just really got him excited. Maybe it was her throaty voice. Not a cigarette voice, but just a little sultry. He again had to refocus his attention on his line of questioning. He would come back to that.

He then asked, "Kay, who took care of Mr. Robertson's transportation?"

"Transportation? You mean like his car?" she asked in a polite but firm tone.

It was obvious that she was losing patience with him. Chars knew it and he was just going to have to be frank with her.

"Probably one of the secretaries. I am not sure. Why do you ask?"

Chars considered his answer. He did not want to give up the only true piece of information that he had. And he didn't want to ignore that question, but wanted to get back to his original line of questions.

"It seems that nobody in the office knew where Mike was coming from or going to. The office workers were not sure what he was doing out in the middle of…" he paused for a second, and then said, "Nowhere. He was driving a white Lexus. Do you know if that was his personal car?"

"Mr. Reynolds, you are beginning to really annoy me. I did not handle his transportation. I have no idea what car he owned, or was driving. You could have found that out from his office. I have not been there for quite some time," she said with frustration.

Then to Chars' surprise, she signaled the bartender to bring her another drink. There was an uneasy silence. Chars again noticed the man at the bar. He had ordered and finished a beer. He slid off the bar stool, dropped some money and left. Chars gathered the courage to ask her another question.

"Did you ever attend any of the meetings with Mike and the Freedom Organization or its founder—was it an Algiers Banger?" Chars asked, but he was sure he butchered the guy's name.

"Kay breathed out a surrendering sigh and said, "No Mr. Reynolds, I was not involved in meetings that Mike had other than to arrange the time. I believe that the Freedom Organization may have been a contributor, but you could have also looked that up in Florida. Usually if a potential donor wanted some private time with the Senator, I would handle the scheduling. I remember the Freedom Organization and I recall that Mike did meet with them. I don't recall how often or what the result was."

"Would Mike have had to prepare for these meetings?" Chars asked.

"Maybe, but that would not have fallen under my umbrella of responsibilities. That would have been done by Justin Crawford." Kay took another drink and said, "What is Chars, some sort of nickname?"

For the first time, Kay did not appear adversarial. Chars said, "Short for Charles."

"Chars, I would like to know what happened to Mike. What is it that you are not telling me? It must be important enough for you to come all the way up here to chase this string."

Chars did not believe that this lady was involved. She was tough and politically savvy, but she wanted to get to the bottom of this too. He was just not sure how much he should tell her. Her phone beeped just loud enough to be heard over the restaurant crowd noise and the clinking out of the kitchen.

Martha excused herself saying, "I'm sorry, I have to take this."

She moved to the back of the bar into a hallway that led to the bathrooms. It was Ben Thomas. He usually did not contact Martha—or Kay for that matter.

"Are you able to talk?" Ben said.

Martha took another look around and said, "I am having dinner with the reporter, but he can't hear right now."

"Good. Martha, we really need to know what he knows and where he going with this. He has somebody else trailing him that might take care of him. If they think that he is about to solve the Robertson murder, they might just take him out. Can you go with him and see what he knows?"

"What if they do try to take him out?" Martha asked.

Just at that moment, Chars came around the corner. "I am sorry. I had to use the restroom; did not mean to interrupt." He smiled and moved past her and into the men's room. Martha was trying to figure out if he had heard anything and was mentally kicking herself that she was not paying better attention.

"Okay," she said to Ben.

"Depends on what you can learn. We don't want it linked to us. Just use your best judgment," Ben said.

"Okay, I had better go," Martha said, flipped her phone shut and quickly went back to the table.

Their drinks had been cleaned up and she wondered if she had been gone that long.

Chars came back around the corner and said, "Oh there you are."

Martha smiled and said, "I haven't eaten yet; let's go somewhere a little quieter."

Chars was taken aback. "Sure, I bet we can find some place. Did you drive?"

"Cab," she responded untruthfully.

"I've got a car," Chars said brightly. They made their way to the front of the bar and as they got to the front door they realized that it had started to rain very hard. "Wow that moved in quick. Let me run out and get the car. I have an umbrella in my briefcase. I can pull up and you can get in without getting too wet."

Martha smiled an appreciative smile and said a simple, "Thanks."

Chars was out the door quickly and around the corner, pulling out his keys in a swift stroke and hitting the remote key entry. Even though he had moved fairly rapidly, he still got a good dousing. He started the vehicle, backed out and swung the front end toward the door where Martha stood just inside. He had to park a little ways down; but close enough. He opened his brief case and pulled out a short-barreled umbrella. He stopped and jumped out. He raised the umbrella and pushed the automatic button and walked quickly to the front of the restaurant.

As Chars reached for the door he was hit in the back by the force of a huge explosion. The force was terrific and caused the front plate glass windows to shatter, but the tinting helped keep the effect from being worse. Fortunately for Chars the restaurant's front door was open enough for him to pass through when the explosion knocked him forward. Otherwise, he would have probably crashed through the glass. The impact was felt up and down the block. People that were walking stumbled a bit before regaining their footing. They were astonished having been rocked by the explosion, and now were assessing the damage from flying glass and falling debris.

Chars landed unconscious on top of Martha. She was momentarily dazed, but slid out from under him and checked his pulse. He was alive, but lay motionless. Martha realized that she had a scrape on her face and was bleeding slightly. She stood shakily and used a napkin that lay on the floor to dab her injury. She did a quick check of Chars to see if there were any major injuries. The sound of sirens increased in the background. and people were now starting to peek out of the surrounding stores and make their way down the street. All that was left of Chars' car was a burning carcass. Martha could hear someone yelling that they needed help. Fortunately, nobody had been sitting at the window tables. Evidently someone had been hit by some glass, but it not serious enough to be life threatening. Martha moved toward the back of the restaurant. She needed to wash off the blood from her face. She went into the bathroom, washed her face and appraised the damage. It was a minor scrape and would not need any further attention. She exited the bathroom, but instead of going back to the front of the restaurant, she took a left and went out rear exit door that led to the alley. It was the same door by which she had entered. She went around to parking garage that was one block down and got into her car, started the engine and drove in the opposite direction of the Brickyard. As she turned onto High Street, she paused involuntarily as an ambulance and a fire truck were motoring toward her in the oncoming lane and she moved over to the side. Sirens filled the air as Martha continued on and merged onto Highway 670.

Chapter 33

Will Oliver woke up the next morning and drove to the Senate offices. He had called Martha last night, but she did not answer. When he got into the building he checked Martha's office, but she had not come in yet. He looked at the clock and figured it was a little early. Martha usually came in around 9:00, unless of course there was some meeting or something. By 9:15, she still had not arrived. Will thought that she might have had an appointment and was coming in later, so he dialed her cell phone number. He received a voice mail message, but Will did not leave a message.

Lucille entered and said, "Did you hear about the explosion outside the Brickyard yesterday?"

Will looked up with a puzzled look on his face. He had not read the paper yet and went to bed without the watching the news. "Downtown?" he asked disbelievingly.

"The press is saying it was a car bomb."

Lucille handed Will the paper. "It made the front page."

Will took the paper and said, "I would think so." He looked at the burned out shell of a car. "Was anybody hurt?" He continued to stare and began to read. The sub headline said, *Miami Reporter the Target of Explosion*. "Wait a minute. This is the reporter that was here." He looked up at Lucille with his astonishment unconcealed. Lucille was just nodding. She had already made the connection.

"I guess he really upset someone," Lucille said as she moved toward the door.

"Lucille, have you seen Martha this morning?"

"No, I haven't, but she does not usually arrive till after 9:00," Lucille said as she was now almost completely out of the door with only her head protruding back through.

Will checked his computer clock "Well it is after 9:00 and I wanted to ask her a couple of things. Could you check with some of the other people to see where she might be?" Will asked, but continued to look at the newspaper article and did not look up.

"Yes Senator, I will check around," Lucille said and closed the door behind her.

About ten minutes later, she opened the door, "Senator, you better come out here," Lucille said through the doorway.

Will moved around the front of his desk still looking at the picture of the burnt up car.

"Senator, Laura needs to tell you something," Lucille said turning the floor over to Laura who was looking a bit apprehensive.

"Yes, Laura?" Senator Oliver said with an inquisitive look on his face.

"Well, I am not sure about this, but I think that Martha had an appointment with that reporter."

Oliver looked like he had been slugged in the stomach. He closed his eyes and sat back on the edge of a desk. "That son of a bitch. Do we know if she was there?" Oliver asked.

No answer.

"Has any one checked with the police or the hospitals?" Will asked quietly.

Everyone looked at each other.

"I assume that means no. Laura, could you get that started?"

"Yes sir," she said quickly and turned toward her desk.

"Lucille, could you check her personnel file and get me her address and phone number?" asked Will.

Lucille nodded and headed toward a filing cabinet. She thought for sure that the Senator had Martha's address and phone number, but did not want to seem presumptuous. Will walked back into his office and began reading the article again.

Chapter 34

"The police are waiting outside to talk to you Mr. Reynolds. Do you feel up to talking to them?" a nurse with dark red hair asked, while removing a blood pressure cuff off of Chars' left arm.

"I suppose it is inevitable," Chars said while buttoning his shirt sleeve.

A plain clothes police officer and a uniformed officer were waived in by the nurse. The detective was a rather small man somewhere in his forties by the look of his slightly graying hair. He pulled a badge out of his suit pocket and introduced himself as Detective Arnold Smith.

"Mr. Reynolds, you have had an interesting few days."

Chars took a deep breath and smiled slightly. He had momentarily forgotten that he was at the police station just a few hours ago.

"You were booted out of the Senate offices, picked up as a possible terrorist and now you car has been blown up," Detective Smith said with a bit of amusement.

"Well, the first was a misunderstanding and the second was a case of mistaken identity," Chars said as he reached for a cup of water that was on the side of the emergency room bed. He glanced over at the officer and returned his attention to the detective.

"And someone blew up your car. Was that a misunderstanding or mistaken identity? The detective asked.

Chars raised his eyebrows and let out a breath. He raised his arms, shrugged and opened up his palms in an "I give up" gesture.

"Do you want to tell me what you are working on that has caused such interest in you?"

Chars said in a less than genuine tone, "I am working on an illegal immigration story."

The detective rolled his eyes and said, "If you are not going to cooperate, I don't think we are going to be able to help you, Mr. Reynolds. Normally, I would not care if someone were to rub out a Miami reporter, except for the fact that the bomb destroyed an entire business front. That concerns me greatly."

Chars asked, "Was there anyone else hurt?"

The officer said, "Fortunately, only a couple scrapes."

Chars let out a sigh of relief. The detective continued, "Were you alone when this happened?"

Chars thought a moment. He had not asked about Martha, but he did wonder if she had managed to escape injury. "Yes."

The detective did not even bother to feign surprise when Chars answered.

"Mr. Reynolds, I consider this an investigation and the information that you give me is going into my report. I would be willing to take you in again if I thought you were obstructing justice. So let's make it the truth, ok?"

Chars did not respond. The detective looked over at the officer and motioned for him to close the door. "Mr. Reynolds, I am not sure what or who you are trying to protect, but I know from the witnesses that you were meeting with a woman. You went outside and returned with your car to pick her up, presumably because the rain was so heavy. When you got out of your car to escort your lady friend to the car, it went boom."

Chars still did not answer. "I gave a Sergeant Jerry Collins a call before I headed over here. It seems that he helped to clear up your other…mistaken identity problem. He said that you are working on a story regarding the death of a Florida Senator," said

Detective Smith.

Chars asked impetuously, “If you knew all that, why are you asking me questions to which you already know the answers?”

Both men stared at the reporter and after an uncomfortable pause, Detective Smith said, “I wanted to see if you had a propensity to lie.”

“I see.”

“Mr. Reynolds, we are going to need to take you to the station until we can clear this matter up. Until you become a little more forthcoming, I am going to report to the business owner that you will personally be responsible for paying for the damages to his business.”

Chars looked to the side of his bed and touched two painkillers that the nurse had so considerately left in case he needed it.

“Mr. Reynolds, shall we try again?” The detective said and pulled out a pen and a small spiral notebook.

Chapter 35

"Lego, what happened?" Pat Lewis said into a cell phone, while chewing nervously on a toothpick. Lego was leaning on a pillar next door to a locally owned Mexican restaurant. One hand was massaging his temples as he was shaking his head slowly.

Lego said in a heavy Puerto Rican accent, "Boss, it was on a 30 second timer. It was unfortunate that he got out of the car. Do you want me to make another go at it?" Paul Gallegos eagerly asked.

Lewis ignored the question and said, "This guy is getting to be a real problem. The boss is not going to be happy. Reynolds has managed to stir up an unwanted investigation. If he gets any closer on the Florida job, the FBI and who knows who else are going to get involved."

"I know boss; let me try again," Lego was not quite pleading, but close.

Again Lewis ignored Lego and asked, "Who was he meeting with?"

Lego ran his hands through his hair, and said, "It was some lady from a Senator Oliver's office. I think she came in and left through the back door."

After a moment, Lewis said, "I think we should follow him and see where he goes next. If he heads back to Miami, which I think he will, I will put Bostic on him." Lego's shoulders sagged knowing that he was not getting a second chance. Lewis continued, "He should be finished up with his current assignment."

Then Lego had a thought and said with a sly smile, "Maybe

this Oliver is also a candidate, no? You want me to kill him?"

"No Lego," Pat said firmly, "we do not want to be impulsive."

Paul's head dropped a little in disappointment.

"Lego, if I get the go on Oliver, you will be the first I call," Pat said.

"A smile is returning to my face, Boss," Lego said.

"I am sure it is, Lego. Talk to you soon," Paul Gallegos clicked off his cell phone and pulled out of his driveway into traffic.

*****

"Chars, what the hell is going on?" Jerry said seriously concerned.

"I think someone tried to kill me," Chars said with a tone that belied his fear.

"You think? You THINK?" Jerry said with exasperation.

"I just need to know if my contact was in on it."

"Chars, you are in trouble. You may need to disappear for a while."

"Have you gotten anything else that helps put this together?"

"We did get the passenger airbag removed and tested. It shows DNA. We have run the DNA and there were no matches, but it was a woman. If we ever catch up with that person we could at least place her at the scene, but it probably would be thrown out in court," Jerry said.

"So we know that there was a passenger?" Chars asked.

"At the very least, it is enough to put some people on it. And what have you found out?"

"Not much," Chars said, "My contact here used to work in the Robertson campaign. She evidently got married and moved to

Ohio. She started working for a Senator here. That all could be a coincidence, but the fact that someone try to blow me up at our meeting may mean there is some connection. It could be nothing, but if she did in fact have something to do with the Freedom Organization, then I might have the connection I was looking for. Could you do a background on Martha Hall and a Kay Moore?" asked Chars.

"Sure can. But I'll have to get a friend of mine from the FBI involved," Jerry said. "What else?"

"As soon as the CPD's finest here let me go," Chars glanced up, but did not receive any acknowledgement, "I am coming back to Miami. Could you meet my plane?" "Sure can. Anything else?"

"Yeah, here's Detective Smith," Chars said and handed his cell phone to the suited man standing next to him, waiting impatiently.

Chapter 36

Oliver picked up a phone and started to dial Martha's cell phone again. The television caught his eye. There was a picture of the former Vice-President, Lancaster Smith in the corner of the screen. Oliver pushed the mute button to allow for sound.

The announcer said, "Smith was 58 years old and will be remembered fondly by his contemporaries. Here's Gloria Sonta with the reaction of the President."

The picture shifted to the Rose Garden. There were several people lined up behind President Parker. Parker adjusted the microphone up a little and said, "We are all saddened to hear of the death of Lancaster Smith. He served his country proudly as a Marine and public servant in the political arena. I will miss him as a friend. I urge prayers and encouragement for the family during this difficult time," Parker said solemnly and paused.

He evidently was not going to take questions, because he turned and stepped away from the podium. He was visibly shaken. The announcer came back on and broke for commercial. Oliver was shaking his head in mild disbelief. He tried Martha's cell phone and again was answered by voice mail. He did not leave a message. He wanted to track down that reporter and ask him a question or two. Instead he picked up his office phone and dialed the police station. Normally he would have Lucille call, but he really did not want her to know that he was doing any checking.

The desk sergeant answered the phone. "Sergeant Murray."

"Sergeant, this is Senator Will Oliver."

Murray was not sure whether to believe the caller or not,

but did not want to get in any trouble just in case it was really the Senator.

"Yes, how may I help you?" he paused, looked over to his partner Stuart, pointed to his phone and mouthed, "Senator." He had a smirk on his face as if the caller were playing a prank on him and he was going along.

Oliver knew that he might run in to this so he said, "Sergeant, I know that this is not standard protocol, but I am looking for some information and I would like you to help me get to the right person."

Murray was starting to take this guy seriously and just answered, "I will help if I can."

Oliver figured the guy probably still did not believe that he was in fact the Senator and began to regret making the call.

"I understand there was a car bomb at the Brickyard," said Will.

Murray said, "Yes there was.".

"I would like to speak to the person in charge of that investigation. Could you have him or her I suppose, call me at my office as soon as possible?" Will said.

He gave Murray the office number, who dutifully wrote it down.

Murray stuttered and said, "I, I will pass this along and the detective will be back in touch with you."

When he hung up he let out a big sigh and said to his partner, "Thank God I just played that straight. That was actually a State Senator."

Stuart looked over and raised his eyebrows revealing that he was impressed.

Within 10 minutes, Senator Oliver's phone buzzed. He punched an intercom button.

Lucille said, "Senator, are you expecting a call from a

Sergeant Smith of CPD?"

"Thanks Lucille, put him through."

The phone rang this time and Oliver picked it up and said, "This is Senator Oliver."

"Senator, this is Sergeant Smith of the CPD, I had a message that you wanted to talk to someone with regard to the car bomb incident."

"Thanks for getting back to me so quickly, Sergeant. Can you brief me about what you think happened and where the investigation stands?"

The Sergeant leaned back in his swivel chair and considered where to begin. He was feeling some pressure speaking to a State Senator, as anyone would. He wanted to give a professional summary and of course not give anything away that would compromise the case.

"Well actually, Senator, you were on my list of people to call," said Smith.

Oliver stopped his doodle of Donald Duck and asked "I am?"

"Yes sir. We feel that the target of the bomb was a Miami reporter named Charles Reynolds. From the information we gained from him, we know that he was meeting with a lady from your office," the Sergeant said.

Oliver was not sure what to say, but finally came up with: "I was advised of that as well."

The Sergeant smiled a thin smile and hesitated for a moment. "Senator, when were you aware that Mr. Reynolds was meeting with your Ms. Hall?"

Oliver did not like the tone in which that question was asked. He responded with a cautious, "I was told this morning by a staffer. You see, Ms. Hall did not..." He stopped and stated it differently. "Well, what I meant to say was that she is running late this morning."

Oliver's throat was tight and he feared that something very bad was wrong. He did not want to say anything that might get Martha in trouble and yet he was concerned that something the stupid reporter had done had gotten her somehow involved.

"Has Ms. Hall, in fact shown up for work?" Smith asked.

"Let me check." Oliver put Smith on hold and buzzed Lucille.

"Has Sergeant Hall, I mean Ms. Hall shown up, Lucille."

"No sir and she's not answering her phone. Is that why the Sergeant is calling?"

"Well not exactly, but yes. Thanks Lucille, I'll let you know what I find out," Oliver said and then returned to his call with the Sergeant. "No Sergeant, it does not appear that she has come in. Is there anything that I should know?"

"Senator, what exactly is your relationship with Ms. Hall?" Smith asked.

Taking exception to the question, Will asked shortly, "What is that supposed to mean?" Smith scribbled sown that there was likely a relationship going on between the Senator and Martha Hall.

"What I mean is, did she work in your office? What was her job title? Did she report to your directly or through someone else that we might need to talk to?"

Oliver thought to himself that he wished he had not responded so short. "Oh, I see. Well, Martha reported directly to me. She was, I mean is a campaign advisor."

"Senator, did Reynolds come in to see you yesterday about the murder of a Senator in Florida?"

"No. I mean yes, he came in, but it did not have to do with anyone's death. He came on the pretext of writing an article about my new Education Bill. I am sorry Sergeant; you are going to have to clue me in." Oliver was feeling very uneasy not knowing where this was going.

"Senator, I have confirmed that Reynolds is working on a story about the Florida Senator that was killed in a car accident a few weeks ago. It appears that the accident may have not been...well, an accident." The Sergeant paused.

"Well, all I can tell you is that he said he was doing an education story. We did not discuss any Florida Senator."

The Sergeant leaned forward with pen in hand ready to write. He was going to hit the Senator with a question that he wished he was in the same room in order to see his reaction, but he let it go anyway.

"Senator, you say Reynolds saw you on the pretext of writing a story about your Education Bill. Why did you have him removed from your office?"

Oliver was tapping his pencil harder and harder on the side of his desk pad. This had gone quite far enough, but he did not know how to make it stop. It was if he was being accused of something. "I had him removed because he was disingenuous about what he asked to see me about." he said in an agitated tone.

"So how did you find out that he was not there about the Education Bill?"

"When he started asking questions that had nothing to do with the Education Bill."

"Questions about the death of the Senator from Florida?" asked Smith.

"No, not that. Sergeant, I see where you are headed with this and I am not real pleased with the insinuation. If you were not aware, there is a story in the papers that implies that I took some kind of payment from a group that I did some consulting work for."

"Some consulting work?"

Will was getting quite upset now at having to explain all of this to a Sergeant. "Yes, consulting work."

"So, he said he wanted to talk about your Education Bill,

but then when he asked you about a bribe, you had him removed from your office?"

"It was not a bribe!" Will said, almost out of control now. "Look, Sergeant," he said in a condescending tone, "I called you."

"Yes sir, you sure did. I appreciate that, but I am going to need to get a statement from you—this afternoon if possible.

"I am not meeting with you this afternoon, for God's sake. I have Senate meetings to attend! I just wanted to know whether Martha was involved in the accident."

"Which accident are you referring to?"

Oliver was red in the face now and said, "The car bomb accident."

Smith thought that this guy has something to hide or knows something. "Okay, the car bomb. Involved how?"

Oliver paused a moment to gather his thoughts then said in a very deliberate and calm voice, "Was Martha Hall there when the car bomb went off? Was she hurt?"

Smith was shaking his head slowly and had a smile that said, *I am not sure what your game is buddy, but I am going to find out.* He said, "As far as we know, Senator, she was at the crime scene and she apparently left. We don't think she was seriously hurt, but nevertheless she should not have left the scene. Therefore, she is currently listed as a person of interest with regard to this explosion. Senator, where were you yesterday evening, at around, oh say 6 o'clock?"

Chapter 37

Chars arrived at the Miami International airport at 9:10pm. He retrieved his luggage and sat down in a common area. His head was aching, but he wasn't sure which event had caused that. He knew that he had not had any caffeine for the entire day and in the past that had resulted in a horrific head ache. He started to pop a couple of the pain pills that he got from the D.C. hospital, but decided on a couple of aspirin instead. He stopped at a hot spot and plugged in his computer. It seemed like days since he had checked his messages. He had 314 new messages. Chars shook his head and took in a breath. It would take too long to go through all of these. Jerry was supposed to meet him after his shift ended. He would pull up at about 9:45, if Chars had figured correctly. He skimmed down through messages to find the most important ones. There was no e-mail from MR_Friend, but there was one from Priscilla White. He opened it up and read that the names listed in the incorporation papers were Algiers Banger, Gloriette Banger—Algier's deceased wife—and Nathaniel Banger, a deceased uncle. He hit delete and perused the remaining messages.

His computer binged. Mr. Friend was online. Chars signed on as available for conversation. He received the first message.

"Where have you been?"

Chars typed in and hit send: "I had some business in Ohio. Delayed for a couple days."

Mr. Friend was typing: "What did you find out about the Freedom Organization?"

Chars typed back: "That they don't like people who ask questions."

The message came back: "The Freedom Organization killed Robertson."

"What motive?" Chars instant messaged back.

Mr. Friend typed back: "To keep him from being elected. I don't know. Maybe Robertson knew them and was concerned with what they were doing."

Chars typed back: "Did he say he was scared of the FO or say that something was going to happen to him?"

Mr. Friend responded: "I can't tell you how I know. But if you can find out who the FO is, then maybe their motive would become clear. I know Robertson was killed, and I am certain that the FO had something to do with it."

"You are leaving something out. How do you know that Robertson was killed?"

The answer came: "I was there."

Chars was stunned. He could not type anything. He just sat there with his mouth open. "Who are you?" He finally managed to peck out.

The reply came quickly: "I am the link that you have been looking for."

Chars blew out a long breath and folded his hands back behind his head. He accidentally touched one of his wounds and winced.

He typed: "What else can you tell me that I can use?"

Mr. Friend typed: "I can tell you that the FO was responsible for Smith, Scott, Mitchell, and Robertson. Algiers is no longer, but someone has taken his place."

"Responsible for what?"

Mr. Friend answered: "I thought you had done your homework. We need to meet."

Chars' brow furrowed. That was strange he thought. "Okay, when and where?"

"Terminal F, Miami Dade Port," the response came.

“When?” Chars typed.

“Tomorrow night 8:00p.m.” Mr. Friend signed off.

Chars slumped down in his chair and let out a sigh. He packed up his computer and luggage, and went to meet Jerry.

Chapter 38

"The Senator will see you now gentlemen," Lucille said to the detective and his two companions.

They looked grim and all business. Two were dressed in dark suits and the third was in a police uniform. Lucille figured that could not be good. She was thinking that they must have information on Martha's disappearance. The Senator rose from his chair and shook hands as each introduced himself. One of the men in suits was the Detective Smith that Oliver had talked to earlier. But Smith was not visibly in charge. It was Detective Adam Brock, a 15-year veteran of the Columbus Police Department. He carried himself rather erect and his expression was completely serious. Brock's hair was cropped close with just enough to part on the left hand side. Oliver was dressed conservatively as usual, but had his tie loosened and his jacket was draped on the edge of a couch toward the side of his office. He was sipping on a glass of water with a lime. He did not offer the policemen any refreshment as he wanted them out of there as quickly as possible. The men took the seats that were arranged around the front of Oliver's desk. Adam Brock sat back in his chair and pulled out a small spiral notebook from his jacket pocket. He reached in his other pocket to retrieve a pen. He searched around for a short time and then looked over at his partner and signaled that he needed something to write with. It was obvious that he was in charge of this entourage.

"Senator, thanks for seeing us. We understand your need for discretion," Brock said trying to relax the Senator.

"If you were trying to be discrete, I hardly think you would have brought a uniformed officer with you," Oliver said quite boldly. "No; I'd say you are going for maximum effect here."

Brock visibly stiffened. "Well Senator Oliver, I was in favor of hauling your rear end downtown to the police station for this interview, but my Sergeant Smith, here, said that it would be more beneficial to meet you where you felt comfortable. So I hope he is correct and that you are going to cooperate."

Oliver looked over his half glasses in an attempt to intimidate. It did not seem to be working. "I don't like being addressed as if I were a suspect."

Brock snapped back, "What you have told us and what you have refused to tell us, indicate that you need to be ruled out as a suspect. That is what we are doing here. The only thing that kept us from listing you as a person of interest in our media report was that you are a State Senator and a report like that will be very detrimental to your career. So, Senator Oliver, I would suggest that you get off your high horse and answer the questions that my colleagues and I have and give us any information that you think would be beneficial in figuring out the truth about this crime."

"Before you go any further with this, Detective Brock, it is Detective, correct? Let me suggest something. Back the hell off or I am going to start making phone calls and I think you are going to be very uncomfortable with the heat that will be turned on." Oliver was red faced and was using his index finger to direct his anger directly at Brock.

Brock stood up. "I can see that this interview needs to be in our office and that our initial consideration will not be necessary." His eyes narrowed. "Will we need to make this official with a warrant or will you be willing to voluntarily come in yourself?"

Oliver picked up the phone and said, "Lucille, get me the Chief of Police on the phone, NOW!"

The other two men now were looking very uncomfortable. The uniformed police officer was leaning in his chair, chin in hand, partly covering his mouth, head tilted forward, looking at Brock as if to say, hope you know what you are doing. However, Brock seemed just as confident. He actually seemed bolstered by the Senator's tactic. What Oliver did not know that Brock did know, was that the Chief of Police was out of town attending a law enforcement conference. He knew that he would not get through.

"This is Senator Oliver, is Harry in?" Oliver glanced over at the collection of men in his office and waited and listened. "I see, and the Deputy Chief as well?" There was another pause as Oliver was looking like he had just taken a bite out of a lemon and was slowly moving his head from side to side in disbelief. "I see. I would like you to get a message to the Chief as soon as possible and ask him to call me." Oliver again paused. "I understand that. Just give him the message to call me." Oliver was again turning an angry red.

Meanwhile, Brock looked at his notebook as if reviewing some important entry. But he was still there waiting for Oliver to finish his little show of power and conclude his tantrum. This had deteriorated into a pissing match, but Oliver was going to have to answer questions. Brock did not want this to get to the Chief's desk because it would not be pleasant. He would come out all right, but would be chastised for letting the relationship become adversarial. Oliver had something to hide or was being an A-1 dick. He had heard good things about Oliver being a normal guy and all that. *Seems like the pressure or circumstance has brought his real colors to the surface*, Brock thought. When Oliver hung up the phone, Brock gazed up from his spiral notebook with a brief smile and then moved on as if the conversation were starting all anew.

"Senator Oliver, we have a duty to find out what happened at the Brickyard. I assume that you have an alibi for that time period, is that correct?"

Oliver was visibly incensed. He let out a simple, "Yes."

Brock continued, "I am also assuming that you have not

had any military training and have no expertise in the building of bombs. Is that also correct, Senator?"

"That is correct." Oliver said with a steely stare that did not leave the face of Brock.

"Would I also be correct in saying that your only contact with Reynolds was the day of the bombing?"

Oliver nodded yes. The other two men could be seen relaxing a little bit.

The phone beeped and Oliver punched the intercom button, "Yes?"

Lucille said, "Senator, the Chief of Police is on line 3."

An almost imperceptible smile crossed Oliver's lips. Brock crossed his legs, but otherwise, showed little or no expression. The other two glanced briefly at each other then returned to gazing at the wall or the floor, but said nothing.

"Thanks Lucille." Oliver punched the button for line 3 and said, "Hello Harry. Sorry to bother you." He paused and listened for a moment. "Thanks, I hope it does go forward." Another pause and he said, "They are fine, thanks." Oliver was now wishing that he had not called the Chief. The three men were watching him and presumably following his conversation with their boss, the Chief of Police. "Have you been briefed on the explosion that happened yesterday?" Oliver listened and turned toward the window slightly. "I see…Good… Me too."

Oliver had the phone between his shoulder and ear while apparently taking notes. "The reporter came to see me earlier in the day. I think he was after a story on the Cattlemen's, so I had him removed." Oliver listened for a while and then said, "Harry, I understand, but I think he had just finished a meeting with one of my staff and now she is missing." Oliver waited for the obvious question and he answered, "It was Martha." He again listened and then said, "I am sure she is fine, but, well you know, I am worried." After another pause he said, "Harry, I have a Sergeant

Brock here in my office who is saying that I need to go downtown and answer some questions. That is very unrealistic with my schedule and potentially very embarrassing." Oliver leaned forward with his elbows on the desk. "Okay, sure will. Thanks Harry, see you when you get back."

"Okay Gentlemen, your boss reminded me that you were just doing your job and that everything should be able to be taken care of in my office. In return, the Chief told me to tell you that what I am telling you about should remain completely off the table for the media. Therefore, let's start again on a more civil basis. Martha and I are having a relationship. I have not heard from her and she is not answering her cell phone. Obviously, I am concerned with her safety. I had never met Reynolds before and thought he was just a less than scrupulous news reporter. I did not know Martha was meeting with him and I really would like to know why. I think he was probably following her in the hope of getting some big scoop. Very few people know about Martha and me. Neither of us is married, but I wanted to be discreet. I am worried about her and would very much like to talk to that reporter."

Oliver finished and gave the officers with a look of finality. No one said anything for a moment. Brock took his time finishing up with what he was writing. Whether he was just making Oliver wait or he was really doing something important, Smith did not know. The detective did recognize, though, that the pause was irritating Oliver.

Just before Oliver was about to explode, Brock said, "We have talked to the reporter. He says that Martha is actually Kay Moore. She is married and took the name Martha Hall; Hall being her husband's name."

Oliver's mouth dropped open and a shocked looked took over his face. His head was involuntarily shaking slowly side to side. "No. That can't be. She lives alone. He must have been lying."

Brock had Oliver reeling. He appeared to be genuine, but Brock thought to himself that you could never be sure because some of these guys were great actors. Just take Bill Look-You-In-The-Eye Clinton. He went on national television and said he never had sex with that woman. Later, of course everyone found out that the woman had been on her knees giving him head in the Oval Office.

Brock continued, "It appears that Ms. Moore worked in the Mike Robertson campaign. It also appears that Senator Robertson was likely the victim of foul play. The reporter said that he made an appointment with you to try and find Ms. Moore. Does any of this ring a bell with you Senator?"

"No it doesn't, but she was here with me when Robertson was killed." Oliver was solemn and had lost any sense of defiance. He now had an almost melancholy look that showed confusion, hurt, and betrayal. Sergeant Smith finally said something, but Oliver was really lost in thought.

Smith repeated the question again. "Senator Oliver, you have had no contact with Martha Hall or Kay Moore since the day of the explosion?" Smith asked.

Oliver returned his focus and said, "No, I have not."

"Senator, if we need anything else from you we will be in touch," Smith said.

All three men stood in unison and exited quickly. They left a disheartened Oliver at his desk, distraught and confused.

Chapter 39

Ben Thomas was at his computer in Key Biscayne, Florida. His hazel eyes were drooped and his hair was disheveled. He was checking the Internet for news stories about the Robertson accident. The papers had not published a story in three days. The last mention was that the FBI and the State Police were cooperatively investigating the matter and were looking for potential witnesses. The lone witness had left the country on vacation and had been unreachable. The Freedom Organization was not mentioned anywhere. He Googled Charles Reynolds and came up with a number of hits, but the most recent one was regarding a story on the Immigration Bill that was being discussed in Congress. The last report from Marley was that Chars Reynolds had not been seriously hurt in a car explosion in Columbus. He did not give a great amount of detail, but said he would call back later when Reynolds was released from the ER. Ben thought to himself, *I don't know who is after Reynolds, but they need to get their act together.* He had received two calls from Oliver, neither time leaving a message. He had not heard from Kay, but he figured that was not unusual. He typed in Will Oliver and drew a number of hits. The first one read, "Local Senator to answer questions about payment from Cattlemen's Association." He typed in Lancaster Smith and got the latest information about his passing. One article's headline read, "Smith's heart attack serves notice of need for annual exam." Ben thought to himself, *get an exam and stay out of politics*. Ross had not called either and Ben was feeling that he was left out of the loop. He was fidgety. He pulled a draw from his Heineken and then called Ross, but got no answer, so he left a cryptic message. Ben then called Oliver's private line. Oliver answered immediately while trying to remain calm, but he was noticeably on the edge. Ben could tell from his voice that he would need some calming.

"Ben, I have been trying to reach you," Oliver said.

"Sorry Will, I have had several fires happening at once. What's up?" Ben asked with his usual level demeanor, leaving out the obvious that Will was right in the middle of one of those fires.

"There is a lot going on here as well. Did you hear about a bomb that was detonated in downtown Columbus?"

"Yes I did. Terrorists of some sort?" Ben asked.

"I don't think so. I have been in with the police. They said that someone was trying to kill this Miami reporter. It was the same reporter that was in here talking to me. I thought he was after me on the Cattlemen's story, but the police said that he was working on a story about Mike Robertson." Will paused for a moment.

Ben was just listening and said, "I understand."

"Ben, Martha was meeting with him when the explosion occurred."

"What was she doing with him?" he asked and wondered if Marley missed that part. Or, he thought, *it could be that Marley never had an occasion to meet Kay or Martha.*

"I don't know, but I intend to find out." Will stood straight up off his chair and began to pace back in forth. "Ben there is also this." Will was talking as if he was trying to give Ben enough information to solve this puzzle. Of course he had no idea that Ben was the architect of the puzzle.

"The police seemed to think that Martha may have had something to do with the accident of Mike Robertson in Miami."

Ben was now confused. "You are joking. What could she have had to do with that?" he said earnestly.

"Not only that, they said that Martha was married and that her real name was Kay Moore. They said that she used to work with Robertson on his campaign and that since she left the bomb accident or whatever you call it, she is a person of interest," Will said quite excitedly.

And Ben knew why. He knew that Will was in love with Martha. That love is maybe the only thing that is keeping him from really figuring out the situation.

"Okay Will, let me do some checking. The police have obviously made some mistakes here. Are they saying you are a suspect?" asked Ben.

"No they are not saying it, but they sure implied it with all their questions. I called the Chief of Police to try to get them to lay off."

Ben drew in a breath, put his hand on his face and closed his eyes. Oliver was just like a broken gumball machine. "Will, you are over reacting. Do not try to throw your weight around! That just makes you look worse. You need to cool your jets. I have told you before that you are not shrewd enough to try and manipulate people. You do not have it in you and you are better off just being yourself. You did nothing wrong, so stop acting like you did. The more you react to this the more people are going to want to take a deeper look. So just chill," Ben said with a parent's voice.

Will was usually able to control his emotions a little better, but he needed to get a grip.

"Okay," said Will with a slight pout on his evident in his voice.

Ben thought he must have looked like a child that had been corrected.

"Look Will, I am sorry, but you are in the big time now. We cannot afford to have you flying off the handle and calling in the heads of departments when someone asks you a question that you do not like. You can't just throw people out of your office.

You are going to have to get tougher—like Teflon; you know, the heat is turned up, but nothing seems to burn or stick. You need to be like that," Ben said and remained silent to see if Will was absorbing the idea.

"Ok," he said. "What about Martha?" he asked.

"Let me get started on finding her. I am sure she's ok."

"Ben, do you know anything about Martha working for Robertson?"

Ben took in a breath and thought quickly about how to phrase this, "It is possible that she worked for Robertson."

Oliver was nodding his head in resignation. "Ben, did Martha work for you?" Will asked, before he could think better of it. As soon as he'd asked, he wished he hadn't. He did not want to know and he had that sick feeling that his relationship with Martha or Kay was a set-up. He did not even give Ben a chance to answer because he already knew the answer.

Ben started to say something, but Will said solemnly, "Ben, I need to go to the Senate meeting. I will call you later." He was about to hang up.

"Will, Martha had nothing to do with Robertson dying. She was working for you."

Will thought a moment and said quietly, "Ok, ok. I got to go." He closed his phone, went into the restroom and threw up.

Ben's phone vibrated and he answered in the usual code. The voice on the other end did not identify himself.

He said, "Algiers had a friend. He's from the old country. His wife's maiden name is Stephens. His daughter used her name. Pat Lewis is the man. We need to send a maid to clean up the house."

"I understand," said Ben.

The voice continued, "We need to terminate the organization and leave his friend as one of the founders. I will draw up the necessary paperwork."

"I see."

"We need a contact to whom we can deliver the information."

"I've got the exact person in mind," Ben said.

He disconnected and then dialed the Miami Express. The receptionist would not give out a number for Charles Reynolds. He would have to give a number and Reynolds would call him back. Ben asked to be put into his voice mail. He left a message from Dr. Thomas Ellerman of the Freedom Organization.

Ben called Marley, "Get on your boy Lewis. I want to know when he moves."

Chapter 40

Chars was driving and Jerry was following a few cars back. They were making their way at night down Highway 395 toward the coast. Jerry was on the cell phone and was reminding Chars what the back-up plan was and how they could escape if things went wrong. Jerry had insisted that Chars pack a small caliber Taurus pistol. Chars had it sitting on the passenger seat. He looked over at it uncomfortably. He had shot a shotgun at a range once, but he had never used a handgun. He did not know if he could actually shoot somebody. He really did not like the idea of putting it in his sock and was trying to come up with an alternative. He had seen on television that the cops often stick a gun in the back of the waistband. That did not seem very comfortable. He decided to do as Jerry advised when the time came and just stick it in his sock.

They took the Biscayne exit and headed south past the Southwest Airline Center that used to be the American Airline Center. They proceeded to 5th Avenue, which turns into Port Boulevard. This was a huge facility and Chars was not really sure where to go. He looked in the rear view mirror and noticed that Jerry's vehicle was gone from sight. That made him stop for just a second, but then he proceeded on cautiously. He flipped his high beams in order to get a better look at some of the signage. He did not see well at night anyway and this place was so dimly lit, Chars was having to squint to see.

Chars moved his way past the administration building. There was surprising little activity. He could see sparks at the far end of one of the dock areas. Someone must have been doing some repair work with a commercial welding unit. He continued looking for a sign that read "F." He made a left and parked. He was somewhat away from the complex, but figured he could walk. Jerry was still nowhere in sight, but Chars figured he must be out there somewhere. He moved around the corner slowly and along to the side of a corrugated metal building, trying not to look as scared as he actually was. They had discussed additional back up, but decided that it might cause Mr. Friend to rabbit—or worse, this was a trap. Jerry insisted on Chars wearing a police Kevlar vest and Chars put up no resistance at all. He was nervous about meeting this guy face to face. Even though he remembered that a meeting was exactly what he had wanted in the beginning—but now he was not so sure.

The wind and surf provided a tranquil setting to an otherwise tense amble down one side of the pier and around to the other side of the huge dock that housed dozens of businesses. They were mostly shipping companies, importers, and brokers that the normal person would never know existed unless they worked there. Large boats lined the northern-most side of the port. Chars figured that this would be a great place for someone to disappear and never be heard from again—and that person could be him. The thought made the hair on his neck stand up. He knew that Jerry was out there somewhere and that would even up the odds. He came around a large pylon-looking thing. Chars saw a figure move from behind one of the large sheds. It was a clear night with a half moon, which would make it difficult for anyone to hide. It could have been Jerry, but Chars was not sure.

Over his shoulder he heard a muzzled shot and instantaneously a bullet whizzed by his ear and struck the side of a metal storage building. Chars instinctively ducked and dropped to the ground. Just in time too. As he dropped, another shot sped overhead. Another fraction of a second would have been fatal. Chars was glad that Jerry had insisted on the Kevlar vest now.

Chars wished he had a Kevlar helmet too. He rolled over behind a concrete parking abutment and covered his head. He reached down for the gun in his sock and it was gone. He had forgotten to put it in his sock. He was cursing himself under his breath. "You stupid s…." He heard another shot that had a different sound to it. It had a louder pop than the first two Chars realized, and because it did not hit him he figured it was probably Jerry returning fire.

He decided to take a peek over the concrete. He lifted his head up to look over and as soon as he did, another bullet hit the side of the abutment and sent fragments of concrete flying in every direction. He dropped back down. Chars felt the sting of being hit with concrete shrapnel in his deltoid, the side of his face, and the top of his ear. Chars realized that the bullet had come on the angle rather than straight in front. The shooter had either changed position or he had two people shooting at him. He checked out both injuries and when his hand returned from his ear, it was covered with blood. Chars fought back a wave of panic, trying not to think whether his ear had been blown off. He carefully followed the edge of his ear around from the lobe to the top. To his relief, the ear was in tact, but bleeding. He found the cut with his finger and removed a handkerchief from his pants pocket. He rubbed his shoulder with the other hand while holding the handkerchief against his ear. The projectile hit him hard, but his protective clothing must have covered enough of his shoulder so as not to allow penetration. It was aching as if someone had hit him with a fist using full force. Chars thought about how his brother used to do that. He would come up from the side and do a full punch into his arm. Sometimes Chars was hit so hard that he could not help but cry. That would always get a parent involved and nobody wanted that. When Mom yelled from downstairs wanting to know what was going on, Chars would say through sniffles, "Nothing, Mom." Then Chars would summon his courage and hit his older brother back as hard as he could. His brother let him get a free shot in and that way the fight would be even.

He heard another two shots and someone cried out in pain. Chars was fairly certain it was not Jerry that he had heard, but he needed to go check. He could be wounded and need his help. Chars belly-crawled, staying as close to the ground as possible. He crawled through a puddle that had an oily scent to it and he pulled back, but his knees and elbows were already soaked. He tried to ignore to petroleum smell and continued to the other end of the concrete barrier. He carefully looked out from a low vantage point. He could hear sirens coming from the highway. Jerry was still nowhere to be found. Chars gathered himself and charged toward the next abutment and covered up quickly. No shots had been fired for about 30 seconds, but it seemed like an age to him. The sirens were getting closer all the time. Chars could see the shadow of people from the very end of the deck looking toward him. They were most likely spectators, trying to see some bloodshed and were probably the ones that reported gun shots. They did not venture any closer for fear of becoming victims themselves. Chars' attention had been distracted just long enough for someone in a dark green pair of coveralls to slip up behind him. The man pulled his head back and raised a 7-inch blade to Chars' neck. The blade had just begun to penetrate the skin when a shot was fired and the top of the assailant's head blew off. Blood and brain matter exploded, the knife dropped out of the man's hand and the body began to slump to the ground like a sheet that had lost its clip on the clothes line. His legs crumpled and the rest of his body necessarily followed. The force of the shot caused Chars to be pulled back and he landed partially on the dead man's chest and rolled off. Chars had blood on him everywhere. He looked around for the handkerchief that had momentarily dropped to the ground. He returned the cloth to his ear and could feel the blood running down his neck, back, and chest—and now he had the assailant's blood on him as well. Chars was shaking as the adrenaline started to subside from his system. Jerry stepped from the shadows and ran over to Chars to see if he was all right.

"Where's your gun?"

"I forgot it." Chars said. "It's on the front seat of my car."

Jerry rolled his eyes. "Just as well. Ok, I will take care of that. Give me your keys."

At last, the patrol cars were pulling around the corner. The police cars lights were almost blinding and the two officers came to a rolling stop and assessed the situation quickly. They both exited the car while drawing their weapons and using the doors as protection. Jerry was already standing with his badge held up in one hand and his department issued, Glock 22 in his other. He identified himself.

"The scene is clear!"

The officers were still wary and had not holstered their weapons.

Jerry said in a growl, "There is another one over behind that barrel next to the gray building. I don't think you'll need an ambulance for him either. This is Chars Reynolds. He was the target."

Within a few minutes an EMS unit had pulled up and they were making their way toward the scene. One officer checked out the man that was lying prostrate in front of them. The front part of his skull was in tact; however, the back, where the bullet exited, was completely missing. The officer was careful not to disturb the scene.

He told his partner, "Go check the other guy."

Two more sirens could be heard and almost instantly pulled around the corner with lights flashing. The officer looked at Chars suspiciously, but slowly put his gun away. Deciding he would not need handcuffs, he snapped the container positioned at the small of his back. More squad cars arrived and another EMS vehicle pulled up. After giving a brief statement, Chars rolled up on the EMS gurney that the technicians had popped up for him. They loaded him in the back and motored off toward Aventura Hospital.

It was almost midnight now and Jerry was waiting just outside the emergency room, smoking a cigarette. Jerry had his cell phone on his waist band and sported an ear module. He did not particularly like the apparatus, but it did make him look rather high-tech. He finished one conversation, crushed out the cigarette and called another number. He returned to where Chars waited for the doctors. A nurse frowned at him for being on the telephone, but nodded when she saw his badge. Jerry was finding out the latest about the procedures for his mandatory administrative leave. Following a shooting involving any police officer, that officer was taken off duty. This one should be quick, the detective had told Jerry, because the two men were obviously professional thugs. The only hitch was that it was an unofficial meeting with the bad guys. That could be accounted for because of the friendship between Chars and Jerry, but it would still draw some unwanted attention.

The emergency staff had made quick work of Chars' ear. It only took four stitches in the lobe and a nice sized patch. However, the shoulder would be a three-hour ordeal.

They waited and waited until a worn-out intern in hospital scrubs poked his head into the holding station and said, "Mr. Reynolds, Mr. Charles Reynolds?"

He was a scrawny bespectacled young man that looked more like a high school student than a real doctor. Nevertheless, off they went, Chars on a hospital bed under a sheet and Jerry tagging along, talking the entire time. They took Chars to a room through some double doors, which had a sign that read. Orthopedic Wing: Authorized Personnel Only.

A tiny little doctor with close cropped hair and a green scrubs came into the room and greeted everyone with a hearty "Hello."

His name tag read, Herman Mathews, Doctor of Orthopedic

Surgery. He took another look at an x-ray and motioned for Jerry to follow him outside.

As the two left, the doctor said, "Mr. Reynolds, you are going to fine. The nurse will get you a shoulder immobilizer, which you will need to wear. Limit your activities that would cause your shoulder to hurt. I have prescribed a pain killer, should you need one."

He moved on outside and addressed Jerry. He introduced himself again, shook hands with Jerry, and said, "Our staff closed up the cut on Mr. Reynolds' ear. And the bone scans show a slight proximal humerus fracture in the shoulder. Surgery will not be necessary. It will heal up if Mr. Reynolds wears his immobilizer for three to four weeks. He will need to have it checked again and his doctor will decide whether or not to move him to a standard arm sling."

Jerry was nodding while wondering if he was supposed to be remembering this or taking notes or something.

The surgeon continued, "What is a concern to me is that Mr. Reynolds seems to have been rather unfortunate in the last couple of weeks. It is fairly obvious that he had stitches in his head to close up a sizable gash."

Jerry was listening, but knew where this was headed and was just being polite, nodding his head.

"It seems that he also had some other trauma, maybe to the back of the head; possibly a concussion. I understand you are a police officer and his friend?"

Again, Jerry nodded his head.

"Is there something you need to tell me about?" the doctor said with all sincerity.

Jerry smiled and said, "Doc, I appreciate the interest. We know all about Mr. Reynolds. I am placing him under police protection in the hopes of no further injury. He's got someone trying to kill him, that's all," Jerry smiled as his phone rang.

"Excuse me Doc, I gotta take this."

The doctor's mouth dropped open at the "that's all" comment and gave a short look of disbelief, but shrugged his shoulders and headed on to his next case.

It was a detective from Jerry's office. "We got the initial report on the two guys you iced at the port. Both were clean and had no I.D. But the first, you know the White guy; we got a print match on him. His name was Bostic, a former Chicago cop. We are looking for more stuff on him, but that's what we got so far," Bernie Frey said.

"What about the other one?" Jerry said while taking notes.

"He is not going to be so easy to track down, but we sent his face to the FBI for their face recognition program and they said they would get back to us mid-morning."

Jerry walked back into the emergency room. Chars was buttoning up is shirt and gave a tired smile to Jerry.

"Chars, how you doing?" Jerry said softly.

Slowly shaking his head in disbelief, Chars just looked at Jerry and laughed at little. "Man, I have had crap knocked out of me. There is no part of my body that does not hurt," he said.

Jerry looked squarely at him, trying to detect any hint of deception. "Know anything about an ex-cop from Chicago?" he asked.

Chars thought hard. "I can't think of anything. Was that who was after me?" he asked.

"Well, he was the one that someone who is after you sent. I don't know what the Chicago connection is, but that would be a place to start. Do you recall if Robertson had any ties to Chicago?"

Chars thought and said, "No, I did not come across any."

"Well, he could just have been a hired hit man; not attached to any group. I'll take you back to the police station. Maybe when we get there we will have some information from the FBI on the second man," Jerry said and scooped up Chars' personal belongings.

The nurse a came in with a wheelchair and despite Chars' protests, she wheeled him out through the entry. Jerry had already pulled his unmarked police cruiser up and he opened the front passenger door for Chars. Chars looked like an old man, moving slowly and carefully. He had a bandage on his ear and his arm was in a sling. Jerry shut the door for him and moved around to the driver's side.

Chapter 41

Jerry was sitting at Chars' kitchen table. Chars was standing at the counter and called in for his messages for the first time in a couple days. He had 12 messages. The first four were from his office inquiring about his latest round of injuries from the bomb attack. It must have made the news in Washington and Miami. Marsha Lincoln had called, very concerned. The FBI had called and left a message to contact a Field Agent Mallory. Another message from the FBI was telling Chars to expect Agent Mallory to be stopping by. Chars was writing down the numbers and making notes beside them.

Then he listened to a message from a Thomas Ellerman of the Freedom Organization. He signaled to Jerry that this one was important. Jerry came over to where Chars was standing and watched as he took the message and wrote down a number. This may be the break that he was looking for. He went over to his computer and searched for Thomas Ellerman. There were no direct hits.

Jerry's phone beeped. It was Sergeant Bernie Frey. "They think the second guy was Salvador Entioli."

"Central America?" Jerry asked.

"No actually, not. They think he may have come from Central Europe, maybe Italy. Wherever he's from, he has links to the Chicago Mob."

"Really?" Jerry said with surprise. "What in the hell did Chars get himself into?" Jerry said aloud to no one in particular.

Chars looked up from his computer with a bewildered look

on his face.

Frey continued, "That's not all. Salvador matched a DNA hair sample in the FBI file. It linked him to a death of an unidentified woman in Puerto Rico just a few weeks ago. It may be the witness to the Robertson accident."

Jerry's face changed into one of pain. "Freda," he said with sadness.

MR_Friend was signed on: "You were in the news. Are you all right?"

Chars typed in: "No, I am not all right. You set me up."

MR_ Friend was typing: "I did not set you up."

Chars was hammering the keys so hard that the table was rocking back and forth. "You sure did you son of a bitch. You set the time and the place and the two gorillas almost took me out."

MR_Friend was typing: "What meeting?"

Chars typed: "You know exactly what meeting. You set me up to be killed and when I find out who the hell you are, you are going to jail."

MR_Friend was typing, and then sent this: "I did not arrange any meeting. I have not had a conversation with you in two days."

Jerry was looking over Chars' shoulder and said, "Maybe someone at the FBI could track this guy, but I don't know how."

Chars leaned back in his chair and said, "This guy pisses the shit out of me. How can he carry on like he did not set me up?"

Jerry looked at the screen again, and said, "Because maybe he didn't set you up."

Chars' face flashed with anger. "You were there, and you know what happened. How can you say that?"

MR_Friend was typing again: "Reynolds, I did not arrange any meeting. How were you contacted?"

Chars was still fuming and typed in: "You contacted me, Mr. Friend. You said you were at the accident."

MR_Friend replied: "I was not at the accident." Who did your contact say he was?"

Chars was banging the keys again: "YOU, YOU, YOU. Mr. Friend. My good, good, Friend. You set me up. And I am going to find out who you are."

MR_Friend typed back: "I never said I was your friend; I don't even know you. I was trying to help catch the ones that murdered Mike. I am Mike Robertson's friend, not yours, asshole. Now, I don't know who contacted you, but it was probably the Freedom Organization—they must have intercepted my screen name or something, but it was not me. Have you checked your house for bugs?"

Chars' eyes grew wide and Jerry immediately looked up at the light fixture.

Jerry put his finger to his mouth and said, "Chars this guy is a nut case, just let it go."

Chars understood and said, "I guess so—but I want to know who this guy is."

Chars checked his message history. Chars now realized MR_Friend stood for Mike Robertson's friend. He had thought MR had stood for mister. MR_Friend had not set him up, it was Mr. Friend. Someone must be listening to his conversation..

Chars typed in to MR_ Friend: "We need to check for bugs. Will get back to you."

Chars signed off.

In Florida, Justin Crawford signed off as MR_ Friend.

Chars stood up and walked over to Jerry, who was standing on a chair almost directly under the light fixture. He was on his tip toes trying to see over the top of it. He could not see anything, but cussed to himself for not thinking to check this sooner. Jerry figured the guy that broke into the house probably was not there just to check for notes. He would have to get a Clean Sweep Wand from his office. It looked sort of like a magic wand with a mini-

LCD screen at the handle. It could be moved around a room and would pick up any kind of listening device.

Jerry looked at Chars and said, “Hey, I’ve got to run over to the HQ. I’d feel better if you went with me.”

Chars agreed and they left. Once outside, Jerry explained what he needed. He also let Chars know that this could be their way to find out who is behind all of this. They might be able to bait them into to making a mistake.

Chars looked at Jerry with a pitiful look and said, “And I am going to be the bait, right?”

Chapter 42

Will had finished his Senate meetings and was driving back to Blue Ash. Surprisingly, Clanston had approached him and offered what Oliver considered to be as close to a truce as he was going to get. Clanston had complimented Oliver's contribution to the Education Bill and looked forward to working with him. Oliver tried mightily not to let his mouth drop open. Clanston went on to say that he was glad that the Cattlemen's deal had been cleared up. Again, Oliver looked at him unaware that anything had been cleared up, but went along with Clanston anyway. Considering the grief Clanston had caused Will, it felt strange, but he thanked the elder statesman and walked out of the Senate Hall wondering what happened. He was completely puzzled.

Will was grateful to finally have the weekend to think about all that had happened. As he drove home he knew that what was making sense to him now was the fact that Martha had not been in love with him. That was why she did not want to meet his family. That was why she avoided intimacy. She had made love to him not out of devotion, but duty. Will was devastated. He had fallen in love with a Freedom Organization plant. He wanted to call Ben back and ask him why. But he knew why. The FO wanted to monitor their boy. What better way than to have someone in the middle of it all. Martha was Kay Moore and the reporter somehow had tracked her down.

Then Will stopped in the middle of his thought. Reynolds was working on a murder investigation. Kay Moore worked for Robertson. Reynolds said that Robertson was killed. Did Martha have something to do with that? Did something go wrong with the

Robertson campaign and she somehow killed him? *That's ridiculous,* thought Will. *Nobody kills anybody for stuff like that. That's all in the movies.* He still wanted to find Martha. As he pulled into his neighborhood, he had a sense of relief. He drove into his garage and closed the door, shielding himself from the rest of the world. He had two days to hide and figure this thing out.

Will Oliver had slept in and had almost forgotten about all the events leading up to his current hiatus. He had experienced the toughest two weeks of his political career and the turbulence was not over yet. He decided that he would take a ride on his motorcycle. He pressed the start button and the bike came to life. He put on a helmet that he had worn since he first bought the bike. He thought the heavy tinted visor and a shiny black lacquer finish made him look a little like Darth Vader, but he had gotten used to wearing it—although at first he had to stop and take it off to get a breath of fresh air. It was just like when he played football. He did not know why but the helmet caused some type of claustrophobic attack. He would have to take his helmet off and then hide from the coaches. If they caught anyone with their helmet off even on the sidelines, running would be the consequence.

He pulled out into traffic and headed out of Blue Ash. He opened it a bit when he got on the highway and pushed his speed up to 85 as the highway was practically vacant. Will checked his blind spot and began to pass a car, when he noticed a dark sedan in his mirror. He eased off the accelerator as he considered whether it was a smooth-topped state trooper. It was too far back to see the license plate, so Will decided to pull back a little bit. When he did, the sedan seemed to slow down as well. He decided to get off at the next exit. When he did, the sedan continued on past the exit. Will pulled into a gas station and topped off his tank. It was a whopping $6 and he paid cash. He felt like heading back and crossed over the highway and motored back toward his house. He looked in his mirror and he thought he saw another sedan hanging back suspiciously. Maybe he was just imagining it. Why would anyone be following him?

He decided he would watch his speed. It could just be a speed trap, but then a different car, raced by him in the far right lane. If it was a police car, the occupant did not seem too interested in a cyclist that was doing near 80 miles per hour in a 60 m.p.h. zone. As the car passed, the driver looked over at Will. A very uneasy feeling came over Will so he slowed to just below the speed limit in order to quicken the passing of this weirdo. Will thought, *he might have been looking at the bike, but he seemed unusually interested.* The car's windows were tinted and it was even difficult to see any of the person's features. Will looked in his rear view mirror, but other dark sedan was no longer visible and he cursed for not paying better attention. Maybe the car that passed was supposed to be a distraction. Will decided to drive through a fast-food restaurant and just go home. He ordered and placed the sandwiches in his storage box. He drove to his garage and got out to enter his code for the automatic door. He had forgotten to carry his opener with him. When he had the garage door open and returned to his bike, two sedans bounded into his driveway. They startled him and his first reaction was to run, but he held his position as the two men in the front vehicle held badges out of the opened door and then moved cautiously toward Will.

"Senator Oliver, we need to talk to you."

Will had a look of bewilderment, but managed a feeble, "Sure."

"I am Field Agent Scott Wilson, and this is my partner Rick Coombs," Wilson said with a menacing look.

Coombs waived off the two agents in the other car. Will supposed that the FBI was fairly certain that he was not a serial killer about to launch an attack on them with an AK-47 hidden in his shirt sleeve.

Coombs said, "Senator, would you prefer that we go inside?"

Will looked at him still confused and again managed only a weak, "Sure." He killed the engine on his bike and pushed it into the garage. "What do you need to speak with me about?" Will asked looking to clear up his confusion.

He thought to himself, *it must be about Martha, or maybe this was about that crazy reporter.*

Wilson look at Will incredulously, "You don't know what we are here about?"

Will cocked his head about and thought, *are you getting smart with me?* He looked at Agent Wilson directly in the eye, and having regained his composure, said calmly, "I have no idea why you are here or why you were following me."

The FBI agent looked briefly at his partner, giving away that they had not intended to be seen. They followed Will in the front door and through to the kitchen.

"Before you became aware that we were following you, where were you going, Senator Oliver?" Agent Wilson asked.

Will looked at him with utter confusion and a pained expression. He said, "Agent…" he could not remember his name.

Ross helped him out. "I am Field Agent Wilson and this is Agent Coombs."

Oliver remembered now and started nodding his head. "Yes, yes; Ross and Coombs. I am going to give you about two minutes to tell me what the hell you are doing here. Do you understand?"

Wilson's gaze narrowed and he gave a thin smile. He expected this type of arrogant attitude from a State Senator. He adjusted his shirt sleeve under his dark suit coat. He clenched his jaw and said with some distaste. "Senator Oliver, have you seen or spoken with Martha Hall in the last two days?"

Oliver thought, *ok, this is what this is about.* "No," he said flatly.

The FBI agent did not even give that answer a moment to settle. "Senator, what do you know about a group called the Freedom Organization?"

Again, Oliver tried not to show any reaction and stated with little emotion, "They are a political action group."

"So you are aware of the Freedom Organization?" said Wilson.

Oliver gave him a look of impatience and said, "I just told you that."

"Senator Oliver, do you know of any of their activities?" Coombs asked taking his turn, so as not to become part of the scenery.

"You would have to be more specific than that," Will said.

Wilson edged toward Will and looked as if he was going to bump him. "More specifically, Senator, we are looking into an attempt on the life of a Miami reporter. Senator, were you aware that Martha Hall was also Kay Moore?"

Will let a breath out and said, "That is what the police told me. But no, I don't know that for a fact." He was still trying to reconcile that bit of information, but now figured that it must be true.

Wilson continued, "We know that a Kay Moore worked in Robertson's campaign. We believe that Kay Moore became Martha Hall. We are fairly certain she knows about or is a part of this Freedom Organization. We are trying to ascertain what you know about that murder attempt on Charles Reynolds," Ross said and took a slight step back to lean on the kitchen counter.

Agent Wilson was watching Oliver closely. Agent Coombs was looking at Oliver like a Doberman sizing up a meaty bone.

"And you think I had something to do with that?" Will said with disbelief.

"We are simply asking questions. You were intimate with

Martha Hall, were you not?" Coombs asked.

Oliver was enraged but tried not to show it. He thought to himself, did the whole damn world know about my personal life? What in the hell is going on?

Will said softly, "Yes."

Agent Wilson said, "We believe that somehow Martha Hall, or Kay Moore was involved in the group called the Freedom Organization."

Wilson paused, looking intently at Will's expression to determine what reaction that statement would draw. Will looked at the man and then over to his partner.

"That's it?" asked Will looking confused. "And with that information, you think that she somehow planned a bombing of a car to what…eliminate a disingenuous reporter?" Will stood and was shaking his head. "I don't know whether to be incensed or feel pity at your stupidity."

Both were looking at him with little expression. They just looked at him.

"Okay fellows, the only thing you have close is, I was having a relationship with Martha. I did not know she was anything other than Martha. I did not have anything to do with her meeting with the reporter and was not even aware that she was meeting with him until the next day. I would have a hard time believing that she knew about or was involved in any way in the bombing of Reynolds' car. As far as the Freedom Organization, I only know them to be a group that supports candidates," Will said and sat back in his seat.

"Senator Oliver, please be careful about what you say to us. I consider this to be an official interview and you would not want to be accused of obstructing justice."

Wilson again was looking directly at Oliver to read his reaction.

Will looked at him with an incredulous look, "I am sure

that works with some people, Agent Wilson, but I just told you what the facts are. So let's just dispense with the veiled threats."

"Senator Oliver," Coombs jumped in, "We did not say that you were involved in the attempts. I believe you when you say that you don't think that Ms. Moore was involved. We know that you are very, attached, shall we say, to Ms. Moore. But, if you know of her whereabouts or any other information, you should trust us and give it to us."

Will shrugged a bit but the gesture showed that he had no idea.

"Senator, we understand that it would be normal to want to protect someone you love," Wilson said, expectant of a response from Oliver.

When none came he continued, "Martha is not who you think she is, Senator. We have reason to believe that she was sent here," he paused, "to work for you," he paused again. "Senator, we have contacted you because we have reason to believe that your life may be in danger."

Will's mouth dropped far enough to almost dislocate itself. He stared at this man with an absolute look of disbelief.

Coombs continued, "We believe that either the Freedom Organization or possibly, but less likely, some other group is actively targeting specific candidates. We feel that it is no coincidence that the reporter Reynolds, who is working on the Robertson story, has had two attempts on his life."

Oliver let out a long sigh. He did not say anything—he was speechless.

"Senator Oliver?" Wilson asked hoping to get something out of the man who was obviously shocked by all that he had heard.

Will's mind was racing from the thought about Martha and that she was somehow involved in all of this. He was running the events through his mind and it just did not make sense. The

Freedom Organization had helped get him elected and it was very unlikely that they would whack him after getting him into office.

Wilson decided to throw out another bomb to see if that would help the Senator give up his lover.

"We are also looking into the death of former Vice-President, Lancaster Smith. Senator, if you know how to make contact with Kay Moore, it could be in your best interest to give that information to us."

Will closed his eyes and was shaking his head slowly. "I think you guys must be on a snipe hunt."

"Senator, we can't help you if you don't cooperate. Kay Moore has disappeared and is likely in hiding or has been eliminated as potential informant. Chars Reynolds has experienced at least two attempts on his life and has suffered an attack in a hotel room and a break-in at his home. Mike Robertson's accident has several suspicious details that I cannot disclose, but I can say that it is likely that his accident was staged. We believe that this Freedom Organization is targeting politicians. Somehow you have ended up on their list as well. It is possible that Kay Moore was a plant. She worked in Robertson's office prior to coming here. Mr. Reynolds has an informant that has been feeding him information. That information has nearly gotten him killed. So whatever you know about this organization, it would be helpful for us to know."

Chapter 43

Chars checked his voice mail. He had several messages from the office, including one from Thom Stanton.

"Chars, would you mind checking in with me; we have some things to discuss, including your continued employment with the paper. Thanks."

Chars thought that Thomas sounded rather perturbed. He hit the delete key. The next message was from one of the secretaries at work, it was from yesterday afternoon.

"Chars, this is Mimi. You have an envelope that some delivery service dropped off. It does not say who it is from, but I put it on your desk. If you come into the office, oh say in the next month or so, you can pick it up."

Chars smiled a little and said aloud, "Mimi, Mimi, Mimi. What envelope? Probably my pink slip. I think I might put off picking that one up."

He hit delete again. The next one was another message from a Thomas Ellerman. It simply said that there would be some information delivered to him that would help him with his story. Chars had forgotten to call the guy back. He still had the number at his house. He puzzled over that and hit the number 9 to save the message. He needed to get out of his house anyway, so he drove to the office. Jerry presumably would return to his house to run the scan. He would let himself in so that would not be a problem. Chars arrived at the office to a few greetings and several raised eyebrows.

One of the secretaries said, "Hi Chars, Mr. Stanton is looking for you."

Chars looked at her with a wide-eyed expression and asked, "He's here?"

She then gave a knowing smile and a little laugh that made Chars return a forced smile. She said merrily, "He's down here while Cooper is on vacation. He is in Cooper's office as we speak."

Cooper, Chars' actual boss, had taken Stanton's vacated position after his reassignment to Washington, D.C. Chars like Cooper because he let Chars do his work unfettered. Chars did not stop at Cooper's office and in fact took a circuitous route through the office to avoid going by Cooper's office. When he arrived at his little cubicle, the pink that he saw was actually a stack of phone messages. The envelope was in the middle of his desk and apparently undisturbed. The seal was true and Chars looked for any indication of its origin. There was none. It was a full size manila envelope. Chars had almost decided to take it to Jerry for fingerprinting and possible DNA match if it was anything critical. He then decided that it might just be from accounting. He debated a little while longer and his curiosity was getting the best of him. He figured that his prints were already on the package and they could always ignore those. He took out a letter opener and from the bottom wedged it in the bottom fold of the envelope. He slit open the bottom and pulled out the incorporation documents for the Freedom Organization. He had the names at last. He picked up his messages and left undetected by the great Thom Stanton.

"Jerry, I've got something important," Chars said excitedly into his cell phone.

He practically ran all the way to car, looking over his shoulder and around every corner to make sure that no one was following him. At one point he thought he saw Stanton lurking around a corner, but it was just some other stiff-backed boob making his way out of the building. It was as if Jerry had not even heard what Chars had said. Jerry was excited about what the Wand had uncovered.

"We found some interesting vermin, Chars. Looks like someone was very interested in you. I hope you didn't do anything in your bedroom that you would not like to see on the Internet at some point."

Jerry was letting the police team out the door, shaking their hands and nodding his thanks as they left Chars' home.

"Jerry, that explains quite a bit, but I am on the way. You heard me when I said that we caught a break?"

"Just tell me; we've got all the bugs out."

"I received an envelope with the Freedom Organization names on it. I will need to know who sent it though. Can you get a DNA test done on it?"

"Sure if it's something that needs it. You already had the guy's name, didn't you?"

"No Jerry, this looks to be the names that we really needed to find out exactly what is going on here. Plus, there are names of candidates here too. Jerry, it lists candidates like Robertson, Smith, Scott and Mitchell...all the names that were on Mr. Friend's original e-mail."

Chars was accelerating onto the highway now and only about 20 minutes away from his house. He noticed there was a car following him into his neighborhood. He was more fatigued than panicked. He was going to a house with a cop in it and whoever it was did not care if they were seen. Chars pulled into the driveway and got out. A dark sedan pulled up on the street in front of Chars' house. Chars looked at them and immediately thought FBI. He was right.

"Mr. Reynolds?" a man in a dark suit and nicely worn silk tie inquired.

"Yes, but I have already had my visit from the Jehovah Witnesses," Chars said wearily.

"Mr. Reynolds, I am Agent Preston with the FBI and this is

Agent Turner. May we come in?" Agent Preston asked politely.

Chars smiled and said, "Sure. We are having a happy hour at half past, come on in and join the rest of the group."

The two men were a good six inches taller than Chars and made him feel a bit intimidated. Jerry heard the conversation and had thumbed off his safety. He was partially hidden in the kitchen waiting to see if this might be another ambush.

Chars called out to him and said, "Jerry, you can come out now. It is just our friends from the FBI."

"Mr. Reynolds, we understand that you are in possession of some information regarding the Freedom Organization," Agent Preston said.

Chars jerked around and looked accusingly at Jerry. Jerry gave the look of "It wasn't me."

"We are not at liberty to tell you how we know, but it was not the local police," Agent Turner inputted.

Jerry gave a puzzled look at the two agents.

Chars was hacked off now and spouted, "Well you can't have…it."

He stuttered because he just admitted to having what they had asked about.

Jerry had taken a seat and said, "Chars, if they want it, they are going to take it."

Chars glared at Jerry and said, "This is privileged information. I have the right to protect my source."

Agent Preston looked very interested and asked, "Is there something in there," he stopped and nodded at the envelope, "that gives up who the source is?"

Chars gave a frown and said, "No."

"Mr. Reynolds, we are trying to save people's lives here and we are investigating the murder of a U.S. Senator. You know you are going to get your story, but you are going to have to give that envelope to me," Agent Turner said holding out his hand.

Chars reluctantly handed over the envelope. He was momentarily enlightened and said, "You know, I remember you," directing his comment to Agent Preston. "You were following me that day at the Purple Dolphin restaurant."

Chars' comment caused Preston and Turner to look at each other, but neither said anything. Preston was carefully examining the envelope and had taken a peek into the open end. He saw two pieces of paper with names typed out. Jerry gave a curious look at the two agents.

He looked at Chars and said with smile, "You are right, Mr. Reynolds. You are very observant. Was there anything else that you removed from the envelope?"

Jerry announced, "I got to take a pee." He stood up and started walking toward the bedroom.

Chars glanced over with a curious look on his face and said, "Jerry the bathroom is back this..."

Agent Turner looked a bit startled as Jerry stood and began to leave the room. Turner glanced at his partner and said, "Uh, hey, you can't leave."

Agent Preston was reaching in his jacket to pull out a Beretta, when Jerry whirled around and shot him in the right shoulder. Preston pulled the trigger twice, but the bullets sprayed off the floor. Chars was stunned, but had enough sense to dive toward the floor. Agent Turner had his weapon drawn and mistakenly aimed at Chars instead of trying to take out Jerry. Jerry immediately dropped him with shot to the head. Preston switched his gun to his left hand and managed to fire one more errant shot. Jerry put a bullet right through the man's forehead. Paul Gallegos collapsed in a heap on the floor, giving up the last vestiges of life.

Chapter 44

Standing outside a restaurant, beyond earshot of any passerby, Ross Saunders finished one call and then made another.

"Hey it's me. Marley just called; the man is headed to Cincinnati. He is coming after Oliver. You need to get there before he does," Ross Saunders said.

The person the other end said, "I will be."

Ross went inside the restaurant and felt the cool air conditioning hit his skin. A nicely proportioned female bartender noticed the handsome man entering and came over to his side of the bar.

In a Polynesian accent, she said, "Welcome to the Cook Islands; can I get you something to drink?"

Ross looked over the drink listing and said, "I'll believe I'll try the Tonga Special with Maker's Mark."

The young woman gave him a slight bow of the head and said, "Very good, sir."

Will Oliver was trying to catch up on his reading for the bills that would be proposed in the next session. He was an avid reader, but there was so much stuff. He had tried to put all the Freedom Organization information in a neat file, but it kept coming out, flooding his consciousness. How could have Martha been involved? If it came out that he was part of the Freedom

Organization, it would be death for his political career—Clanston would see to that. He thought about calling the reporter. He could probably look him up online or somehow get a message to him. Surely, he was going to make this whole thing public and then that would be the end of the shortest political career in Ohio history.

His house phone rang and Will answered with a short, "Oliver."

An unidentified person on the other end of the call said, "I have some information that you need to have."

Will sat up abruptly in his chair. "Who is this?"

The person evidently ignoring the question said, "Meet me at JeanRo Bistro on Vine St., 8:00pm. Don't park on the street."

"Who is this?" Will asked angrily.

"It is better if you don't know my name," the caller said confidently. "I have information on your girlfriend, so don't be late."

And with that the call was terminated.

"I won't be there," Will yelled in the phone, but there was no response.

Will held the phone to his forehead, trying to decide what to do. Finally a recording came on that said, "If you would like to make a call…"

Will slammed down the phone and grabbed his keys. If he hurried, he could make it to downtown Cincinnati in time for his meeting at 8:00. As Will pulled out of his drive, an observer concealed in a tan Chrysler sedan, pulled out and began to follow.

The driver made a call and said, "We are on the move."

The voice on the other end said. "JeanRo Bistro on Vine Street, 8 o'clock."

The driver asked, "Can you beat him there?"

"Got it covered, I just need to know if he stops along the way or changes his mind."

The driver said, "Will do."

Will was aware of danger of showing up to a meeting that he did not know who he was meeting with, but he had to find out about Martha. Tying to remain calm, he pulled out his cell phone and called Ben Thomas. He received the cryptic greeting of the last four digits of the phone number and then Will could hear the beep signaling that he was in voice mail.

Will simply said, "Call me, I am headed to a meeting that could be trouble, but they say they have information about Martha. Call me."

Will hung up and ran his hand through his hair and rubbed the bridge of his nose. He exited off Highway 37 on the Main Street exit. He cut off on 4th Street and parked a block over on Postal Place. The caller said not to park on the street, but where was he supposed to park? He decided that a block away would just have to do.

Chapter 45

Chars was uninjured and Jerry only sustained a flesh wound on his left shoulder. It was not a clean shot and in fact had been a bouncer that ricocheted off the tile floor. The police were there in almost an instant due to the fact that Ms. Wendell had already called them to report two suspicious men impersonating FBI agents. Chars wanted to know how she knew. He went outside on the patio and asked across the fence.

She said, "I heard them identify themselves as FBI, but did they show their ID?"

Chars shook his head because he had not noticed. Ms. Wendell let out a small sigh of disgust for Chars' lack of observation.

She asked, "Did they have government tags on their vehicle?"

Chars again gave her a blank look.

"Chars, how can you be this great reporter, when you have the knack of a knucklehead? She turned from the fence and was walking back to her house. "Besides, the real FBI had already been here and it was not the same guys."

Chars turned, went inside his house and pulled the patio door shut. "Ms. Wendell knew that these guys were not FBI."

Jerry smiled. "Sharp old coot, isn't she?"

Chars sat down; the smell of gun powder and the copper smell of blood were still in the air. The crime scene had been marked and there was still an investigator and a photographer finishing up. This would be a crime scene for many days to come and Chars began to think about the next few days. He thought there must be a service that would come clean up crime scenes.

Finally he asked Jerry, “How did you figure they were not FBI?”

“First, neither one of them asked me who I was. So I figured they must already know. Professional courtesy would have dictated that we establish who is on whose turf. Second, the guy’s shoes did not go well with his suit. You wear a suit like that; you don’t wear casual dress shoes. Then when he reached for the packet, I saw his gun. The FBI switched exclusively to a 40-caliber Smith and Wesson two years back. It caused quite the uproar, because the agents used to have some choice in the matter. Then finally, when you said you recognized him from the Purple Dolphin, it smelled bad. The FBI had not even gotten involved in this back then.”

Chars leaned back on the sofa a little to see the two police officers in the kitchen.

“I guess I was just worried about that envelope. How did they know about that?”

Jerry took a swig from a Shiner Bock bottle, draining the last bit. “My guess is that if you take a look at your cell phone, you got a nasty little critter in it. What was so special in the envelope?”

“It had a name that we had not come across before. And then it all made sense.”

Chapter 46

Will moved around the car and looked down toward the direction of the restaurant. He decided to play this a little cautiously, so he headed out in the opposite direction and then decided to double back around the block. He would be a little late, but he was not sure he wanted to be here anyway. He thought that a gun would have been a good idea, too bad he just had that thought. He could not even remember where is little .38 caliber was, much less the key and ammunition. He took out his handkerchief and wiped his brow. The sun was almost set and he saw once in a Clint Eastwood movie that it was better to approach with the sun to your back. He was headed the wrong way for that to work. He would have to go past Vine and then come back. Will chided himself; he was definitely overreacting. He came around the corner and an alley ran the distance between the backs of several businesses and restaurants. *That's it*, thought Will, *I will come into the restaurant from the back. That way I can see who it is before they see me.* He moved down the alley and then he heard a voice from behind him.

"Are you lost or just trying to get some exercise?"

Will swirled around and saw a woman with her back to the sun. Smart lady he thought, but then he realized it was Martha.

"Martha?" Will asked with a puzzled and hurt voice.

Martha's eyes dropped and she said apologetically, "I guess I should apologize for leaving on such short notice, Will."

Will just stood there motionless and speechless.

"It was just getting a little complicated with that reporter, that's all," she said with very little emotion.

Will finally recovered and asked, "Where did you go?"

Martha fidgeted and said, "Where it was safe."

Will was feeling the wave of emotions come back and the overwhelming feeling of betrayal. He looked down and then back up at Martha. "You want to tell me who you really are?"

Martha had closed the gap between them and only stood about 15 feet away. Will could now see that she was wearing a light rain coat.

"Will, it is really something you are better off not knowing."

He sounded like he was going to cry. "I thought you were dead."

"I know and I am sorry. I just had to leave," she said quietly.

"Are you married?" asked Will.

"No, I just told the reporter that to get him to look somewhere else. But Will, I am not—I cannot come back."

"Why not?" asked Will.

"Because there may be a lot of questions; questions that we cannot afford to have you answer. So, one of us has to go away."

Will saw a change in her face and a cold look come in to her eyes. She reached into her raincoat and pulled a .45 caliber handgun. She aimed it directly at Will and pulled the trigger. He flinched as he registered that Martha was actually trying to kill him. He quickly fell to the ground and went into some sort of instinctive fire roll. The sound of the shot reverberated in the alley. He checked himself over quickly. He thought, *she had missed; from 15 feet, she missed.* The bullet went right by his head. Martha did not shoot again, in fact, she had left the alley by the time he looked up. He heard a sound of running water behind him and he slowly turned to look. A man lay dead in a puddle of blood, and his bladder was emptying into a storage drain. Will stood and walked over to see the man's face. There was a single bullet between his eyebrow and scalp line. The man was still holding was a silenced revolver in his right hand. Will stumbled, but managed to walk quickly out of the alley and back the way he'd come from his car. Tears were flowing down his face. He realized that Martha had saved his life and… he would never see her again.

Chapter 47

Heinz Innsbruck sat in the back corner of Glunz Bavarian Haus. He'd eaten at this North Center restaurant in Chicago, Illinois, every Tuesday for the past five years. He had dined on the pork tenderloin with a bacon mushroom sauce along with ethereal herb spaetzle. He liked the dim lighting and the staff always gave him his favorite table. He had finished off his meal with an order of fried cinnamon apple rings with a crème anglaise. Heinz leaned back in the corner booth and appreciated his work of the past year.

He had avenged his daughter's death and derailed the benefit that would have been enjoyed by Algiers Banger and his minions. He had, in effect, changed the course of history back to where it should have been going. Heinz had learned a tremendous amount from Banger's exploits. Heinz had always shied away from politics, preferring to hand out a few well-placed payments to cops and local officials. After seeing what Algiers had accomplished, Heinz was really excited. He knew that he had not exactly ushered Brett Swain in to the Vice-Presidency, but he did get Smith out and actively promote Swain through his contacts. Heinz could hardly believe it. He actually knew the Vice-President of the United States personally. And now that Parker had decided not to run, perhaps he would be close friends with the President. The Lincoln bedroom was a possibility thought Heinz.

With his meal complete, he needed to use the men's room and he sent Nicky ahead to check it out. While Nicky checked the stall Heinz stood and brushed the bread crumbs from his shirt. When his attention returned to the restaurant, a man in a brown suit had appeared next to him.

He reached out and slapped him on the shoulder and said, “Mr. Innsbruck, how are you? Algiers Banger sends his regards.”

Heinz felt the sting on his shoulder but did not realize what had happen. He stiffened and a scowl came across his face. The man turned and walked into the kitchen and out the back door. Nicky was returning just in time to catch Heinz as he stumbled and began to fall.

Chapter 48

Will's cell phone vibrated and he quickly picked it off the coffee table. He had driven himself home after his alley encounter with Martha and was still visibly shaking. He'd tried to calm himself with a beer.

He answered with a weak, "Oliver."

"Will, this is Ben," the voice said with an element of enthusiasm.

"Ben, do you know what happened?"

"Yes, I know," he said calmly.

"What in the hell is going on!?" Will almost yelled into the phone.

"Will, I know you are upset," Ben said with the patience of a parent.

"Upset? Upset? I don't know what the hell is going on and I was going to be killed!"

"Will, get your wits about you; everything has been handled."

"What was handled? A man tried to kill me, and Martha or Kay or whoever the hell she is shot him first! She shot and killed a man!"

Ben still remained calm and said, "Yes, she killed a man who wanted to kill you."

"Why would someone want to kill me, for God's sake?"

"I will explain it to you if you calm down, but it is over now," Ben said.

Will was pacing up and back in his living room. Whipping around each time that Ben told him to calm down.

"Ok, ok, I am calming down." He paused and then said, "No, no; I am not calm, BEN! How am I supposed to be calm when someone tried to kill me and I thought she..." he stuttered, "She was going to kill me!"

Ben let out a breath. He knew that Will was fairly sheltered and this would shake anyone. He thought that he just needed to keep working on getting Will past this and then everything would be fine.

"Will, I wish I was there to help you through this, but let me explain what has been happening. Then we will determine what needs to be done from here on."

Will had sat down on the couch and had his head in his hands. "Ok," was all he could manage.

Ben thought, *right, now we are making progress.*

"Will, we have helped several other candidates get elected. There was a group of people that took over the organization."

"The Freedom Organization?"

Ben was nodding and said, "Yes, the Freedom Organization. They were systematically undoing everything that we were able to accomplish. Will, they were responsible for the death of Mike Robertson."

Will stood up and took a drink of his Boddingtons beer. "They killed Mike?"

Ben smiled knowing that he was making progress. "Yes, and they have been trying to kill that reporter."

Will was processing all this. "The bomb?"

"Yes, the bomb."

Will paced back across the room and asked, "But why?"

"It is very complicated, but the reporter connected the Freedom Organization to Mike and when it was determined that it was not an accident, he began putting the pieces of the puzzle together. They could not afford to have him getting any closer."

Will stopped pacing and sat down again. "And they were

willing to kill him and….me?"

"Yes," Ben said sincerely.

There was silence for a moment.

"Ben, this is way more shit than I can handle."

"It is right now. But you are going to wake up tomorrow and the papers will have the story about the Freedom Organization. The people responsible are now out of commission. The reporter will break the story and you will not even be mentioned. You are still an up-and-coming State Senator."

There was only silence.

Ben continued, "Will, I know you are confused and scared, but this is going to be resolved and you are going to be able to move along with the work that you set out to do."

Will was just shaking his head in disbelief and said softly, "Ok."

There was another moment of silence.

"What do I do next?" Will asked.

"You get your Education Bill passed and then…and then you get ready for the next election."

Will looked up and asked, "The next election?"

"Will, the Governor's election will be starting in two years."

THE END

Epilogue

Chicago Mob Boss and Architect of the Freedom Organization Dies

Radical Left Group Allegedly Killed Florida Senator

By Chars Reynolds with contributions from Priscilla White
Miami Express News

Deer Park, IL- Chicago Mob Boss and the likely architect of a clandestine and violent Freedom Organization died Thursday of an apparent heart attack. Heinz Innsbruck allegedly targeted a variety of conservative political figures and candidates with smear tactics and even orchestrated Senator Mike Robertson's deadly car crash. FBI officials are investigating the death, but issued a statement that Innsbruck died of a massive heart attack late Thursday evening at a Chicago restaurant.

Information on Innsbruck is murky at best, but according to a variety of sources, Heinz Innsbruck had grown up in Austria and did not arrive on the shores of the United States until his 21st year. He stood a little over five foot nine in his early days, but had shrunk to just under five six. A local vendor said Innsbruck had "dark brown eyes that could look at a person and immediately engender fear and dread." "Physically, he was anything but intimidating, but as soon as he looked at you, he commanded your attention," said one family friend who wished to remain anonymous.

Arriving penniless in the United States like so many other immigrants, Heinz started honing his skills as a bag man for a mobster in New York City. Within a couple years he had moved up the organizational ladder and made his first hit. Despite his success, he saw the fact that only family members were moving into the most important positions. He decided to strike out on his own. Using funds he had stolen off a competing courier, he set out for the Windy City. He learned that Chicago was in fact windy, but that is not how it got its name. The Windy City was a name that the New Yorkers had given Chicago because of the people's boastful ways. Innsbruck did not like Chicago and returned to New York for a short time. However, the mob now saw him as a threat and Heinz retreated back to Chicago. Heinz was not purported to be a talker but a doer. "He did not say much, but if he did, you could be sure it was going to happen," according to another anonymous source. Heinz had quickly learned the ropes and made a name for himself as a good handicapper and very efficient problem solver. Problems that he dealt with best were those that left the other person dead. His network became substantial and his ruthlessness had become well-known. He was a doting father to his two daughters, but had very little affection left over for anyone else. Persons who crossed Innsbruck were short for this world.

Evidently, Innsbruck's hate of conservative candidates manifested itself shortly after his daughter, Mira Stephens, was killed in a botched robbery and car jacking attempt. He reportedly learned that she had been having an affair with Lt. Governor, candidate Karl Scott. Upon learning of the affair and subsequent dismissal of his daughter, Innsbruck orchestrated the downfall of Scott, by leaking another affair that Scott was having. Innsbruck also established a nefarious connection to the late Vice-President, Lancaster Smith. That relationship's disclosure led to the resignation of Smith. The subterfuge that caused an FBI investigation into the Freedom Organization was the highly publicized car accident that killed Florida Senator Mike Robertson. Investigations by the Secret Service, local police organizations, and the FBI continue. The initial investigation into Senator Robertson's death that sparked this wider investigation was led by Jerry Reynolds of the Miami Police Department. Sources in the Robertson campaign and the immediate family members have been unavailable for comment.

Check out other books by Daniel Reed on-line at

ReadReedBooks.com

Front Cover: ©BigStockPhoto.com; Kevin Kangas, Miraco

Editing for "The Cleaning" by Ruth Blaikie rblaikie@xtra.co.nz

All characters in this novel are created purely from the imagination of the author. No character is based on any real person, dead or alive. Any similarity is purely coincidental. Names are fictional as well and have no relationship to someone bearing the same name.